MORE WORKS BY SUSAN MERSON

Dreaming in Daylight

When They Go and You Do Not

Your Name Here: An Actor and Writer's Guide to Solo Performance

OH GOOD NOW THIS

Susan Merson

[blocpress]

Oh Good Now This is a work of fiction. Some incidents, dialogue, and characters are products of the author's imagination and are not to be construed as real. Where real-life historical figures appear, the situations, incidents, and dialogue concerning those persons are based on or inspired by actual events. In all other respects, any resemblance to actual persons, living or dead, events, or locales is entirely coincidental.

Cover design by John Phelps, Image Faucet

ISBN: 978-0-578-78758-9

Library of Congress Control Number: 2020920562

For my mother
Sura Rifkeh Sara Rebecca Shirley Feldman Fields Rubenstein Merson Lubin

"Therefore choose life.
So you and your children may live."
Deuteronomy 30:19

Acknowledgments

This book was a long time coming and I have many people and places to thank for its final appearance.

So many thanks for the counsel and patience of Wendy Rohm and the Paris Writers Workshop. Stays and readings at Belize Writers Conference, Cuba Writers Conference and in Iona, Scotland, with Angela Locke, the gracious and welcoming.

Thanks to Jule Selbo for always setting me straight on my path in so many ways. Liza Monroy for helping to dig out the story from its landscape. Shane Howard for a dance. Ellen Parker for listening to the garden with me. Sheri Meyerhoffer for listening most nights. Barb Levinson for reading with an open heart. Karen Richardson for her easy and excellent facilitation of this book's production. John Phelps and Image Faucet for the years of beautiful images and friendship.

The inspiration of my daughter, Sofia and my husband, Tony. These two are my generating and sustaining lights in all the dimensions. So very grateful.

And even the people who said no after time and money and vision were spent and spent. These shall remain nameless here but are ever present as impetus for taking back my work and putting it in the world.

The NY Writers Bloc—oh yes. Especially Milton Washington and his kind support that sent me to the next step, and Cassandra Garbus, such an articulate and caring reader. The L.A. Bloc, too, with Barbara Bottner ever kind, smart and right on target with alliance, wisdom and such enveloping kindness on this and so many projects and life events.

The Bloc has been and continues to be my supportive home in all its iterations and I am grateful to all and everyone over the years who has listened, nodded or nodded off—giving me the feedback I needed. May we all be blessed with such caring circles.

Chapter 1

Til Death Do Us Part. Not.

"Not many opportunities for someone with your skills around here. And your age, after all," Cheryl McGuin says, glancing at Vivi's application, over her eye shadow and half glasses.

"You can't use age to discriminate against a qualified employee!" Vivi sits up straighter, hoping her small spare tire doesn't show under her tee shirt. Cheryl looks up, hoping no one else had heard that remark.

Cheryl is playing hard ball, dangling the Home Center garden job in front of Vivi. The cold weather is coming in. There are exactly zero other jobs that will pay her enough to cover the rent in this little town, if only, just—and she's already had to ask her landlord for an extension on the rent for last month. She doesn't really have anyone she can borrow from, certainly not her friend, Vikram who works at the college. He will just lecture her that she needs to be more responsible for herself. Vivi understands what it is to have little power and she has seen lots of bullies use that power, profligate. What woman doesn't? She can face this small-town manipulator.

"I'm qualified, I just turned fifty and my age and gender are not the issue," she says again, a little louder.

"Relax! No need for harassment law suits. We all watch the training videos." Cheryl looks around again checking no one is near them at the Contractors Service Desk.

"It's just, I'm good at what I do." Viv smiles a little, trying to reel Cheryl in and be an ally. "I've been a landscape designer and garden consultant in California for several years. I even had a cable garden show. I will confess to knowing more about succulents and sustainable desert landscapes than East coast perennials but I am a fast learner. I kept Sandy's shop running until the estate got settled and his cousins closed it up."

Vivi had learned quickly when she had first come to town and worked briefly for Sandy Gilford's Exotics. She tended the orchids and water flowers until Sandy died of cancer and the shop closed up a few months ago. Now, her savings are almost gone. Vivi needs this job.

"I promise I will be an asset to the Home Center garden department." Vivi visualizes her own orange vest with maybe half of the Employee of the Month pins on it that Cheryl's vest featured. She has learned this on You Tube. Visualize success! Visualize success!

Cheryl watches Vivi construct her case, hold her own against her rough edged, country versus city bullshit. Vivi is enough of a scrapper for her so Cheryl decides to soften a bit.

"I'm not discriminating. It would actually be good for me if you take the job. We need to keep our diversity numbers up. Too bad you're not a person of color." Viv isn't sure how to respond to that one.

"I am sure I can keep those philodendrons happy enough to attract my commission. And your approval." Cheryl doesn't look up. "I can handle a few philodendrons," Vivi sniffs firmly, finding her footing.

Cheryl gets straight to the point. "You sure you can haul dirt?" hefty Cheryl asks. Her greasy bang hangs over her right eye in defiance of the strict job codes she lives by. "We're not a gourmet taste. Right?" Cheryl fingers her work medals, making sure they are all pinned upright above her left breast.

Vivi nods.

"I mean, the rich guys only come here when they're slumming and you probably have to do shifts in paint and lighting. That work for you?"

"Sure. I've done a bit of decorating. I think I can handle it."

"Not decorating. Carrying boxes to the forklift. Getting stock from the back warehouse."

"Right." Vivi needs this job. She wishes she didn't feel so out of her element. But then, she often does and pushes through anyway.

"Okay. You start ghost shift," Cheryl says. "10:00 p.m. til 6:00 a.m. You get a lot of contractors coming in those hours. Setting up big orders. You handle it?"

Vivi was not going to be deterred by the late night hours or even try to claim ageism again. She was fine and needed to clinch it.

"Ghost shift? Well, okay. Yes, I can handle ghosts."

"We haven't seen any lately," Cheryl says dryly.

Vivi's smile is weak. "Joke! I can also help with garden design if that's ever something folks need around here."

Cheryl gives her the fish eye. "Fork lift, hauling dirt, working warehouse. Got it?"

"Yes."

"Oh, and see this gal." Cheryl hands her a card. "She'll be the final decider, unofficially that is." Cheryl turns in her swivel chair . "She's actually a great gal. She'll be a good friend to have in a new place." Cheryl slips her a card. It says TARA'S TAROT. WALK INS WELCOME.

Cheryl watches as she reads it.

"Go see her," she says with a smile. "You won't be sorry."

It's been two years since Vivi settled in Rhinecliff near the hip college where her old friend Vikram teaches. At first, she sought work as a landscaper, but this is New England and planning a garden in L.A. isn't the same as shoving back years of poison ivy and long established trees in the green of the eastern countryside. No one needs clever irrigation tricks and not even the rich clients who come up to weekend really care what species of forsythia they plant. Instead, locals want to know if you have a mower you can ride and if it has a plow attachment for winter. Gardening is seasonal work in the land of four seasons. "Home Center is a good break," she thinks, "Safe haven for the winter."

Vivi arrives at four at Tara's place, still trying to figure out why she has decided to do a reading with the local mystic. She knows Cheryl wouldn't really fire her if she didn't consult with Tara.

"Well, my days aren't exactly full," she thinks to herself as she walks across the squeaky floors of the converted house on Main Street. Tara's parlor is in the former kitchen of the house, and the old linoleum groans in welcome as she steps through the door. A small bell sounds and the smell of the old wood and long ago floor glue welcome her as well.

"Hey!" A friendly voice calls out. "I'm in back. Out in a minute."

Vivi can't figure out where the voice is coming from. And then an ample woman about forty years old steps out to greet her. Tara is short and round with straw blond hair piled on top of her head. She's wearing a flowery polyester top, the kind that is supposed to hide the carb bingeing of the weeks before, but instead just heightens the affect. She is carrying a large cardboard box which she shoves onto the counter.

"Hey! Knew you were coming. You like my place? I consulted the cards before I rented and it showed a 4 of Wands, so I knew I was good."

"I'm . . ."

". . . Vivi. Cheryl told me to be on the lookout for you."

Tara hums a little tune as she straightens the box on the counter. "Have a seat, Viv." She says. "I just got a new box of stuff I want to put out. Cool, huh?"

Tara opens the cardboard box and takes out a couple of dream catchers and four or five decks of cards. Vivi can see that they aren't new.

"I get everything on eBay for the store. Why pay the going rate? I have to make a profit somewhere." She continues to put out the decks in no apparent order and hang the two dream catchers on the knobs of the cabinets above the sink.

"There! That should work."

In a grand gesture, Tara grabs a curtain and pulls it across the sink and appliances and it creates a cozy space for her table, lava lamp and two chairs.

"Magic," says Tara. "Here's where I do my readings."

"Clever," Vivi says, beginning to admire Tara's pluck.

"I'm open Monday through Thursday eleven to seven though I mostly work online on that Psychic website during that time. Even though they take more than half of what I earn, I do okay."

She sits and settles. Takes a deep breath and turns her full attention to Vivi.

"So, Cheryl sent you here," says Tara, making small talk. Vivi can feel a shift in attention in the room like she is being warmly scrutinized by lovely aliens.

"She told me it was a requirement if I wanted to work for her. Said

Home Center workers need to 'be in the know,'" Vivi says this a little embarrassed. She's never been to a reader before despite all her years in California.

"She's just trying to keep me in business. Otherwise I'd move in with her and the cousins and the parents and she'd have another mouth to feed!" Tara laughs loudly, shaking her head. She is jolly with her belly and flowered top and draping blue skirt with stars and moons on the hem. "And you might guess, this mouth likes to be fed!"

Tara laughs again. Vivi smiles despite herself. Tara asks, "You like plants?"

"I was a gardener in California. But here, I have to toe the line," says Cheryl. I am committed to hauling mulch, selling houseplants and earning a living. And I faked my way through the computer training. Ready to go!"

They have settled into their chairs and Tara is tossing some cards, shuffling them and getting a feel. She flips over three cards.

"Oh, my dear. Some bleak times, past, yes?"

Vivi is startled by this pronouncement. "Well, it's been a time of change, I'd say."

"Change?" says Tara. "You betcha. This Tower card is about the whole thing coming crashing down. But it's in the past position. See here? This is the present," she shows Vivi the 7 of cups. It's a picture of a man taking a look at a whole gallery of possibilities. "Look at him," Tara says. "He's got lots of things to choose from."

"Well, that sounds good," says Vivi tentatively.

"Not bad. Don't get over infatuated with the possibilities. And the last one . . . here. The Hermit. Yep."

"What's that mean?"

"Oh it's fine. Just a time to go inside and let things percolate. Inner wisdom and all that. Not a bad sentence!" Tara laughs again. "Now. Anything specific on your mind?" Tara continues to flip cards. "So," she says. "Who is this guy? This King keeps showing up. King of Cups? He fell out of the deck twice while I was shuffling. "Who is this guy who won't leave you alone?"

Vivi is mystified. "How did you . . . ?"

"Oh, it's not magic. The cards just know, that's all. They pick up what you bring. Who is this guy?"

"Well . . ." Vivi is not eager to give away her secrets.

"Did he wear a baseball cap? My head's itching like crazy."

"It was red. Yes. Jake." says Vivi, reluctantly. "It's probably Jake. My husband. Well, he was, he is . . . he's dead." Vivi shrugs, unsure if she is being casual or displaying psychosis.

Tara laughs again. "Well, he may be dead but he's not a shrinking violet. The guy won't stop talking!"

"That doesn't surprise me."

Tara nods her head and closes her eyes. "So, he tells me, he's sorry, please forgive him . . ."

"You're kidding." Vivi shifts uncomfortably as she recognizes the phrase that Jake offered in the note he left. It's hard to think of it as his suicide note. But, he put the note in a bag of pills. And he didn't wake up that morning after their fight.

"Yep. He says that to identify himself." Vivi is startled and gathers her ire as a flak jacket.

"Well, tell him to leave me alone! He can't come with me! He's dead and he's still driving me crazy. I mean it! I'm done with it! He shows up in my dreams . . . as my . . . He keeps showing up and I'm done. I'm done!"

Vivi is getting panicky. All this hocus pocus stuff is not part of her bury-and-conquer plan for the future. She thought this was behind her and she is none too happy with images of Jake being stirred up as she's working so hard on making this new life.

"Okay. Okay now. Not to worry. Just talk to him."

"Talk to him?!"

"'*Talk to me, Vivi,*' he is saying. Did you help him figure stuff out?"

"He used to say I told his story to him. Explained him to him. But he's dead. Forget it. This is crazy."

"He needs you to keep doing it." Vivi shifts in her chair ready to rise. Tara is steady. She knows what she knows. "He promises he will leave you alone but every now and then, he still needs you to talk to him. He's trying to figure out why he came in to be with you in the first place."

Vivi is ready to bolt. "I'm not sure I'm comfortable . . . with . . . I thought I was done with this!"

"Relax," says Tara. "There are no real mistakes. So, this guy, this Jake, he wants you to know he's sorry and well, he'll be around." Tara closes her eyes to listen. "You know, to help out. He can't seem to make sense of . . . well, he says he loves you still but he can't figure out why really."

"What is that supposed to mean?"

Tara listens quietly. Then, she says, "Was he a story teller?"

"Well, he wanted to make movies. I mean he made bad movies."

Tara smiles. She says quietly. "He says he never wrote a love story that worked. He says maybe you will tell him why."

"I have no idea what that means," says Vivi, a little too fast. She can feel herself being crowded and she just hates that she can't be cool and let this roll off her back.

"That's okay. You will." Tara says simply.

Vivi looks around the shop. She sees the blue curtain and the silly folding table and chairs. She wants out, but before she bolts Tara says, "Just acknowledge him when it's right. You can always come and talk to me when you're confused. I mean til death do us part, but he's not really totally dead yet. So, technically . . ."

Vivi finds it remarkable that she is sitting in this shop with this chatty gal in a flowered top, discussing the intricacies of her marriage and its vows, which apparently are not fulfilled quite yet.

"Thanks so much, Terry. I'll be heading out now," Vivi says firmly, her heart beating a little too fast.

"Tara. And you'll be back. That's fine. Listen, if you feel like leaving an online review you can go to this website . . ." and when Tara turns to get her card, Vivi stands and walks straight out of the shop, down the stairs to the parking lot and into her car. And hates that her heart is racing and hands shaking. Again.

Vivi slams out of Tara's shop and gets into her Saab station wagon, a remnant of her L.A. life. She is not due at work until ten at night so she jams the car into gear and heads to the mountain road up near Route 6. The views of the mountains up there remind Vivi of her drives along Mulholland in L.A. as she was trying to make sense of Jake's death, the fact that there was no money, and that she would have to start a whole new life.

No matter, the new life has started. She's been east for two years. She's not having dreams about Jake anymore of him trying to come back to seduce her, make her laugh, or find a way back into her heart. She's no longer furious about the way he squandered their money on stupid movie projects and how he took a lover who then managed to take everything they had together. She's through it! She's done. The radio coos Beach Boys at her. "I wish they all could be California girls."

"Forget it. What good did that do me? I made it. I'm here. I'm . . ." Vivi arrives at the pull out at the top of the rise. She turns in, breathes deep and gets out of the car. "Safe."

Here high above the town Vivi feels better. She floats naturally into the landscape easing her boundaries and the chatter ceases.

The view is misty even at this time of day. The blue of the mountains rise to hit haze. The pamphlets at the Visitors Center said there used to be a small community on that rise long time past. She sits and gazes and lets herself travel into that hollow where something good is always waiting for her. She can feel how easily she can leave her body, float out and dunk herself in the mist, allowing herself the luxury of being washed by light. The image of a young woman, naked, lithe, and easy comes to her. The woman is washing in a river. She has a child playing nearby. The image is not separate from her. It seems to be her, or once was. Vivi leaves it at that. Simple, this reunification. It always seems to rise from that hollow and surround her with the possible. This is her safe place. She calms, gets back into the car and sits for a moment gazing out at the light as it shifts.

A small bird shoots like a dart from a pine and sails in the current, confident and showy. He swoops down near her and comes close enough for her to see the gray and blue of his round strong body. Vivi notices him and how he masters the down drafts and makes it all look easy. It was mention of Jake that sent her here to this place of calm. If only Jake had been that deft, she thought. But she prefers to leave him and that bird, out of her thoughts.

She starts her car, appreciates the way the sky is giving way to the next color coming in. She stops at the big Topper's grocery store on the way home for chips and guacamole, and allows the fluorescent light to bake her back into her shell. Then, she heads to her small apartment in town to prepare for the night shift.

Chapter 2

On That Morning. Two Years Earlier.

The sun was hot for seven in the morning, even in L.A. Vivi sat on the green bench in the garden. She had opened their bedroom door and seen Jake not moving. She had grabbed the plastic bag full of his pills from the side table and gone to the garden. She could hear her mother's firm but quiet voice in her head. "Vivian. Go back to the bedroom. Open the curtains. Look at your husband."

Instead, she looked at the plastic bag in her hand. It was moist. The slip of paper inside was softening. She reached in and read the note. Her tears dropped one by one onto the cloudy mess. She didn't move, burning, burning in the light.

"I'm sorry. Please forgive me. Thank you. I love you." Vivi read the note nestled in the sleeping pills. They had quarreled the night before and she had slept in the guest room.

Her life swelled up around this violation, choking her still. But she did something though she did not remember it later. She saw him, shook him, called his name. She reached for her cell phone, hot and burning, and dialed her friend Ellen. Vivi wouldn't remember anything or what she said but then Ellen was there.

"Oh Christ, honey," Ellen said. "You're burned to a crisp. How long have you been sitting here?" Ellen hurried inside and got a cool cloth for her friend.

Vivi sat on the couch in the living room while Ellen made the calls from the kitchen and then Ellen opened her arms and Vivi, red-faced and lobster-clawed, wept and wept and wept.

After Ellen left, Vivi sat up on the sofa, not moving until dawn.

At first light, Vivi scanned the room searching for something to root her. She landed on the picture of Jake on the beach, in a small plastic frame. The one with sand dripped on his head. He looked like a happy Buddha, she thought. Or, as Vikram would say, an Indian sadhu. Jake had always found that picture annoying.

Next to the picture was the small Indian statue that Vikram, Jake's Hunter College roommate, gave them as a wedding present. And a picture of the three of them, Vikram, Jake, and Vivi at a family party many years earlier.

She picked them all up and held them in her hands. The statue of Vishnu and Lakshmi, celestial lovers, came alive. Lakshmi's legs twined around her lover like snakes, his four arms flinging out to conduct the cosmos. All those arms made her feel safe. Vivi fell into them and finally closed her eyes.

Jake's parents had insisted that Jake's remains be buried in New Rochelle despite the shiva in Los Angeles where everyone in the "Business" lived.

"Shelley," Ellen said on the long distance call. "Vivi needs to do this here in L.A. The shiva in L.A."

"But we can't bury him in L.A! He has to be here in New Rochelle!"

"Shelley. Jake wanted to be cremated. You can have the remains. And have whatever you want when this is over."

"Where's Vivi? Why can't I talk to Vivi?"

"Vivi asked me to help her. Her husband just died. She needs to do it her way."

"Oy. You think Bernie and I aren't bereft? My only son! So young . . ."

"Shelley. I am asking you to do this. Jake would have wanted it here as well. Then, Viv will send you the remains. You can bury him there."

"Cremated? What kind of a Jew gets cremated . . . willingly?"

Ellen paused hoping this was a rhetorical question.

"Shelley, for Chrissakes." Bernie spoke in the background. "Shut up, already. Let's go bury our son."

"We can't bury him! He'll be dust." There is a long dense quiet that almost crushes the connection. Bernie took the phone. "We'll be there," said Bernie. "Tell Vivi we'll stay at the Commodore. Tell her not to burn him til we see him."

"Yes. Thanks, Bernie. I will."

Shelley and Bernie had grudgingly come out for the week. They were happy with the deli platters from Nate and Al's and had a few friends locally connected with Bernie's factory where Jake had worked for several years, so they were not completely at a loss. Vivi handled that week to her own liking. It was a good strong stand. Her friend Ellen supported her. Still, Vivi remembered it only as moving through toxic rooms of crushing haze. Later, she would not have one image to soothe her as she navigated her healing.

Chapter 3

The Shiva and the Shiva Plates

The morning after the shiva—the Jewish week of mourning where family and friends gather to support the bereft—ended, the garden was still strafed with food and errant prayer books stuffed in clefts of the towering butterfly bush. The house was quiet and straightened, but straightened by friendly folks who wiped the sink down with Vivi's linen napkins and put the serving platters on the living room sofa to dry. She wrestled with Jake's mother's punchbowl, retrieved from a dusty closet, impossible to fit back in its place. Maybe it sensed that things were different now. No way Vivi could keep the house with all the debt that Jake left. Unless there was a windfall from somewhere. She already had her eye on the realtor who could help her get the best price.

She wiped cleanser off the radio cord and threw out the stiffening challah bread and an entire aluminum tray of coleslaw and pickles. Her red napkins were basted with crushed raisins and chocolate chips. She heaved the whole mess into the sink and watched as the last crumb yielded to the growl of the disposal.

All those movie types, Jake's pals with the baseball caps and bellies who had swapped stories and dreams of movie greatness at the coffee spot at Farmers Market came to the Shiva. The food was free and they stuffed it, trying to digest the fact that dreams can end before they are completed. No one who came by could sit in that truth. It made the house itchy and full of discontent. Vivi longed to get on with her life.

Jake's "business partner," Carol, trying to make things better, apparently had come in when Vivi wasn't home and taken away her favorite plates, the blue ones from the thrift store, replacing them with a brand new set she found on sale at TJ Maxx. Vivi had come back from making the funeral arrangements looking for the comfort of green salad against blue willow and was faced with a pattern of black and white oblongs instead. Carol left a note, "Jake liked things black and white." Screwball.

Carol had been especially distraught. She had not aged well, Carol. At least, that's what Vivi had always thought when she watched Carol at the back table conspiring with Jake over some movie treatment they were sure was going to finally make millions. The whole thing tired Vivi out. *"All that hoping and dreaming, all that panting after things that should have come years ago"* kept Vivi off balance and irritated. Her dreams ran to simpler things like doing the possible and making peace with what came. She had learned from years of 'making do' that being happy with what came along was an easier road. Life was bumpy enough for Vivi. While her single mom worked, she did her homework in their shared bedroom at Aunt Shirley's house. "It didn't kill her to not scotch tape pom poms to the flocked wall paper," she said. So, she worked at the corner drug store on Saturdays and never considered a day without trying to earn money through her teen age years. For Vivi, it was easier to accept going to the local college than pining for the scholarship to Rome. Things were as they were. Life was good enough. Making do with the gifts that came along built the survival muscle that her mother was always talking about when she would explain to Vivi once again why things are not always like a movie, but they are still good enough.

Vivi heard a car rumble up to the house. She opened the door to see Carol standing there in the morning light looking feral, like a hungry coyote come down from the canyon for a last chance at a tasty kitten before her retreat to the lair. Carol stood in the driveway.

"I want my plates," she said.

"The ones you left me?"

"I want my plates. The oblongs. The black-and-whites. I know you have them and I know you hate them and I want them."

"Um. Sure. Come on in."

Carol looked as if she'd been dunked in ashes.

"Carol. You okay?" Vivi stepped carefully, her path strewn with cracked porcelain before she even reached the kitchen.

"Okay?" Carol looked at her. "What the hell does that mean?"

Carol's eyes brimmed over. Tears tumbled past clumped mascara and sunspots and dribbled all the way down her face to rest on her cheek jowl. She was a mess.

"Just give me the plates!"

"Carol. Let's sit down. Have a cup of tea. It's a rough time for both of us."

"I hate tea. I hate it. I love coffee. And so did Jake. He loved coffee, strong and hot. And you never made him coffee."

"He has terrible acid indigestion. Can't digest anything. Like a baby with all his allergies and hives and . . ."

Carol stopped short and looked at her rival.

"Had," Carol said. "He had. He's dead. In case you didn't notice. He's dead. Goddamn it!"

"Breathe," Vivi said. Being in Vivi's kitchen with Jake gone was too much for Carol. Carol began shaking her head, desolate. Her eyes came up to find Vivi's. The two women balanced on a fine thread of ownership of a man neither of them fulfilled. Carol blinked first.

"I gotta go," she said. "Your blue ones are in the closet. I hid them."

"I found them, thanks."

Carol nodded and left the kitchen, walking slowly across the living room, out the front door, and into her banged up Jeep Cherokee. The engine caught. Carol put on her aviator glasses and pulled away from the curb.

The oblong black and white dishes sat embarrassed on the microwave, forgotten, trying to disappear, like a kid whose parent came to pick them up from a playdate, drunk. Vivi opened the kitchen cabinet to check again that her Blue Willow was in place. She went to the linen closet and folded the towels three times, lining them up with each other. Ellen called her twice during that process and finally ended their last conversation with ironic praise.

"Boy, you're really in charge of that linen closet."

Vivi took her favorite cup, a sturdy mug from her uncle's drugstore back in Columbus, and poured just the right amount of water over garden fresh mint to let it steep. She felt sure she would find her potholders soon. She looked down to see a small worm fall off the mint leaf, swimming in circles for its life.

Chapter Four

Carol Redux

Vivi needed to make peace in some way with Carol. She told herself she was doing the right thing. The modern thing, to come to détente with her husband's lover. Carol was a partner in all the film properties she and Jake had pitched that might sell and help keep Vivi afloat. Vivi needed those black-and-white oblong plates out of her house.

Carol lived in the Vine Hills. That area of L.A. full of odd and charming cottages built as love nests for the paramours of would-be movie moguls. More than one young chippie getting off the train from the Midwest found herself happily hidden behind bougainvillea, awaiting her Big Boy to show up.

Carol had lived up there for twenty years, Jake had told Vivi. Waiting for romance and life to find her, Carol loved the beauty of hiding until she realized she had made herself so obscure that no one cared to find her. She had to figure out how to earn money after she was dropped from her low-level development job at a small production company. There was some temping at the studios and a stint answering phones at an architectural office in Beachwood. Then, a lucky death of an aunt in Illinois left her enough to buy her cottage and start pitching movies. She met Jake at the Farmers Market gatherings. She had been dating Marty Fein at that time. He dropped dead of a heart attack, and then there was Jake. Carol was not born under a lucky star.

"Carol? Carol, you home?"

Vivi managed to parallel park her car on the incline and jam on the emergency break. She found a couple of big rocks and wedged them behind her back tires.

"Carol? It's Vivi." Vivi knocked on the door. No answer. The curtains were drawn but there was a radio playing back in the kitchen.

Vivi placed the big box of dishes on the front porch and leaned into the window.

"Carol, if you can hear me, I left the dishes here for you. I thought we could visit. I have some of Jake's things. His baseball cap, maybe a sweatshirt. Let me know if you'd like anything . . . Carol? Carol? I'm . . ."

The door opened. Carol was standing there with a cell phone at her ear.

"Oops, sorry . . . I . . ." Vivi whispered.

"I got somebody here now, Ned. I'm sure we can make a deal at Fox. They loved the idea." Carol lifted her chin. "I'll call you back." She looked at Vivi.

"Hi, Carol." Vivi smiled weakly.

"Hi."

"I left you . . ."

"Yeah. I heard you. No need."

"I brought back your plates."

"Not now, Vivi. I am trying to finish the deal on the script."

"The one you worked on with Jake? You sold it?"

"Stranger things have happened."

"That's wonderful. You know Jake cashed in his life insurance to make the last movie. I can really use the money." Vivi tried to smile, looking for a bridge to the woman in front of her.

Carol eyed Vivi and could not focus as a hurricane of ownership swept over her. Blown to her own island of "I, me, mine" with no travel junkets granted, Vivi was nowhere near paradise.

"Talk to your lawyer friend about that, Vivi. This screenplay is mine. He gave it to me. You're on your own."

Vivi shifted in her sandals but decided to stay put. "Carol. Isn't there some way we could talk?"

"What? So you can take what's mine. What Jake and I made together? What did you two ever make together? I gotta go."

"Carol. Stop" Vivi somehow needed Carol to know she never owned Jake. Neither of them did. "You know, Jake killed himself. Official. He left a note."

The wind immediately was sucked from the doorstep. Carol's eyes are stunted and fixed.

"You came here to tell me that? On my front porch? What kind of piece of shit are you?"

"Carol . . ." Vivi gathered her breath. She had not said that out loud before. She had not meant to be cruel. "I'm sorry. It's all so confusing."

"You killed him. He told me! He told me how you were killing him. Always criticizing him, never accepting who he was. Hell, you didn't even like him!"

"This is too crazy, Carol. I . . ."

"Why did you come here?"

"I thought you should know. I thought we should know. We should know it together!

Neither one of us could save him. He was on his own journey."

"Oh, fuck. Fuck this. Fuck you, fuck Jake." Carol stands stone still and closes the door.

Vivi can hear Carol's body slump against the door and heave moans.

"Holy Christ," she murmurs. "Holy fucking Christ."

Vivi stands there. No feeling. Nothing to say. No movement to make. Finally, Vivi hears Carol pull herself up and clump away against the wooden floors. Her voice faint from the kitchen.

"Ned. Yeah, I'm back." Her voice is wobbly. "Some piece of shit salesperson trying to sell me a bill of goods at the door." Vivi stood listening to this report of her nonexistence. "Yeah, at least a Jehovah's witness would leave something worth thinking about."

Vivi knew part of this performance was for her. For a moment she was fascinated how Carol's version of the truth was through a lens to which Vivi had no claim. Then, Vivi turned and found her way back to the Saab.

When she got back to her house she called Ellen. Ellen spent the next two weeks trying to secure Vivi's rights to the films Jake and Carol had pitched together. In the end, it was a no go. They could not prove to the Writers Guild that anything they wrote ever had Jake's imprint on it. All his notes were destroyed, nowhere to be found in the house. And Carol coughed up a note from Jake saying, "how brilliant you are. Everything we write you write and I have no part in it." Some deluded love note perhaps?

The bank account was empty. The life insurance long ago cashed in for the film in Jamaica. Even the safety deposit box that had his mother's pearls was empty. Vivi was broke and the only thing she had to sustain her was the house, already mortgaged, but with enough left to give her a bit of a new start. She could fight Carol and live on food stamps or she could take the next step. She put the house on the market.

Chapter 5

Puffing Up

The night before the first open house, Vivi paced the halls, hoping for a sign or something that might confirm that she and Jake had lived there as a couple for twenty years and that he had died in that bedroom. That their lives here were part of the place even though it was time to leave those things behind. The house was resistant to change, she knew it, and it had held some tough times. But she hoped it would forgive her sudden abandonment.

The house wanted to rest, too. She knew that. She knew it was a stretch to ask it to reconfigure itself for someone new, some new gathering of energies, it wasn't her fault. She had to sell it and move on. She was grateful for the years of shelter and how the house bent and embraced them both when they moved in to make their L.A. life. But after the first thrill of feeling young again, at the prospect of sheltering a new family, the house turned on her.

The house itself, just like Jake, was sick of Vivi and her contempt for ease and blue skies and a successful life. The house wanted to get back to the business of being beautiful and sincere and uncomplicated like the rest of the city. The house put its best foot forward, thrust its chin job into the night and tossed its Bosley curls. It wanted to live the good life with someone who wanted to live it well.

Vivi was surprised when the broker brought a huge platter of moo shu chicken from the chicest Thai place on Melrose for the brokers open house. She didn't think that food would entice the crowd, everyone so focused on their slim figures, but the Jags and Caddies, BMWs and Mercedes coups lined their cul de sac in search of a free lunch. The top brokers in L.A. nodded approvingly of the work she had done to keep the place looking great in between bites of rolled moo shoo held out far from silk blouses and Brooks Brother ties.

She had staged it well, getting rid of knickknacks and lots of black plastic bags of clothes and old magazines. She had changed out the old tile in the kitchen for granite, added under cabinet lighting and gotten rid of the original linoleum that Jake always hated. She replaced it with bamboo. Cabinets were refaced, showers refitted with steam and multiple shower heads. But once she completed the facelift with those fancy floors and trendy counters, the kitchen virtually spit at her when she crossed through the room.

The house was ready to go. Nasty and aloof and ready for its screen test, Mr. DeMille. It was lifted, puffed, scrubbed and sculpted. It sold in multiple offers and within ninety days, Vivi was homeless and solvent.

The night before she left L.A., Vivi went out to the garden. She walked from the butterfly bush she planted when she got the garden show on cable TV, to the poinsettia tree that grew despite itself after Vivi left the Christmas plant discarded near the mulch pile. She moved from corner to corner, touching the leaves, murmuring that she had no choice, that she couldn't take the entire garden with her wherever she was going and that she was grateful for the beauty that the garden had shared with her. The Dutch hornpipe was in bloom. That huge bulbous balloon of a flower was all puffed up and ready to burst into an elephant ear of color, reflecting all sound, all smell within its radius. It was an outrageous creation. It dripped like flesh when it opened, had no smell of its own, but instead an ineffable ugly wisdom that affirmed the truth that "as you sow, so shall you reap." It was an extraordinary product of the garden and Vivi respected it, admiring how it took over the fence and nearby trellis with its ganglia.

That was the thing about California. Things grew. And Vivi had thought they would grow, too. She and Jake. They would grow together, like slices of grafted root trees, they would grow strong in one tall ascension. She had been sure that they could make it. But she had to admit, they never did.

There was no light now except far away, behind clouds. Vivi wasn't sure that she'd even see a star once the clouds parted. Still, better to sleep out there with the plants she had some relationship with, than in the empty rooms, the closets and curtain-less window frames staring at her, gasping for air as they adjusted to their new state. There was no forgiveness and, out of respect for the house's feelings, she felt it better to take the garden's offer of a last night lodging.

She pressed the button on the plastic dial of the bed and heard the grind of the pump as it gathered garden air and shoved it into its plastic belly. The bed inflated. Vivi tested it. She went back inside and found her perfectly wrapped sleeping bag ready for the car. She had to admit she was sorry that she would have to roll it again, carefully, in the morning. That was always Jake's task and he did it very well, and with pride. Vivi would rather heap the thing in a corner but this evening, in her new state of moment to moment living, she enjoyed the way it snapped open and spread its down filled self across the slight rise of the mattress.

Vivi did not undress. She slipped into the welcoming pocket and settled in, her head covered, her eyes closed tight. She let her breath slip from her just the slightest bit and like an aching balloon, the air escaped with a moan and a weeping cadence of regret.

"I'm sorry, Jake. So very, very, sorry," she heard herself whisper. The words rode on her breath. They had been sitting on her ribs for days as she had scrubbed and tossed and ripped away the fabric of their home.

"Oh my God, what a mess of it I have made." Then, she heard the phrase in her ear. And the soft warmth of something, someone, urging her to repeat its rhythm.

"I'm sorry, please forgive me, thank you, I love you," the voice said.

"I'm sorry," said Vivi. "Please forgive me," she thought. "Thank you."

She paused here and felt the effort, the failure, the one step at a time.

She settled on her back, felt the relief of a cool breeze on her eyelids and above her the clouds parted to show the moon. She did not feel the slight pressure on the mattress next to her, the wrap of arms, the imprint and the way the breeze hummed "Whither thou goest, I go too. For now, anyway." And what was left of Jake and their life entered into Vivi, his new hitchhiker's paradise.

Chapter 6

Cement and Rubber

The road out of L.A. morphed from faux palm tree paradise into the belly of the dry and thirsty beast. Vivi's ambivalence for the wretched beauty of the parched hills had always puzzled her. The hills looked like lumpy giants covered by a scabrous pelt. Vivi had thought that someday she would come to understand why they slept in such discomfort, why the hills spoke so starkly to Jake. The sunlight through the driver's side window needled her bare left arm, reminding her to cover it with her tee shirt.

Vivi planned to head straight through to Vegas but when she did a drive through lunch in Barstow she found herself staring at the world's largest thermometer far longer than her double cheeseburger and chocolate malt lasted. She figured that she should fill up the Saab. It was a long way between gas stations on the freeway. And then, there were postcards she wanted even though she had no one who wanted to receive them. And then, she made a visit to the Ladies Room at the gas station that had lost its key. She waited while the girl behind the counter ran out to her car for the master. It all took longer than she had planned but, she needed the time, needed to shed some of the weight.

Back on the bleak highway to Vegas, she listened to the thrum of her tires against the pavement and then she saw it: Primm, Nevada, loomed like a neon satellite beckoning her to another planet. A concentration of light bulbs flashed against the incoming twilight. Promises winked from the billboard. A stretchy cowboy waved his mechanical hat! A great casino! Family friendly restaurants! Discount rooms and only an hour to Vegas! From the highway she could see a very large water slide next to Buffalo Bill's casino.

A night on the road was perfect.

Chapter 7

Primm Hologram

Vivi checked in and found herself ten flights up looking at scrub brush and bruised hills. Downstairs, the hotel was half dark and the cranky clerk told her they weren't open for the season yet, but she could have a room if she needed it. The relentless party promised by the billboards of Primm was nowhere to be found. Nevertheless, the skeleton crew and dinging bells of the slot machine called her. The place was just weird enough to provide refuge. She grabbed a waxy apple from the bowl on the desk and headed upstairs.

Leaving her overnight bag on the dresser, she felt like Sleeping Beauty falling into a trance. Her dreamless sleep was brittle like the cracking of piled brambles around her castle. The moon hit at her window but there was little else to hear her sigh, or the creak of the bed as she rolled trying to find comfort.

"Hi, Viv." Vivi heard the sigh now clearly, but it was another voice, not hers. "It is 2:42 in the a.m. and I'm wandering over your big wide Vegas bed!" Vivi sat straight up, stock still. "Surprise!"

She shook her head trying to locate what reality she was playing in. She felt a pressure grow around her shoulders, an awkward embrace she did not invite. She shook her head and whispered so only he could hear.

"Jesus Christ, Jake. Is this you?" She felt foolish, yet in full belief. It was so dark in the room. She wondered why she couldn't see anything through the window. But she knew he was there somehow.

"You're right. It's me." Vivi wondered if she heard his voice or felt it. "I know what you're thinking, Viv," he said. "I mean, it's kind of a feature of my current condition."

Brittle, like the creaking bramble around Sleeping Beauty's bed, that was the feeling in her neck, her back, her arms as she strained to locate herself and her senses.

"What do you want of me?" She spoke carefully.

"You can get in a car or go to another state, but even stopping at a tacky Vegas spot will not keep me gone."

Vivi looked toward the window again and now saw a jagged light seep out and spread, creating the figure of a man. The light blinded her, and hit her ears with its high pitched insistence.

"Let me touch you, okay? I mean, I'd really like to touch you and we're here in Vegas and . . . what happens in Vegas, stays in Vegas."

It must be Jake, she thought. Only he would quote a tacky commercial campaign. His eyes, or the light that formed his eyes, grew more round. Cylinders of pleading moved right into her body as strongly as when they made love as young ones. She felt the light seek her darkness, hoping to creep and cradle her once again. She did not melt to that touch. Instead she felt sheaths of ice form around her and, protected, she felt how the darkness lost its urgency. It went limp and resentful, the darkness, passion faded in their marriage. It was a familiar hollowing. He had filled the hollowing in their marriage with Carol. Vivi had ignored it and planted more perennials in the garden. The earth at least had been welcoming and warm to her touch.

"What do you want, Jake?"

The light shifted to a harsh fluorescence. "I'm stuck in the waiting room before the pearly gates," he said. "I can't get into heaven. They say, well . . . those of us who suicide, we have to stick around and figure out what went wrong. Maybe keep visiting til we figure it out. How's that for something to look forward to?"

"Jake, I can't help you. I don't know why. I don't know what I did. Or didn't do."

"Screw it. Let's fuck. Why not? I mean it would be a trip to fuck an angel, right?" She could feel the light pressing in against her. "Wouldn't it? Come on."

Vivi felt herself being pushed back on the bed. She felt the pillows come over and on top of her. A pressure against her stomach and against her jeans.

"Stop it," she said. "Stop what you are doing!" The pressure was growing on her chest, on her legs. "Leave me alone, Jake. I can't help you. I never could. I just wanted to love you and make a life."

"You were claimed by somebody else way before we got married." He was pressing her now. She felt his face against hers. She could feel his hands come alive and try to touch her, hold her head still. "Do you know what that does to somebody? To live with someone who never loved them!"

Vivi was totally confused. She felt her body shoved, she felt a pillow come up and over her throat, she felt the breath being squeezed from her. She wanted to protect what was new inside of her, whatever courage she had mustered since the death and selling the house. She needed that new seed that had lodged itself and would not let go. But, she wasn't sure if Jake was in there, too. Hanging on, riding her new resolve like a bronco.

"I won't let you go, Viv!"

"You decided to check out!"

Vivi rolled forcefully from the bed. She fell hard onto the floor and grabbed for the phone. "Help!" she said into the receiver. "Help! Help me, I don't know where I am!" The ringing on the line went unanswered. Vivi lunged for the bathroom and slammed the door. She flicked on the fluorescent fixture and stared hard into the mirror. There were scratch marks on her face and neck. She backed into the toilet seat and stumbled. The light went off in the tiled and porcelain room. She didn't know where to move. She could see the light from the other side of the door grow strong as it approached the bathroom. Then, she heard the brittle rustle of the brambles again. Like they were cracked and cracking in the wind. Like their thorns were heat seeking missiles, pelting her refuge, ready to destroy the walls she had built that would allow her to survive. Then, the light faded and one by one, like the last popped corn in the popper, the drumming in her ears and eyes fell away.

Vivi didn't move all night. At least she thought she didn't. She woke feeling the cool porcelain of the bathtub on her cheek. Light was hitting the desert.

She crept back into the bedroom, gathered her things and left. Maybe it was the waxy apple. Or a spell from the cranky clerk. Or just plain grief itself. But, Vivi was ready to put Primm and her visitation behind her.

Chapter 8

The Parents Poke Around

Every day, Vivi arrives in the Employee Lounge at Home Center to the smell of burnt coffee and greasy doughnuts. She dons her apron, her hat, and her gloves, and L.A. is eons away. That is fine with her. Cheryl is a fair boss. Jake's parents do not stay in touch after the unveiling of Jake's headstone. Until, a year after the unveiling, Vivi gets a note from Shelley that reads, "I finally found your address. Should we have lunch?" She folds the note, written hastily on a B'nai B'rith notepad, and puts it in her pile of monthly bills. Another debt to fulfill.

Shelley looks worn when she gets out of the car. She has lost weight and it looks as though she is letting the grey come in through the years of blonde. Bernie, cigar in jaw, comes around the back of the car and watches as his wife struggles out of the front seat. He stands there as if he is waiting for her to pass through him and onto the street. She manages, walks up to the door, and comes in. Then she realizes Bernie is still outside.

"Bernie! Come! What's with you?" She is laboring to hold the door open.

Bernie says nothing but steps forward behind his big glasses and his stogie. He sees Vivi first. Shelley opens her arms. "C'mere, Vivi darling.

Give me a hug. C'mere darling!" Vivi stands and they embrace and Shelley hangs on, catching her breath. "Oy," she says. "It's been too long, sweetheart."

Bernie says, "It's been a year. I paid for that stone a year ago."

A year after Jake died, the unveiling of the head stone was in New Rochelle. Vivi called Laura, Jake's cousin, but she couldn't make the trip. Vivi had written a note to Vikram when she arrived in Rhinecliff. Vikram was on a Fulbright.

"Back in the country in several months. Sorry to hear. Glad you will be nearby."

So, she was on her own.

The stone read, "Beloved son, husband, and creator." They had not asked Vivi her opinion. She had Jake's ashes in a Ralph's grocery bag. She handed them to the Rabbi. He waved them away.

"You can put them in the hole." It seemed he preferred not to dirty his hands. Vivi stooped down to place the bag in the hole.

"Oy, wait," Shelley cried. "Take that fahschlepta bag off. You couldn't get an urn? Why didn't we get an urn?"

Bernie grunted. "Shelley. Leave it."

Shelley lovingly took the small cardboard box that held the remains of her son out of the white plastic grocery bag. "It's heavy. I didn't know he would still weigh so much." She looked at the Rabbi.

"Put the box in the hole," the Rabbi said.

Shelley started to stoop down but looked so lost. Vivi stepped forward and put her arm around her mother-in-law. "Here. Let's do this together."

And they did. They each took a handful of dirt from the little pile next to the small rectangular hole and trickled the earth of New Rochelle upon its favorite son. Then, Shelley and even Bernie closed their eyes. The few aging friends who attended in high heels and oxfords shuffled their feet a little, not sure if they should applaud, and then they, too, stepped up to dribble dirt.

Back at the house, there was more deli. Maybe ten or twelve of Shelley and Bernie's friends softly sat around the living room while the football game called the shots.

Shelley did her best but the day was eating her alive.

"I have to rest, Tatehleh," she said to Vivi. "I have to lie down."

"I know, Shelley. I'm going to take off."

"What? Already? Wham bam thank you, ma'am."

"It's been a long day for all of us. I have a two hour ride ahead of me."

"Drive safe, Viv. Stay in touch," said Bernie.

"Good bye, Viv. Good luck. We'll talk." Shelley kissed the air beside Vivi's cheek and headed for the bedroom shaking her head. "She comes, she goes. I don't know, Bernie. This is not a family. We're like weeds. Allergic to each other."

"Tatehleh!" Shelley opens her arms wide. "Great to see you. I gotta sit down."

Vivi leads them to the corner table at the Matchbox Cafe with a view of the Green.

"So, chit-chat!" Shelley laughs with a big grin. She is as uncomfortable with this as Vivi. Even so, Vivi smiles.

"Yes, I know you hate chit-chat, darling," Shelley continues. "Did I tell you that our cat died?"

"Hadn't heard."

"I was driving Laura crazy. She kept talking about some cosmic consciousness thing. Meanwhile, I couldn't stop pishing. Crying all day long."

"But mostly we have forty-five pounds of kitty litter and cat chow," says Bernie. "I'll be damned if I'll throw it out!"

They order lunch. Eggs Benedict. Quiche.

"No lox? Bagels? It's Sunday," says Bernie.

"'Goyische coup'," says Shelley. She smiles at Vivi. "He's a man of creature comforts."

"Yes," Viv lamely offers. "This place is known for its popovers."

"Laura tells me you're working at a Garden Center? You like it?" Bernie is stuffing the homemade popover in next to his cigar.

"It's a Home Center. Actually. A Home Center," says Vivi firmly. She likes to tell the truth when she can find it.

"Really?" says Shelley steadily. "That must have benefits? That's good."

"Yes," says Vivi. "Lots of benefits and vacation hours and all the grown up stuff."

"Nothing wrong with working for a living," says Bernie. "I said that to your husband more than once."

"He worked hard. Very hard. He just had some disappointments. That's all," sniffs the mother. "But I don't understand something, Vivian. It's something that has been on my mind for two years now. I have to say it to you."

Vivi looks up. She can feel herself ready to launch if Shelley comes at her.

"It's just that, we didn't know he was sick. He was a young man. We didn't know."

Vivi smiles vaguely. "Yes. It was a surprise."

"And," Shelley says vaguely but with intent, "It has come to my attention that the police actually investigated his death. Is that true?"

Vivi looks at her quiche and wonders how many eggs it takes to make it that yellow. "Yes. It is true. You reading police reports?"

"Come on, Vivian" says Bernie. "He was our son."

"How come you didn't tell us?" Shelley is holding herself especially upright.

"I didn't tell you because nothing came of it." Vivi says. "There was no foul play. Did someone tell you otherwise? Carol maybe?"

"Carol," says Bernie. "Who's Carol?"

"Jake's writing partner," says Vivi. "The one who refused to share writing credit for Jake's screenplay. The one who forced me to sell the house, to have to move on."

"Actually it was the lawyer. You had a lawyer. We asked her why."

"Ellen is my friend," Vivi states, as if confirming the fact for herself.

"Yes. I know. A friend who told the truth. We called her when we were trying to get a hold of you!" Shelley is beginning to bubble over.

"You said that you needed money. But that house was worth a great deal of money, Vivian," Bernie is on it now.

"How come you're working at a Home Center? What happened to all the money? The life insurance? The house? We helped to pay off that house," Shelley says.

They are a tag team with a double bone in their maws.

Vivi swallows. "Shelley. Bernie. Please don't ask questions that you don't want the answers to."

"Bernie, did you hear what she said? What are you talking about? We are his parents. What the hell is going on?"

"Jake was a good provider, Vivi. I know that. I paid him." Bernie is exercised now, breathing heavily and even poking that cigar in Vivi's face. That was something she had rarely seen.

"Bernie, please."

"I mean my son was maybe a dreamer, maybe not the best business man, but he made money. This I know." The cigar comes out of his mouth and Bernie waves it through the air.

"He made money. He spent money. What's the difference? He's gone and nobody is happy about that." Vivi is not sure how to steer this conversation. She hates that she sounds so tough, is so leathery in the face of the truth.

"We want to know what's going on. Why are you broke? Did you pay someone to knock him off? It doesn't make sense!" Shelley is beside herself, but she is talking low and fast and hot into her cold coffee.

"Shelley, for Chrissake!" Thank God that Bernie is disgusted.

"Excuse me," Vivi says, "I'm going to the Ladies . . ." Vivi needs a moment to figure out how to play this one. She doesn't want to lambast them with the facts. Who knows why Jake did what he did? Maybe it was just drama. Maybe the whole thing was a mistake. Shelley grabs at her hand and pulls her back in her seat. A glass of water tips.

"Shelley. Stop!" Bernie, again, having no luck with his wife.

"What are you doing?" Vivi is surprised to hear herself so loud and looks around the restaurant. There is no one there except the one waitress and the cashier who is reading the Sunday paper.

"Problem, Miss?" The cashier is interested now and she comes to the table. "Sorry, but you're gonna have to take it outside if you're not gonna play nice. What's wrong with you? It's Sunday, have a Bloody Mary and chill."

Bernie gets up and throws a fifty-dollar bill on the table and storms out. Vivi escapes to the bathroom, leaving Shelley alone, clutching her cold cup of coffee.

Vivi marches to the back of the restaurant and then turns and comes back to the table. She sits down and grabs Shelley's hand. She talks urgently, like her words are merciless acid, and speed will lessen their impact on everyone.

"Shelley. Your son committed suicide. Your son spent all the money we had. Your son was in terrible debt. Your son was having an affair with Carol. Your son was a mess and he didn't have anywhere to turn."

Shelley's eyes look as if they are going to explode.

"He had you! Where were you? You didn't love him enough!"

"Jake stopped looking for me a long time ago." Vivi is vaguely aware that this scene is feeling like a Thursday night family drama. Jake would like it. Neither woman moves. The repulsion they feel for each other binds them. Vivi can see Bernie walking the street in front of the restaurant sucking his stogie, twisting it. Shelley cocks her head and looks at Vivi.

"I don't understand you, Vivian. I never have. But Jake loved you and so we made it all work, as a family. He was all we had. So his death is ours as much as yours. It is cruel of you to think of his death as yours alone." Vivi meets her gaze. "If he did commit suicide, and you did not save him, help him, throw him a line, then shame on you. And keeping that from us . . ."

"I didn't want to hurt you. I didn't really believe it myself."

"Never mind," says Shelley, as clear as a bell. "You kept this secret from us. You kept it for your own. But mothers come before wives. They are the beginning and the ending of the story. I'm sorry you will never understand that."

Shelley reaches for her purse and finds a small compact and her lipstick. She opens the tube and smooths the light pink across her lips, cleansing them, closing them for now. Then, she gets to her feet and takes her purse in her hand.

"I have your family china," Vivi says. "When I get the boxes shipped from L.A. I will make sure that it goes back to your clan. Right now, working at the Home Center is about all I can handle."

Vivi takes Shelley's hand as Shelley stands there. She can't look at her but she holds her hand.

"Every day I try to plant something," Vivi says. "I really do. I try to grow something new. Every day I try to put a seed in the ground, or pinch off a dead leaf, or fertilize a failing plant in Jake's name. Every single day I do what I can to make life."

Shelley looks down at her.

"You two should have tried again. You should have made a baby."

Vivi's eyes catch the clock as it ticks to the next minute.

"I water philodendrons. Keep them shiny and placid. If you want grandchildren that's the best I can do. That is all I can do. That's as much life as I can muster at the moment."

Shelley lowers her head so the waitress and cashier cannot see her tears. Vivi counts to ten. Having a baby was never an option after the first week of their marriage. Vivi lets go of Shelley's hand, stands up, and walks out to the street, does not acknowledge Bernie, and keeps walking. Maybe she'll scrub the floor when she gets home. She looks forward to having her body in contact with solid ground.

Chapter 9

The Birthday Party in New Rochelle. When They Got Engaged.

"Is it a paperweight? What the hell is it?" Jake smiled, playing to the crowd as he opened the small birthday box Vivi handed him. Cousins, aunts, uncles, a few friends were gathered in his parents' dining room for Jake's birthday.

"It's a vajra, an Indian meditation object," Vivi said softly, keeping an eye on Jake for his approval.

"Ooh, Indian!" said Shelley, overhearing. "Really? You know Jake's roommate is Indian. He's here somewhere."

"Yes, Shelley. We've met." She shifted back to her fiancé. "I liked it. I thought you might like it."

"It looks like one of my napkin rings!" Shelley offered, on to the next thing. "Vivi darling, help gather up the wrapping paper. I want to get the dessert on. "

"What is it, Vivi?" asked Laura, Jake's cousin, through her oversize tortoiseshell glasses. "I didn't hear."

"We can use it as a paperweight." Vivi smiles with chagrin. "For all those pages of screenplay Jake's going to write."

Jake's eyes twinkled as she stated their marriage plan. He would write movies and she was going to support his genius. Well, maybe she'd get a job to help out.

It was Vivi's third family gathering since they announced their intention to get married and move to California two months earlier. Shelley had been summoning the family together whenever possible to make sure they approved of Jake's choice, or at least this is what it felt like to Vivi.

"Don't get paranoid, Viv," Jake had said to her. "My mom is going to miss us!" He grinned "I mean, me!"

"She just can't bear the thought of losing her darling prince! And to me! Her rival!"

"That's what your Psych degree gave you? Psychic insight!"

He was always smiling as if he knew something nobody else did and was enjoying a joke that maybe he'd let you in on. She liked that about him. Being included in his jokes. Being part of his certainty that the world was fun and funny and easy to navigate. Things were not so smooth for Vivi. She was always trying to figure out what it felt like to be her and so far, when she could locate herself, she wasn't often sure.

Vivi sneezed violently and looked down. "Oh, Jake! The cat!"

"You remember Rufus, mom's house cat? He's very protective."

Vivi immediately felt her eyes begin to fill with liquid.

"I thought you told me your Mom would leave the cat in the basement," she whispered.

"He loves me! What can I do?"

Vivi looked down to see a huge growling tom at her feet. The creature grinned like his Cheshire cousin, circling, preparing to mark its territory at her feet.

"Shelley, your cat is ready to spray the room for Chrissakes!" boomed Bernie, enthroned at the head of the table, deep into his second single malt scotch.

The crowd laughed. Vivi sneezed. Laura cried, "Kick the cat!" God bless Cousin Laura. "Get that thing out of here!"

Laura, white wine in hand, hooked Rufus with her foot and heaved him into the kitchen.

"There, Vivi. You're safe." Laura smiled at her through those glasses that saw more than most. She was about to throw her arms around Vivi and give her a squeeze but Jake sidled in on the conversation as if realizing he had some loyalty issues to resolve.

"Sorry about the cat, Viv."

"Jeez, Cousin Jakie, choose sides and Vivi better win!" Laura moved toward the kitchen. "You need help, Auntie Shelley?"

"Yes, darling. Can you get the cake plates out?"

Jake stood awkwardly with his fiancée. She wished he'd taken her in his arms in front of everyone and hugged her and told her he loved her and the gift. Especially with her eyes running and her throat closing up by the second.

"It's silver, Jake," she croaked. "You can always sell it when you need money for your next feature." She sneezed for emphasis and Cousin Laura handed her a paper napkin as she passed back toward the dining table with all the cake plates.

"Hear that everyone? There's a supportive wife, Jakie!" said Laura. "Maybe if I had given Billy more gifts he could've traded in for cash, our marriage would have lasted longer!" Everyone laughed.

"It's great!" Jake gave Vivi an air kiss and lightly draped his arm over her shoulder as if to show her to the assembled. The crowd clapped and laughed.

"Watch out," Bernie said. "That 'fahrshtoonkeneh' cat is rubbing against your leg again."

"Oy, Jake," called Shelley from the kitchen. "Pick up the cat and kiss it a little. I won't have anyone peeing on my birthday party."

"Jake, I'm so allergic."

"The cat is whining! It needs some love." He bent down and gathered Rufus next to him. "C'mere you big fur ball. You love me, don't you? You know it's my birthday!"

Rufus purred. Shelley called from the kitchen. "Cake, everybody!"

"Happy birthday Jake, my handsome son!" she says as she enters. "Here, Jake, make a wish!"

Jake turned away to swallow his scotch and to go for birthday cake on the table, burying his fingers into the cat's coat as the crowd sang.

Vivi slunk to the corner of the living room. She schlepped up on the train to New Rochelle to celebrate the day with family and friends. It wasn't her first appearance as the "fiancée" but she was nervous and the cat complication didn't help.

Jake had goals and dreams and Vivi wanted to impress his family as a worthy part of them. She had been in the Village and there was this little store with all sorts of old things. When she saw this silver ornament she'd thought that it was just right for them: stable, silver, and solid with the weight of a past.

"It is an Indian holy object. It is beautiful. I don't think Jake knows that."

Vikram handed her a napkin for her nose and eyes. The distance from the cat was beginning to help. Vikram's eyes were deep. Maybe it was the dope he'd been smoking, or the shadow in the corner of the otherwise thrillingly bright dining room. While Jake liked the spotlight, Vikram preferred to inhabit corners and wait for the right people to find him. Vivi had ended up hanging with Vikram more often than she realized during his visits back from Berkeley.

"But you chose well," he said. "My mother would be happy with this gift."

Vikram always had a way of being when he was close to her. The kind of close that caught her breath. Or maybe it was the allergies. Or the cloud of marijuana smoke that surrounded him, dilating his eyes and unnerving Vivi in his presence.

"How's life in Northern California, Vikram? You settling in to your grad program?"

"I am majoring in ecstatic religious states as induced by peyote, marijuana, or whatever Carlos Castaneda can provide," he joked.

And then he wasn't joking when he said, "You look beautiful, Vivi."

"Thank you, Vikram. And very funny." She made a last wipe at her finally-subsiding runny nose. They hadn't seen each other since Vikram went west and Vivi decided that she would marry Jake and have someone to take care of her.

"And you are marrying Jake," he said without a missing a beat.

"Yes. I am marrying Jake."

"Lucky man." Vikram smiled.

"We will not have pets," she said.

"I love you, Vivi. Invite me to the bris of the first born child." Vikram laughed deeply. "The munchies are calling me to the chocolate cake. Will you join me? But perhaps we should make a stop on the porch. This sweet, sweet weed might help you happily through the party."

"Oh, yes please."

The two of them eased past the glass storm door to the porch without making it rumble. It was dark and quiet in New Rochelle at night but not at all profound.

The dope helped the whole evening. It was easy and buzzy when they stepped back into the vestibule.

Jake was happy with his aunts and uncles. The prince was making his star turn and receiving praise. He waved to Vivi as she stepped in with Vikram, his mouth full of chocolate cake, relieved that he could handle his celebration without having to balance Vivi as well. She waved back. He still had Rufus in his arms.

"Come Vivi," Vikram said. "Let's walk. He has another love at the moment. Yes?"

They grabbed their car coats from the back bedroom and headed across the crusty snow. He lit up another joint and she enjoyed the pleasing red glow coming from his warmed hands.

The sign on the Donut Shop on the corner of the Main Street winked at them as they turned the corner.

"Look, it's flirting with me, Viv. Come, let's lick frosting off a bear claw."

They headed straight to the counter, entranced by the colors and textures. The painfully white donut girl was noticeably impatient.

"Wow," Vivi said. "These donuts look ama-a-a-azing!"

"Yes, it's true. This one in particular. Look, Viv! Look it's round, like a mandala. It will tell your fortune."

"Yeah. Ri-i-i-ight," she said slowly, amazed at how profound the donut in front of her had become. Somewhere in her snappier brain she wanted to ask what the prediction for her future would be but those words just floated and bubbled around the curls on Vikram's handsome face and so all she could do was grin at him.

"We're closing in about two hours. Think you can figure out what you want by then?" says Dot, the donut girl, according to her nametag. She was a townie and not happy about her greasy apron and hair net, especially in front of stoned New Yorkers.

Vivi looked up. "Dot?"

"Yeah. My name is Dot."

Vivi stared at the girl with round glasses and a round name tag and a kind, round face. She couldn't stop herself. She started to see the small circles on the donut shop head band rolling around like marbles. Dot was in matrix mode, and as this occurred to Vivi, she began to laugh.

"What's so funny?" Dot asked.

"Well, I mean. Your name isn't really Dot, is it? I mean there are dots on your uniform, and you have a little dotty smile on the O on your name tag. And you don't look like a dot. Or even a DOT. Are you sure your name is Dot?"

"Don't judge a book by its cover, lady. What are you having?"

Vikram, smiling wide, moved up to the counter.

"We're so sorry, Dot!"

It was all he could do before his wonderfully placid face began to crack and his eyes crinkled. He did everything he could to keep the waves of laughter from over taking his breath.

"Look you two," Dot said, angry. "I have two more hours on my goddamn feet and excuse me if I don't sympathize with your stoned out druggie asses. Either order up a donut or give me some of what you are smoking. Right now."

Vivi attempted to regain some composure. "A dozen please! We'll take a dozen. Right?" She turned to Vikram, who was gazing slack-jawed into the case, attempting to be dignified.

"Yes. A dozen at least. Two dozen. Cheaper by the dozen, isn't it? Aren't they?"

"Straighten up you guys. I mean I have had a helluva day. My dogs are barking!"

"Ha!" Vivi started to smile again, close to dissolution. "Dogs are barking?"

"Rowrf! Rowrf," said Dot, getting into the spirit of things.

"Oh, Dot! I love you," Vivi said. "And two dozen, okay? Whatever you have. You have money, Vikram?"

"Well, some money. Some rupiah, some dinar, some shekels, some francs, some lire, some inti, some . . ."

"Dollars and cents." Dot said. "And seriously," Dot leaned over the counter. "Do you have any more weed? My manager is gone and it's just me until we close. And, if you guys buy two dozen . . ."

Vikram dug in his pocket and handed Dot a joint.

"Donuts on Dot," she said happily, starting to fill up two pink boxes. "We don't really have a full two dozen donuts left. How about some holes?"

Vivi, grinning happily, stepped over to find the perfect fluorescent perch for them as they examined their booty.

"Oh yes," she said. "Negative space. We'll take all you have."

Dot handed them the boxes and ran the joint under her nose. "Thanks, guys."

"Don't mention it," said Vikram, happily opening the boxes at the table in the window and deciding what to eat.

"I'll be right back," said Dot. And she disappeared into the employee rest room behind the fryer.

Soon the sweet sound of tinny Christmas muzak filled the shop.

"It's March," said Vivi. "Isn't it March?"

"Yep, too cheap to get the next season. This is all we got," said Dot.

Vivi and Vikram sat counting the donuts when Dot emerged.

Dot makes a show of lighting the joint and takes a big inhale. "Now, we're talking," said Dot. "We could play checkers," she said. "I mean it depends on how hungry you are but we could play checkers." She referenced the donuts and the holes, some stacked like Kinged checkers already on the tray Vikram was organizing.

"Oh, I'm good at checkers! Jake hates it when I win."

"Who's Jake?" Dot asked, carefully laying out plastic tissue on the biggest table, to make their checkerboard, and passing the joint to Vikram. He takes a nice big hit.

"Her fiancé," Vikram said.

"His old roommate," said Vivi. And now it's Vivi's turn.

"You getting married?" Dot has the joint back and she has no intention of sharing anymore.

"Yes Dot. I am. In a few months. Jake asked and I said yes."

"She is getting married, Dot. Yes." said Vikram, with his dark wise eyes. "She will have no pets."

"Cool," Dot said. "You pregnant?"

"Not pregnant. Just getting married."

The two women looked at each other.

"Good," said Dot." Good luck to you."

Vikram finished lining up the donuts on the makeshift checkerboard.

"Your move, Viv," he said "You have to eat every donut hole that's left on the board when we end."

"I'm in," said Dot. "I really like the sugar jelly ones. Can you avoid jumping them?"

At two in the morning, Dot said they had to go.

"I gotta open at seven," she said. "I'm already wiped for tomorrow night, too."

The dope was gone and they definitely had had their fill. Vikram and Vivi thanked Dot for her hospitality and left the shop, heading back to Jake's parents' house.

They saw no lights and no cars left on the street as they approached.

"Oh shit! Jake left without me. He's going to be pissed!"

"Well, maybe he'll make you cook for him for twelve years and then I can come pick you up in my chariot and we can go off back to God and Goddess land."

"Huh? I'm a terrible cook."

"It's a myth. Lakshmi and Vishnu. Never mind."

Vivi smiled at him. "Can you pick me up earlier?"

Vikram heard her and opened the door.

"Get in. It's too cold out here."

They climbed into Vikram's old Volvo. The dope had worn off but the sugar high had not. Vikram reached into his pocket and took out a little statue of an Indian god and goddess he then handed to Vivi.

"A wedding present."

"Gosh, this guy has four arms."

"Yes," Vikram said. "Doesn't she look happy?"

Vivi blushes. "Never mind," she said.

Vikram slid his arm along the top of the seat and pulled her close. Vivi watched how the space on the dashboard between them, shrunk.

"Don't worry. It's freezing. We can keep each other warm."

Vivi slid closer, feeling his warmth. She snuggled in. He was so tall and it felt good to be smaller-than, surrounded by.

"Jake is shorter than you," she said. "I'm not used to being surrounded."

"The more to keep you safer, my dear." Vikram said with a soft smile.

"So, tell me about this," she said, referring to the small statue he had given her. "Who are these guys?"

"It's the perfect wedding gift," Vikram said. "Vishnu and Lakshmi are devoted to each other. She is the goddess of prosperity, purity, and generosity. The embodiment of beauty, grace, and feminine charm.

"Just like me," said Vivi.

"Just like you," he echoed. "She accompanies her lover in every incarnation on earth. The mysterious capacity to become daughter, wife, mother, lover, mistress, maiden, and sister all at the same time for her lover."

"And what does he do for her?"

"He is stability and strength. When there is injustice on the planet, the other Gods ask him to incarnate into human form and right the wrong."

"A good friend to have."

"A brilliant lover." Vikram moved closer and kisses her. She tastes a trace of sugar at the corner of his mouth.

"Um, I don't . . ."

"Sh-hh," said Vikram. "Just rest here in my arms."

Vivi moved her head to see the moon out the window.

"We can sleep and watch the sun rise," Vikram said.

"Yes, okay."

"Remember to get mad at Jake when you see him tomorrow. He was a real asshole."

"Yes." She took a moment and then turned to her friend. She remembered the last year of dating Jake. She remembered meeting Vikram and how both of them recognized each other. She said, "Am I making a mistake? Marrying Jake?"

Vikram smiled and kissed her again, this time deeply, as if saying goodbye.

"Vikram, I mean . . . Vikram . . . how come you and me . . . ?"

"Sh-hhh-hhh. Quiet now."

He kissed her once more and put her head on his shoulder. She opened the car door on her side and Vikram watched as she came around the back of the car, opened his door and invited him to climb into the back seat with her. She lay down and he lay on top of her. The dope had made them very hungry. Later she remembered his hands under her breasts, and the way he moved up and down her body, being everywhere at once, a sweet and welcome coming together.

They slept deeply and Vivi dreamed of a small village where she and Vikram were other people. She could see them from above as they rolled together on a wooden bed, her nightgown over her head, his face in silhouette against a strange frozen moon. Her body moved closer to her lover, twining itself with the many arms that braided them. The woman in the dream gasped for breath and received it from her love. They were two parts of the same body. Then she floated upward, full, rich, and bursting. Vivi woke, belly full of doughnuts and dope, breasts aching, slit by the sunrise. She had a headache and Vikram had bad breath. He cranked the engine and they left the scene of that crime.

Chapter 10

The Tuna Fish Fight

Vivi rattled the key in the lock before opening the door to their apartment. Rattling chains came to mind, only Vivi was looking to get into this relationship, not out of it. No longer stoned, she was newly aware of her 'humiliation' the night before. The ease of being with Vikram outlined for her the discomfort she often felt on the outside of Jake's circle.

An abandoned tuna fish sandwich, six chips, and a garnish that had been delivered by the deli downstairs sometime in the last twenty-four hours sat on the table. Jake sat there, too, smoothing his napkin and preparing to wrap it around a cold mug of ice cream. The clock reads 6:45 a.m.

When Vivi appeared, Jake focused completely on this task. His scent, separate from tuna and ice cream, floated to her—Dial soap and furious. His hair was still wet. The drift of steam from the shower had come into the living room. He must have showered three times to calm himself down and not slept a wink all night.

Vivi was prepared for the confrontation before taking off her coat but she decided to head towards the bathroom. She needed to figure out just exactly what she was so pissed about.

"Won't you sit down?" he said.

Vivi turned to face him.

"I beg your pardon," she said, not startled but rather incredulous that he was playing this like an injured Lord. Nevertheless, she sat.

"Thank you. I love you. I'm sorry. Forgive me," he said. Problem solved. But not for Vivi.

"You love me? You're sorry? You make a fool of me, you choose an asthma-rattling cat over your own fiancée—in front of your family!" Vivi wasn't really sure what she was fighting for.

"I love you. I'm sorry! Forgive me," he says again, as though it were enough. He carefully angled his spoon beneath his chocolate-chocolate chip. "How was your night with Vikram? Get laid?" His voice was even.

She watched as her hand flung the folding chair across the room.

"Nice work," said Jake.

"What about that goddamn cat? You abandoned me for that god-damn cat!"

"Oh, fuck the cat! Which cat is that, daddio?"

"Right, fuck the cat. Leave me fumbling for a foothold in front of your family. What the hell, Jake? Who abandoned who?"

"Vivi! Stop screaming at me. I can't listen to you when you start screaming at me."

Vivi wasn't screaming but her fury felt that way to Jake. She knew him well enough. He needed her to explain to him how they got off track the previous night. Why couldn't he drop the cat on the floor and embrace his new fiancée, the woman with whom he is embarking on a real life? Vivi knew he needed her help because he really got her when she talked. When she told him what she knew and how she saw the world. When she looked off and somehow came back with just exactly the right something to get him off his ass and back into what needed to be done.

He needed to hear her voice tickling pathways, past the visual and landing somewhere he was not used to going.

"It can't be about being pissed about that cat!" Jake said.

Vivi sputtered and could not bring herself to help him with this. This was their marriage. He had to come through.

They had gone to therapy. Just a few sessions but enough for Vivi to know how Jake wondered sometimes how he could be turned on by her, who she was, what came out of her. She was not who his dream girl was supposed to be. She was not a ballerina. Not like Lily from the NY City ballet who was so light he thought he'd crush her when he came. No. Vivi knew this was an issue with Jake. Needing someone to crush. Her body was sturdy, as wide across as his, and smooth. He could sink into her body and go somewhere he hadn't been before. She knew it scared him.

"I love you," Jake said again.

"It's not enough! You can't say you love me and leave me for a cat."

She wasn't pretty when she cried. She knew he wondered why she couldn't be simpler. Why she had to cultivate that part of her that he didn't understand and never would. Why he loved every part of her and was so terrified at the same time. How the cat was a safer bet and kept him separate and protected.

His ice cream had melted. He couldn't kiss her. He spooned the ice cream into his mouth like soup.

"Maybe I'm wrong," he said. "Maybe I love you, but I don't like you. Don't like you at all. In fact, fuck you!"

Vivi could find no words that would help. She found herself in the kitchen instead, filling their largest pasta pot full of water. She headed back to the table and dumped the contents over his head. Boy! That was satisfying. And she slammed the door on her way out.

Or at least this is what she remembered happening. She came back. Somehow they found their way to each other. He went to the bathroom to take off his wet clothes and she found him there. She was dumbfounded at what she had chosen to do. She was sorry but even more curious about what Jake would do with her fury. How would they find their way through these treacherous waters?

"I should say I'm sorry, Jake," Vivi said, willing to go that far. He stood there, bedraggled and almost laughing. "Or wait, no, you should say you're sorry. Or."

"I'm sorry. Forgive me," he says again. "Try that?"

He looked at her and started to laugh.

"I'm sorry," she said. "You're a mess. We're a mess."

"Thank you," he said. "Please forgive me."

"Please forgive me," she parroted, checking out how they were navigating the waters.

"I just . . . you can't . . . I mean . . . !" she sputtered.

Jake grabbed her and pulled her into the stall shower. He turned the water on full steam. She screeched, first with horror and then delight, and they made love. It was then they decided to go to California sooner than planned and be married by a Justice of the Peace at L.A. City Hall. It was the last good fight they had for a long time.

Chapter 11

A New Beginning

They found a great apartment in Hollywood. Lots of windows facing out to an inner courtyard. It was all jungly with banana palms and agave, huge succulents competing for sun with the overachieving bougainvillea trumpeting its winnings at the top of the wall. "I'm the tallest, I'm the prettiest, I'm the only thing to look at and I win," the sassy vine said with its own pair of Foster Grants. So L.A. They got a reduction on the rent when they moved in because Vivi promised to tame the beast and cut back palms, give the aloe and jade plant their due, and prune the bougainvillea.

She loved the cocoon quality of the courtyard. She loved how all the green made oxygen. She breathed deeply in her new garden and rubbed her belly. The click of the cool metal rocker beat out as it moved forward and backward with the shift of Vivi's weight, tipping her more deeply into this new home. Her first, really. A home of her own. And with Jake, a good partner. She rubbed her belly again for good luck. And something gurgled, or tweaked, inside her. A gurgle, she decided, saying hello. Better than a tweak.

Bernie and Shelley came out for the wedding. Vikram sent a book on tantric sex to their California address. Cousin Laura sent a book of romantic love stories. Vivi wore a white muumuu and a garland of white roses. Jake, at the last moment, decided to don a yarmulke.

On the wedding day, Bernie and Jake drove down Franklin from the new apartment onto the 101 Freeway going south in Bernie's rented Cadillac. Shelley stayed behind with Vivi, ready to ride in the bride's town car she has ordered to take them to City Hall. Maybe it was the pot holes on Hollywood Boulevard that exacerbated the problem.

"You look beautiful, darling. So fresh and full!" Shelley said.

Vivi smiled wanly at her new mother-in-law. At almost ten weeks pregnant, Vivi's morning sickness had subsided, replaced by a rosy glow and a roundness that made Vivi uncomfortable in her skin. She felt as if she had been invaded by troops of hormone soldiers building storage outposts in every latent mammary gland lying secret and undiscovered. Every part of her body had become a balloon of expectation. There was nothing to do but give up and give in. And, she confessed secretly to herself in the bathtub, she enjoyed leaving her body to the army to run. All she had to do was vacate thought and be the landing pad, the fertile soil in which the grand garden was going into mulch, fortification and preparation mode.

Vivi liked slipping the big silk muumuu over her body, feeling it lightly cradle her curves. Yes. The Lilliputians were busy underneath but she, the Walrus Gulliver, could cover everything and sail on a cloud.

"It's probably the first time I'm not in charge of me," she said the night before their wedding, adjusting the pillows behind her head. "I mean, I've always had to be the one to make things happen. Take care of mom, avoid Uncle Allan and Aunt Shirley, grab the scholarship, take a leap and land in New York. Now I get to open the spigot and let everything drain out. Just let the hormone soldiers, and you, fill me up again. I like it." She smiled at Jake. "I kind of like you, too," she said.

"Likewise, I'm sure, Viv."

"I mean, thanks for taking care of me. You really do. I mean, you're taking this awful job."

Jake had agreed with his father that he needed to make money and agreed to manage the family factory in L.A. "Five years, no more," Jake had said. Bernie twisted his cigar in his mouth.

"I'll introduce you to Alan Siegel. He'll get you started."

"It won't be awful," he said. "It's good for a papa to earn a living."

"Papa," she smiled softly. Jake sat up and pounded his chest. The tiny Lakshmi figure fell off the bedside table, and his kisses covered hers and they held on and held on and held on to each other, ready to plunge the very next day into everything they never knew they wanted.

"Here, sweetheart. Will you wear these? From Jake's bubbe." Shelley held out a string of lustrous pearls. "There's an F on the clasp." Shelley ran her finger along the row of tiny diamonds. "All diamonds. It broke the bank when my dad got it for her. I remember that."

Shelley lifted the pearls and asked permission to fasten the clasp at Vivi's neck.

"My mama was Feige. Francis. She would have liked you." Shelley smiled at Vivi and Vivi felt tears in her eyes as she looked at this woman who clearly was doing the best she could on her only son's wedding day, which looked nothing like it was supposed to. Vivi hugged Shelley.

"Thanks Shelley. Thank you."

"I'm sorry your mother . . ."

"Beverly."

"Beverly, is gone. And your uncle and aunt from Detroit?"

"They promise to visit in a few months. They told me."

Vivi went to her drawer and pulled out her mother's full-length white calf gloves.

"Mom's," she said to Shelley as Shelley silently quashed her comments about what piece of clothing goes with what. "They're not blue . . ." said Vivi apologetically, "But . . ."

"Things are seldom as they seem. Skim milk substitutes for cream." Shelley quoted. "Robert Frost. I tried to remember poems so my kid should know a little."

Vivi looked at herself in the mirror, patted the pearls, squeezed the calf gloves tight, and turned to Shelley.

"Beautiful," said Shelley, trying to mean it. "Ready, darling?"

"Let me just . . ."

Vivi headed to the bathroom for the last time before they got into the car. She had been feeling crampy. On her white panties was a splash of bright red blood.

"Shelley!" Vivi called. "Shelley!"

"What darling?" Shelley called from the other room. Vivi reconsidered calling in her mother-in-law.

"Oh, nothing," she said, deciding to ignore the spotting. It was her wedding day and that was drama enough. "Just wondered if my purse is out there."

"Right here," said Shelley, picking up the white crochet purse that Vivi left near her gardening tools in the kitchen. "I'll just wipe the dirt . . ."

"It's fine," called Vivi from the bathroom.

Vivi checked to see if there was any more blood. She grabbed a pad from under the sink and put aside the idea that she could bleed through her white dress and her white pants on this white and sunny wedding day in Los Angeles.

The ceremony was brusque and efficient. Shelley cried and Bernie smoked a cigar through the entire event despite the posted NO SMOKING signs everywhere. Everyone signed the license and Jake kissed his bride. Vivi knew that it should be better than this. But it was just fine anyway. As they stood at the top of the stairs, a Latino couple came up from behind with an entourage of cheering relatives, heaving bags of rice and coins at the couple and showering Jake and Vivi as well.

Vivi turned to Jake and held him close to hide from the rain of rice and good wishes. Her head was aching. She broke into a cold sweat. She held on to Jake to steady herself and then whispered urgently in his ear.

"Jake. Take me home. I'm losing the baby."

Then she crumpled on the City Hall stairs.

"Hi Viv." Vivi heard Jake's voice and then opened her eyes. "How you doing?"

"Oh," said Vivi. "Oh, I better get up."

Vivi was lying in their bed and looked up to see Jake hovering above her.

"Nope. No need to get up. I just took my parents to the airport. You were pretty out of it."

"Yeah."

"Been sleeping for two days now."

"Yeah?" Vivi was groggy. She knew she collapsed at City Hall. That she went to the emergency room. That they gave her an emergency D and C. That she came home the night before and had been sleeping since.

"You lost the baby. That's what happened. On our wedding day. Collapsed on the stairs. Remember?" Jake reported the facts to her as if she had been elsewhere.

Vivi took in the information again. She was strangely numb. She had yet to feel the loss of the quickening, the deflation of the glands, the vacating of the room where she had been holding space for two.

"Sorry, Jake. I am sorry." He looked stiff. She noticed that he had no curves.

"Maybe it's better. Maybe we weren't ready," he said.

Vivi sat upright in the bed. The soft crush of the sheets around her felt comforting. She pulled them across her breasts. "My body was sure ready." Vivi looked over at Jake, "But, now you don't have to take the job with your father. Now you can do what you want."

Jake looked over at her. He was sitting on the bed and she couldn't keep from staring at his collar and the way his neck looked when he took a big swallow, a deep breath. He was forlorn, soft, and knotted.

"Nah. It's better. My folks were pretty clear. They won't help us with cash so, I made a deal to work for five years. Then, I can do what I want. That's what they said."

"Oh," said Vivi, looking at her new husband who looked like a bar mitzvah boy disappointed at the fountain pen that he just received.

"Besides," said Jake, his wind returned. "How would we explain a kid with long black hair and huge Indian eyes, anyway?"

"What are you talking about?"

"That night you stayed out with Vikram. I know you fucked him. I know you got pregnant right after that. I mean we made love but, I mean, it was all pretty close."

"Jake. Why would you say that now? I was only ten weeks pregnant. That was months ago. How can you throw that around now when my hormones are raging and we're both in shock?"

Jake looked right through her, pretty disappointed all round. His parents, his plans, his wife, his choices.

"Forget it, Vivi. Just forget it. I'm going out for a drive."

Vivi felt lucky that her drugs put her back to sleep. Jake quietly left their bedroom. She heard him start up the car and then she heard the quiet. She waited to see if he would come back. He didn't.

Maybe this was just a dream and Jake didn't say what he said. Maybe the image of a small girl drowning in her own lungs, coughing, coughing, coughing—that flooded her brain and had her gasping for air all alone in their bed—was a figment of an overactive imagination.

Chapter 12

Anna Elizabeth

The baby was still dead. That was the first thought that traveled from her icy fingers to her brain when Esther shoved aside the cold wooden coffin top, and the white lace of the neckpiece of the shroud blinked awake and stiff. Attentive to touch.

The child had been in the coffin since February. It was now April and the thaw just beginning. Esther had shoved an axe head into the earth behind the cabin that morning, aching to finish her task before spring. Fearing the sweet smell of spring flowers mingled with the decomposition of her tubercular child, she knew now was the time. That morning she had looked across the back pond to the Smith shop and seen him shoeing horses with the stall door wide open. She could see the fire, feel the air from the bellows and breathe in the steam as he shaped shoes and nails for the feet of the many horses in his charge.

He did not look up when she threw her gaze all that way. He knew she had opened the window and struck him with sight. He knew that would come with the first hint of green spring. Still, he did his work. Slowly, with strength. Methodically, with purpose, he shaped the iron, shod the horses, ignoring their whinnies and head tossing.

As the bell struck seven o'clock, he strode across the path on the far side of the pond.

He knocked on her door and she opened it. Her eyes were red from a day of eyes leaking no matter what she told herself. He walked back to the shed and took the shovel and began to dig a rectangle in the earth, just willing. Then he brought the small box to the graveside and went back inside to Esther. She came silently out with the child's blanket. She carefully covered the pine box where her child lay. As she did, the top slid aside. Just enough for the bald head and lace collar to flare into sight. Esther let a push of air escape from her lungs. Bennett took the box and placed it carefully in the grave.

"Fill it," he said to Esther. "Bury our child."

She grabbed for a fistful of dirt and felt its spring in her hand, so happy to have been released from the bondage of frozen winter. She felt life stir and saw a long strong worm work its way out of her fist and drop to the ground.

Esther laughed gently. Then, she bent down and shoved mounds and mounds into the small hole. He let her do it. When her breath was gone she sat on the ground and patted the earth. He smoothed it with his shovel. She sang a wordless melody. The first star came out. He stood with his leg behind her back and stayed there until she was ready to rise up and be washed.

He washed her carefully. Her hands first, then her neck and her face.

He removed her blouse and washed carefully under her arms and above her breasts. He made her sit in the yellow wooden chair and removed her boots. And her sorry stockings. He washed her feet in a basin of water he had warmed on the stove. She looked at him and went to lay down in her bed.

She slid in and closed her eyes. He covered her with a quilt, brought the lamp by the bed, and sat in the yellow chair. She slept and he watched all night.

And it was done.

Vikram rolls slightly in his sleep. He slides himself up, eyes still closed, and opens them in the half-light to watch Vivi sleep. She clenches her fists, opens and closes them and then laughs lightly. He positions his pillow so he can sleep upright, and places his leg along the curved back of Vivi's body. And they both close their eyes more deeply.

They do not make love. Vikram had spent time in a monastery so wasted the years when he could let his body move into expressive abandon. Then he left the monastery and came back to teach in this country.

Before he found a real relationship with a woman, he continued his romance with Buddha and then he got prostate cancer and was rendered impotent. So, Vikram is a different kind of lover. He holds Vivi when he can. Her arm when they are walking, her face when she is speaking, her foot when she wants to run away from him. He travels a great deal. His work takes him to learning residencies across the world's holy sites and then he returns, gives lectures, smiles more wisely, says less, and sleeps more quietly, and not as often in Vivi's bed as he did when she first arrived.

He has just returned from several months in Nepal. He brings orange robes to wrap himself in when he gets out of the shower and lies next to her.

They have spoken less and less in the last year or so, and he is often gone in the morning when she wakes, but their connection deepens in spite of themselves.

"You were laughing and digging in your dream last night, V," says Vikram softly when she is about to open her eyes. "Do you remember what it was?"

"I was a widow and you were a blacksmith. We had a child secretly and we buried it together in the spring."

"Ah," says Vikram. "Sounds like you are getting even with Shelley."

"I've had the dream before. A few times. But it's always you who's the father. How's that?" Vivi shifts and looks at the ceiling above her. Vikram closes his face when she says this. "Jake always thought that you were the father of the baby we lost at our wedding. You know that, right?"

"You have said that but I don't think so, Vivi. And it was such a long time ago." He bats the idea away from them like a gas-filled balloon. He has had this idle conversation a couple of times before.

"Jake never really wanted kids," Vivi says. "I guess it was Shelley who wanted them. To be a grandmother."

"That's a real longing as well."

Vivi turns to look at him. "Yes," she says. "Longing seems a luxury these days."

"Buddha says—"

Vivi feigns a loud sneeze. She knows enough to avoid conversations about Buddha and what he says about everything that Vivi does wrong in her life.

"Yes, Buddha says Achoo." Vikram enjoys her feint and parry. "Goodbye, my beautiful Vivi. I am off to my own little cell."

"Thank you for coming to be with me."

"Yes," says Vikram. "Happy to be here. Good luck." He wears his benign smile like the shield and armor of a medieval knight.

"What are your plans now?" she asks. "Are you here for awhile?"

Though Vivi knows their time is up, she can't help wanting to stretch the feeling of embrace that comes from his presence.

"I am writing this semester. Some independent study consults. I will spend more time in Colorado."

"Oh," says Vivi. "Sounds busy."

"Open," he says, sensing her longing. She knows it and wants to lighten the rock in her heart that she tries not to make Vikram carry for her, or even with her. But her explanations just pile on the hand weights. Still, she tries.

"I hope you don't mind. I mean the way I lean into you. Need you at certain times. When it seems there is nothing or no one. I hope it is alright that I count on you in this way."

"It is how it is, Vivi. We are old friends. And it is my honor," says Vikram, the unpinnable.

"But you don't love me?"

Vikram's dark eyes twinkle and he throws his head back as he laughs. He is loud. He still has a full head of hair. The gray curl over his left eye obscures it as if hiding half a secret.

"I do love you Vivi. It is what I do. I live in the bath of love. God's love, Buddha's, yours . . . it's all one thing. I'm a holy guy. Stoned on God."

"But you don't want to share the grocery shopping and come home at the end of the day and tell me about it, right?"

Vikram continues to laugh, delighted. She goes on, smiling herself, and then begins giggling. Giggling long and hard. Laughing out loud at the absurdity of her tiny voice and the tiny girl she sees in the mirror of Vikram's eyes. They laugh like they did when they were young and stoned on weed and doughnuts. They laugh like old friends. Finally, the laughter subsides. The waves ebb. They ease and rock back to real time. They are both full.

And then she says, "Sometimes I think that is the biggest part I miss. Since living alone. The idea of being witnessed, even by someone who can't see you clearly." She swings her legs to her side of the bed. Her white nightgown is pretty as it skims the floor in the morning light.

"Eating scrambled eggs from the skillet and talking to the television news shows like my aunt used to do. It builds a wall of invisibility around me. This secret hulking into myself where no one can see."

Vikram gets out of bed on his side and stretches his long legs forward as he listens to her. He bows forward then turns and hugs her from behind. "You are not invisible. I am going now. And Jake isn't really gone, you know. He's around. I can feel him. Chat with him if you get lonely."

"What?! Where did that come from?" Vivi eyes Vikram. Why would he bring up Jake?

Vikram takes her tenderly in his arms and holds her close for a moment.

"You're never really alone, Vivi. Even if I am not here, you know."

"Vikram! You are so . . ."

Vikram gets his back pack and a final swig of his lavender tea. Then he turns and smiles at her once again as he heads out the door.

"Easy does it, Vivi. Easy does it." And Sunday is before her to fill all on her own.

Vivi spends the day doing the unavoidable tasks that have kept her sane. She washes the dishes, and remakes the bed, airing the sheets on her tiny porch. Sunday night, around six o'clock, hits her every week as a particularly hollow time, the moment when one can sink into the weekend and measure the strength that has been gleaned from the break in routine. The week is ahead with its responsibilities. This Sunday night, Vivi is exhausted. She can't help herself and calls Vikram.

"Hi."

"Hi. I was just meditating."

Vivi pauses but then knows that Vikram often uses that as an excuse to keep himself away from conversation.

"Are you done? Can I ask you something?"

She knows he would rather do whatever it is he does by himself at this hour of Sunday twilight, but she presses on. "Why did you say that? About Jake, that is. That he is still around? That you can feel him?"

She can feel Vikram shift and try to decide if he should take a seat or leave Vivi on her own with this one.

"Well, those people we love, those people who love us, they are always around. The boundary is pretty porous."

"Yes. I know. When I first took the Home Center job, and you were still in India, I had to have that Tarot reading with Tara. Cheryl's friend. Did I tell you about it?"

"I don't think so."

"He showed up. At the reading, at least that's what she said. She said he was wearing a red baseball cap and it made her head itch."

"That sounds like Jake."

"He said he never wrote a love story that worked. Said he needed me to keep chatting with him so he could figure out why he loved me, or something like that."

She can feel Vikram smile. "The great mysteries," he said.

Vivi smiles, too. "I'll take that as a compliment. I mean that it shouldn't be so hard to know why he loved me. Or something like that."

She looks out to the darkening sky and hears a cranky motor refuse to roar to life down the street near the Citgo station. "Tara also told me I was supposed to talk to him. But he hasn't been back."

Vivi falls silent for a moment.

"And, you know he committed suicide. Right?" Vivi says. "Did I tell you that? He left a note."

There is real silence on the line. "Yes, you told me." says Vikram. "In your letter when I was still in India. We've never talked about it."

"I've stuffed it all away. I mean . . . I don't think what he did is mine. It was his decision. His way out."

"Yes. But he is still here, Vivi. He needs you to forgive him, to let him go to the next stage."

"What does that mean?"

"He needs to find some peace. Some reason he was here, some reason that he can understand why he chose to leave. He needs to know you are okay."

"I am okay."

"Are you?"

Now it is Vivi's turn to be silent. "Okay enough," she says. "Talking to Jake will not help."

"Do what you think is best."

"I guess I don't forgive him. He wimped out. He was healthy. He had a failure of imagination."

Vivi can hear Vikram moving in his apartment. She knows that she will lose his attention very soon.

"Maybe so. A double whammy for a man who wanted to tell stories."

"I just . . . I just want the next thing to happen. To make a fresh start."

"It's been only three years. It will come."

"I lack comfort, Vikram. Inside of me, it feels like inside of me I am like the princess and the pea, constantly adjusting to avoid feeling that rock that digs into my back."

"It will come, Vivi."

Vivi shifts on the couch. That response is not enough. She knows that, and she also knows there is no other response to be had. "I don't know what to do. I don't know if I should call him to me or keep him at bay. I don't know if I need to keep a space for him as I grow around all that history and take each day as it comes. Or just plow on like I have always done."

She can see Vikram's eyes, and feels like Jake is in a closet somewhere afraid to show his face.

"Call him to you, Vivi. He's always around. Certainly when I am with you. Call him to you and help him find some peace. And then maybe you will too."

She hangs up the phone. She goes directly to her desk and cleans off the circulars and direct mail advertisements that she has thrown there. She finds the Pledge and polishes the wooden surface, rubbing it hard. She can hear the motor at the gas station finally find its voice. It hums, doing the job it has set for itself. Vivi sits in the straight back desk chair and looks through her one window. "Jake," she says. "Jake? Are you there?"

Someone is shoving the top back on a garbage can. "Jake? I told your parents. Almost a year ago now. Help your mother, she is so defeated by your loss." Vivi stops judging how foolish she feels talking to nothing, nobody. She goes on. "I don't know what that crap was in Vegas when I left L.A. Hopefully your angeldom has made you a little mellower." She shifts in her chair and gets up to fold the dishtowels again. And then again. Then she turns and comes back and sits at her desk and says. "I told Vikram. He is a good friend and he can feel you around, too. I don't know how we are supposed to communicate but I am here. I guess I will always be here." This strikes Vivi as the truest thing she has said in a very long time. She settles into her chair and looks out the window as she continues to speak. "Maybe you got lucky and figured out your stairway to heaven by now. I've got a few more steps to climb."

Vivi can hear the echo of her voice against the thickness of the twilight. She closes the door. She closes the windows. She sits on her couch again and looks around the room.

"I don't plant anything new, Jake. I sell crappy wax houseplants—and I don't make anything. Lately, I have been thinking that that is the hardest thing. To not affect the world in any way. To plant nothing, to give nothing, to care for no one or nothing. That is the hardest sentence to face."

Vivi gets up and heads to the kitchen sink looking for dishes to wash and a counter to clean. Her eyes look out at the gravel in the small parking area behind her house. Her eyes feel like the gravel comes right in and sits under her eyelids.

"Once I figure out just how to survive day to day, I promise you I will plant something again and it can sustain both of us. I'll keep trying. Pitch in if you can, okay?"

After her voice fades from the room, she listens for an answer but only feels the chill of sundown. She closes the door, grabs a yogurt from the fridge and switches on Sixty Minutes. Until she gives up and goes to bed, she tries to find an angle on the couch that will allow her to rest. Finally, one pillow on one side gets softer, willing to hold her a bit more easily.

Chapter 13

The Bony Embrace

When Vivi first arrived in the northeast of the country, she was determined to start anew. Yes, she chose this destination because Vikram was here but she had no real illusions about him dropping his spiritual travel schedule and becoming her live in boyfriend. Instead, she was happy to count on him as a friend. She said that to herself a lot. She did not want to be a burden to anyone. Vikram hadn't returned from India when she took her first job at a little flower store on the green. He was still gone a few months later when they had Jake's unveiling. He was not someone to count on, even if they would love each other, in a way to be determined when they actually met again.

After contemplating the smell of the one bar in town, she wrote a snappy upbeat profile for the dating sites, starting with the ones that required payment, figuring those guys would be more diligent and willing. Of course she'd heard the horror stories. But she was optimistic, hoping she would be able to find a new friend. Especially here in New England, so far from L.A. and its scrubbed and lifted sunshine.

Her first encounter was promising. This man was tall and smart. At least that's what it said in his profile.

"I am tall and smart and I volunteer at the Natural History Museum

in Boston. I moved to this area when I completed my book on Unreliable Invertebrates."

It was a great come-on for Vivi. Science geeks did not scare her and she fantasized about long conversations on woodland paths about paramecium and wiggly fish. Not far from her apartment was a conservation area that had several ponds. The word was that it was once owned by a fish scientist down the road and that each pond had a different species of koi or perch or bass or ornamentals. Vivi loved that idea and thought a great first date would include a stroll through the fish ponds to see what made this scientist tick. Perfect.

Instead, he insisted they meet at the corner coffee shop at three in the afternoon on her break from work. She was working at the one flower shop in town and it was always slow. In fact, she knew that the store was closing in a month and she was already looking around town to see what she might find. This coffee with David, tall and smart, was meant as a boost to her social and networking skills.

Coffee was short and stupid. David was more interested in what was happening just past Vivi's right eye than what happened a little to the left, on her face. Nevertheless, he asked if he could walk her to her car, parked in the lot behind the shop.

"Sure," she said. She found optimism in his request.

"Actually, I walked down from my place. My car is in the shop. Any chance you could drop me at my apartment?" He had an open face, she thought. A kind face, even with the straggly beard.

Vivi was happy to do it. She had plenty of time and maybe they would strike up an interesting conversation.

They pulled up to his brown bungalow on a side street. Vivi was heartened that it looked so comfortable and attractive.

"Wow. This looks great!" she said. "So cabin-y. How long have you been here?"

"A while. Want to come in?"

Vivi was intent on making a new friend. She was curious.

"Actually, I'd love to use the bathroom if that's okay?"

"Sure," he said. "I think it's clean." He snorted a little and Vivi got the distinct feeling that a creepy corner had been rounded but she ignored the sign.

They came into a big room with an overstuffed chair and sofa and piles and piles of newspapers and magazines. A large screened TV was obscured by various piles of books and stained t-shirts. As Vivi scanned the landscape, he said, "Bathroom is around the corner. If you can find it."

The hall was lined with more papers and photographs and piles of vintage Scientific Americans. It had boxes from UPS that have never been opened, and when she arrived at the bath room, she pushed open the door and hit a pile of old mail on a rickety wall shelf inside. A flock of dust mites and gnats let loose in a riotous dance of joy.

Vivi shoved the door shut. It isn't that bad, she reasoned, observing that the toilet bowl was mostly white. She did squat rather than sit, however, and quickly washed her hands, letting them drip-dry rather than chance the bacterium and various other microscopic critters on the well-used towel. She had to admit to herself, that despite her best efforts, her social network would not be enhanced by an ongoing friendship with this hoarding pack rat.

"Okay then. Thanks so much," she said, heading to the front door.

"Sure. Thanks for the ride," he answered.

He looked up at her as she moved to the door and then placed all his tallness and none of his smarts in front of it. She wasn't sure what would come next.

"I really have to get back to work. It's been nice to meet you."

"Really? I thought you told me you were a gardener, a landscape designer." His eyes darted past her left eye. She noticed when she was closer to him that he probably had not showered that day. Or was that stale smell from the piles of debris along the walls?

He grabbed at her and snorted that snorty laugh he had previewed in the car.

"Whoa," said Vivi, moving aside quickly. "Whoa. I really should go."

He grabbed at her waist and pulled her toward him. She bounced against his bulk. Her nose hit his chin and her feet slipped out from under her. She was actually surprised he was so strong.

"Feel that?" he said, as he crushed her against his body. "You gave me a hard-on just from the idea of peeing in my house. What do you think of that?"

Vivi shoved back hard, pulling up her knee with a jerk, managing to disentangle herself and hoping she had moved strongly enough to communicate disgust rather than desire as her knee hit his groin.

"Open the door," she said, strongly and calmly. She put her hands up in front of her. "And don't be a creep."

He stepped back and lowered his head. Was he sheepish or just lolling? She grabbed at the door knob which was sticky, but it did turn.

Out the door and a quick pull to get it closed behind her but he stood there holding it open, gazing after her. "Don't come and pee in a man's house if you're not prepared to keep your panties down." Vivi thought that is the sentence she heard. She did not wait to confirm it. Instead she got in the car and headed straight back to the shop, used her key to reopen the door. She went directly behind the counter. It took her a moment to digest her situation. Then, she crossed back to the front door and locked it. She could see any prospective customers through the front window.

Vivi stood behind the counter arranging and rearranging the three orchid plants in front of her. It was the first time she wished that Jake could show up and confirm what a creep this David person was. How pathetic that she gave him the benefit of the doubt. She had to go to more yoga classes. And maybe even take a hike with the Sierra club. Maybe be brave and have a Happy Hour beer with the three people in the bar around the corner. She would consider this after she went home and showered, getting the smell of waxy ears out of her nose.

Finally, it was five o'clock and she pulled the shades in front of the shop. She looked up to see a plump fellow across the street wearing a red baseball cap. He was smiling. Strolling slowly. A tourist, she supposed. She looked at him again as he rounded the corner. The way he lifted his head and adjusted his cap as he headed to an early movie. Confident, jaunty even. But she resisted any attraction.

Why do men in their fifties insist on wearing baseball caps? she thought.

And she lowered the blinds slowly.

Chapter 14

Tara Again

Vivi is afraid she is getting too nutty in her isolation. Vikram comes and goes at will but not often. The only other man that shows up in her life is a ghost, when Vivi is willing to see him. Vivi is willing to admit that Jake is around but, jeez! She feels this is a bridge too far for long-term health.

"Maybe Tara has a perspective on this," she thinks one night as she tumbles round and round the same racecourse looking for an out. *Tara,* thinks Vivi, *no longer suspect. She makes her own choices and they seem to work for her. Her heft would never work in L.A. and thank god neither of them are there any more to face the withering judgements of celebrity. Tara in front of the fake backdrop of stars and planets she hangs in a corner is her own star! It's so great!* Tara's small platform dragged from a construction site holding a kitchen chair is draped with acrylic velvet. When she mounts this Olympian plateau and settles herself, tunes in, turns on the psychic channel—*poof!* she's an oracle. *The power of positive thinking,* Vivi muses. *Not all bad!*

Despite her own diffidence, she has to admit that she and Tara have become friends. They run into each other in the grocery area of the

Home Center. Both women get their paychecks Friday mornings, and by 3:00 p.m. they are cruising the bargain aisles and stocking up for the week. It takes Vivi a couple of weeks to give in to Tara's smile and assumption that they are indeed fated to be pals.

"When you're ready for coffee, the coffee place isn't bad. See you there after checkout?" Tara has a certainty about her that cannot be denied.

Vivi smiles wanly the first week of the offer and the second week, too. Then she finds herself settling in to the coffee shop, hugging her cart of weekly goods to the side of the table and enjoying being off her feet after her shift.

"I got some of that henna dye on sale," says Tara, landing in the chair one thigh at a time. "The kind with the blue tinge! I love it!"

"Good for you," says Vivi. "But be careful the ammonia in the hair dye doesn't distort your psychic messaging."

Tara looks at her unblinking. "Be nice," she says simply.

"Well, tell me, Tara, why are all those old seers plagued with bad hair jobs? Maybe it's the other way round. The ammonia clears the channels."

"I hadn't noticed," says Tara, ignoring Vivi's defensive chatter and fascinated by the directions on the back of the henna box.

At least Tara does not work at Home Center. And she makes a good enough living online. Several times in the last couple of months, Tara has made it a point to tell Cheryl to tell Vivi to be in touch. She warned her about Shelley and Bernie's visit at the Matchbox. She told her not to trust Vikram. She even told her to be patient, that her whole life will change again very soon. Some kind of message from an old enemy.

That last message came two months ago. Meanwhile, Vivi has been trying to be interested in dating and doing her level best to get to the next step, whatever that might be. Today they are not in front of the curtain or even in Tara's shop full of empty birdhouses. Vivi has coaxed Tara out to an early spring sandwich on the lone bench on the green after Tara refused the two lunch spots in town.

"Dating is crap," says Tara. "I don't recommend it."

"What do you recommend then?" says Vivi, almost snarky.

Tara laughs. "Watch your attitude, my dear. I recommend nothing. But, if you are looking for something in the wrong barrel, I am offering you a shortcut away from failure! Where's lunch?"

It was Vivi's turn to bring lunch. Last week, Tara brought peanut butter and jelly and some outrageous chocolate pudding. Bags of Doritos and Coke. Now, Vivi offers her a sandwich from her brown bag.

"I hate fucking egg salad," says Tara.

"You could have asked me to bring something else. I wanted to meet at the coffee shop. We could have had lots of choices there."

"Vivi, I told you, those god damned ice cream chairs scream when they see me coming. Fat people are not happy in delicate shops. A woman needs a good throne."

Vivi looks over at her at her new friend. There actually is a bit of the chubby Queen about her.

"Is that true?"

"True enough . . . for today." Tara takes a huge bite of the sandwich nonetheless. She snuffles.

"Don't eat it if you don't want to."

"It's food and I need to feed the beast."

Inhalation and degustation. Then Tara finds her knitting needles in her plastic bag.

"What do you think? I think I can make some money with these."

Vivi looks over the plastic yarn fashioned into granny squares that Tara holds on her lap. "I'll put some stars and planets on the corners. Drop maybe a mirror in the middle and call them astral baby blankets. What do you think?"

"You'll be under sold by China."

"Buy American!" Tara smiles, pressing on. "If I were you, I'd be happy with the visitor that is still knock, knock, knockin' at your door!" Tara has an actual twinkle in her eye.

"Jake? Vikram? What are you talking about?"

"Jake, of course. He at least loved you. I mean he really did."

"I don't want him following me around, Tara. End of Story."

"Oh stop! He's only company. How's your sex life?" Tara snorts.

"Barren."

"There you go."

Vivi rustles in her bag for her own sandwich. She can already feel her tongue preparing for the thick coat of film that she knows will settle over the membranes when the papaya slips past the tuna and hits her mouth. It is culinary choices like these that sometimes concern Vivi about her own wellbeing.

"I mean, why in God's would you even think that papaya and tuna might be a good combination on brown bread," says Tara as she looks down at the orange slush seeping from the side of the bread, smearing the plastic sandwich bag Vivi holds.

There is a memory of the beach somewhere, Vivi thinks. There is a memory of papaya from another time. Like, maybe, at Olvera Street in L.A., when they drank salty margaritas, and rolled in the crunch of chips, licked up the piquant cleanliness of cilantro and *aguacate*. There it is, she thinks, after the guacamole. The papaya against her tongue, slurping its softness, looking at Jake and wondering if this was how he tasted somewhere below his belly, soft, with a slight smell. Not fresh but alive and complicated. Yes, the taste of papaya, the small black seeds that he chewed and insisted she feel the pepper tingle all the way down her throat and into her stomach where they continued to dance, these small rivulets of taste and insistence. There is the explosion of one or two next to her gut and then, the knowledge that these seeds residing like insects, small stubborn cucarachas, will pass undigested never revealing their worth.

This time, when Vivi's tongue hits the old papaya, shipped from Mexico too many weeks ago it has a slime to it. Her tongue searches for a burst of the familiar, but there is nothing but texture so she cannot taste her own question. Memories lose taste. They retain texture perhaps, they may even touch a photographic response, but the taste cannot tell her if she ever loved Jake, if the slip of the guacamole, the salt on the margarita, the slight scald from the late night coffee created an answer for her. She tasted little these days and the reason she sat with Tara on a bench in the green is because Tara has an appetite and knows how to chew and chew until she finds meaning and a way through to the other side.

They laugh together when the local stray dog sits at their feet and begs for food, and then refuses what they have to give. They laugh, hug, are grateful for the refill that friends offer to each other and head back to work.

Chapter 15

Build

It's Tuesday and Vivi has the day off. She likes how the rhythm of the week is changed up by a day off on Tuesday and again on Thursday. It makes her feel like she's one of those L.A. types who goes to the set when they are called and still has the luxury of a weekday to have coffee at two in the afternoon with no guilt or pressing engagements. She's never had the mother rhythm of 2:00 p.m. being the last bastion of quiet before school pick-ups, soccer drop offs and dinner prep. And the luxury of the small café that sees few working class women reminds Vivi of how fractured and secret her life has become. Half L.A. garden maven, half working class Home Center worker, floor scrubber, still enamored with the dollop of marmalade and cream against her beloved Blue Willow dishes.

Ah! The Blue Willow. She hasn't thought of those for a few years. They remain nicely packed in a storage unit in L.A. along with all the other elements that Vivi couldn't part with in the disassembling of her life with Jake. What could possibly be in those boxes that would fit in her tiny studio? And would she recognize herself when someday she had to open those memories again?

She finishes her tea and leaves an extra tip on the window table. It's the same café in which she and Shelley had their knock-down, drag out fight a few months back and she is careful to apologize with every extra dollar she leaves on the table. She decided she would not give up this one pleasure and slink away after the public spectacle.

She wanders to Kerry's Kettle to pick up her secret vice of a home-made jar of expensive Orange Marmalade. She will use it as a shield against the brash red that she knows will be slamming against the bill-boards as soon as Thanksgiving has passed. She and everyone else will be assaulted with Santa's sleigh and the plastic poinsettias that pass for real in the non-garden section of Home Center soon enough. Marmalade fortifies her for the winter.

Before getting back in the station wagon for the short ride home, she circles the small green in this little town that has become her resting place. The Wishing Well with the VFW announcement and the lone bench purchased by a dead man's estate sit sturdy in the middle of town as they had when she had driven in. It's not a bad place to be. No matter, here she is. She hears the click of her low boots on the sidewalk as she opens the door to the Post Office to check her box. She finds a letter waiting for her.

It is from Ellen, her lawyer pal in L.A. She expects it to contain a scolding for not being in touch. Ellen has been distant in more than miles since it was clear Vivi was not just taking a break on the East Coast but would likely not return to her life in Los Angeles and their regular friendship.

"I mean, I used to set the clock by our lunches, Viv," said Ellen. "But you're blissfully happy out there in all that snow and Home Center interaction."

Vivi would ignore Ellen's digs. She is not blissful in the throes of building something new. But such are the wages of change, at least that's what she thinks. She is often disappointed that Ellen equates their friendship with the convenience of proximity.

"Never mind. I gotta go. Clients coming in." Ellen would sign off and Vivi would sigh knowing that her once solid friend had her own scales to balance. She reminds herself not to depend so much on Ellen for ballast. She reminds herself once again to keep shifting the responsibility for her days back to herself. She knows how to live her life. She knows she has to fill her own hours. She knows that everyone has their own lives. This litany is the mantra of the hours between 8:00 p.m. and 10:30 p.m. when it is too early to go to bed, too empty on the streets to take a walk and the television too full of inane repetitive sitcoms to soothe. It is actually the time of night she has taken to scrubbing floors. Usually she boils some strong Lipton tea and lets it steep in a bucket. She has read that scrubbing the floor with tea improves both hygiene and color and so she is happy to have the experiment to engage in. Fifteen minutes on her hands and knees, the soft smell of tannin and then she can soak in the tub, sleep satisfied, and wake up to Home Center. Balance restored.

Vivi opens the envelope.

Dear Pal.
You are the luckiest girl on the planet. Carol found another beau and got guilty. And the film she and Jake wrote about the mutant crawly things sold, for a Japanese anime miniseries. She has had a come to Jesus moment and is now signing over half of fees received for treatments written etc. by she and Jake. In other words, here is the first installment and a schedule for the rest. Go buy a house.

Sign this document so you get the rights back to Jake's projects and then some.
Your loving, neglected pal,
Ellen

Vivi stands stunned in the little post office. Then, she walks out the door and directly across the street to Al Peavy's real estate office where she has been secretly lingering of late. There is the picture she has been studying.

"That piece of property still for sale?" she says to the woman at the desk in the back of the office. "The one off the rise just up Route 6?"

The woman at the back desk looks up. "What are you looking for?"

"Just tell me the location. I'd like to drive up and take a look."

Down the hall, Tara hears Vivi's voice and watches as she goes quickly past her shop and back out on to the street. She pulls a card and smiles. The Wheel of Fortune comes up.

"Good for you, Vivian. Good for you."

Chapter 16

The Site

The GPS leads her right to the corner she recognizes from the blurry photograph. There is nothing around except the late autumn hay of a neighboring field, a stand of furry cattails, scratchy and stubborn, and a racket of geese and chickens discussing politics. Their high-pitched disagreements end with a piercing scream from the head rooster whose cock-a-doodle makes him the king of the pecking order.

Across the field, there is a winding road leading into brush. The late afternoon sun is reflected magenta at the bottom of the sky. It is a great expanse. It takes Vivi's breath away.

She pulls over the station wagon and begins to pace the field, measuring foot by foot despite herself. She is seeing the garden she will plant, in a circle of terraces around her, her own fortress. The house she will build, open to the sky. She begins to cry as she steps the earth, feeling it say yes. There is something about the angle between the curve of the hill heading down toward the goose pond, the crook of the tree standing alone on the gentle rise that opens the portal, the one to the next step. The ease and breath of a new beginning. She dials Ellen.

"I've bought a site. I mean I found a site! I can't believe it! Oh, Ellen! Is it true?"

"You will be happy! Living somewhere out in the fahkakta country with limited cell phone coverage and not a deli in a 500 mile vicinity."

"It's not that bad!"

"Right. To each her own. I have a client. Gotta go."

"Thank you for your support." Vivi clicks off the phone. Ellen is not the person with whom to share joy about finding a new thread.

Her phone buzzes and there's a text. "Yes. It is true," it reads.

And so, she stands on the hill, crying, for all the reasons she doesn't need to detail.

And the soft autumn breeze and sharp rustle of the cattails tell her to get on with it.

Chapter 17

Home

Vivi snaps on the television as soon as she gets to her rented apartment, as she does every night to bring light to it, to avoid the shadows. She looks around at the little living room that she has tried to make cozy, the sagging Ikea couch and Danish side chair she grabbed from Craigslist when she arrived. All of her furniture is still in storage in L.A. All she had wanted to do when she arrived was get busy on something, anything that might keep her thoughts at bay.

She calls Vikram. She leaves a message, which she knows he is screening.

"You won't believe it. I can't believe it. I'm building a house. A home again. I can't wait." The phone clatters up. Vikram is one of the last to own a landline.

"Vivi. I am meditating . . ."

"So, why did you pick up?"

"I'll call you another time, Vivi."

"No need. No need," she insists. Hearing herself lie. Yes, need. Yes, need. But not so enormous as to drown him. What are friends for? Or better yet, what are friends? She is so sick of feeling like basic human contact is a burden to her enlightened acquaintance.

The rebuke from Vikram is not enough of a smack to dull her enthusiasm. She goes to her tiny bathroom and pours real lavender oil and Epsom salt into the tub and settles in for a soak.

She ponders this idea of what is too much to ask of a human being. About a year ago, she had had another encounter, via the internet, with Denny, an artist. He was short but powerful. He drew mad and crazy women with eyes like corkscrews and he was a great lover. For a lovely couple of months they slept together almost every night and their hunger was inexhaustible. Denny, the painter, had a light touch and a caul settled on them both when they brushed against each other. They didn't talk. Except, when they did, which was only the week before they slept together. Then, they met after work, had a bowl of brown rice, drank some warm sake, ate several cold grapes and went to his bed, a mattress on the floor under wind chimes and a rice paper shade. Vivi thought this was the best possible solution for her loneliness and a great way to evade self-pity and excessive introspection. Exercise, no emotional investment and an excuse to avoid scrubbing the floor on Thursday evenings.

Eventually, Denny got an early morning assignment. He painted houses on a crew with young Latino guys and he got cranky when he realized how exhausted a day of up and down the ladder left him, a white guy in his late 50s.

Soon they were not seeing each other. But he would call a couple times of week and want to have phone sex. That was fun for a while but she found herself having to find online videos to boost her porn chat abilities. And when she tried for some foreplay, like "how was your day," there was a long silence on the other end of the line. Feeling like she should upgrade her abilities, she asked Joe, her coworker at Home Center, if he knew any sites she might check out.

Joe snuffled and guffawed.

"You planning on moonlighting, Viv?" His eyes twinkled. "Those girls get fifteen bucks an hour, I hear. And they get the guy off while they're making soup or oatmeal or something"

"Oatmeal?" Vivi's aural and olfactory sense memories went into overdrive. Joe caught her. "Come to think of it," he said. "I'd ask Cheryl for a raise instead."

The whole thing seemed remarkably erasable in the end. The conversations. The nights of anonymous sex. "No small talk," he said when she whispered goodnight to him on the phone. She wondered how much smaller her talk could get. Eventually, the images of making oatmeal while her lover rubbed his own member dealt the dying blow.

She stopped picking up the phone when the calls came at 11:30 just after the news. She turned off the ringer, the television, and her sexual escapades and went to sleep.

The next day she visits the bank in the middle of town. She sits quietly with Stanley Huber, the investment person, and goes over the numbers again. She has to make sure the money she has is real, and enough to sustain her. They figure the figures up and down, investing the stock market or buying land and it always comes out the same. Vivi has a good chunk to buy the land and build the house. And there is enough left over to invest and even have a small amount come through every month. Money goes farther in the rural Northeast than in LA.

This is real news to digest. She calls in sick and heads once again up Route 6 to take another look at this promise from nowhere. Standing on the rise that will be the perfect place for her view, she throws her arms wide and immediately wraps them back around herself. Vivi is not one for expansive gestures and she realizes her heart has not been so unprotected to the elements for a long time. She feels totally porous.

"Jesus, Jake! If this is your handiwork . . ." She knows how complicated her feelings are around him. She wants to be clear. For herself as well as for him. "If this is a gift from you, then I suppose I say thank you." She looks around the hilltop and ignores the faint breeze that pushes against her cheek and slips down the back of her shirt. "I am not sure why you would give me a new start but maybe things are better where you are now. Easier to be generous. I just know I long to try again and I'm sorry you are not here to try again with me."

She looks over to where she had dropped her purse and sees that her address book, which had fallen out when she rushed to this spot, is now open and the wind is fluttering its pages.

"Oh crap. I have a 3:00 p.m. at the realtor's to finalize the offer. I'm going now. I'm going."

Vivi moves quickly to pick up her purse and her book, get the car in reverse and head down the hill. She shakes her head and hears herself muttering, "Thank you, Forgive me . . ." and cannot put her tongue around the other parts of that chant.

As she pulls away, the site sighs, and maybe there's a nest in one of the trees that is ready to build an addition as well. That darter bird, the one that sailed so close to Vivi when she first was daydreaming about this land, starts building his bigger nest, too.

The next weeks are glorious. Vivi visits the site every day at different times to see where the sun falls, where the best spot for a raised garden will be, to take soil samples to see what will grow. She notices the sound of grass, the smell of the changing winds up on her rise. She even borrows a tent from Joe at work and sets it up next to a $7.99 Home Center folding chair, on final sale from the summer season, and has a picnic for a whole Sunday on the hill. She has never been a good tent sleeper so that part of the fantasy soon gets shut down, but she admires her own ingenuity in the planning of her new home.

In the town library. she discovers that the hill off Route 6 used to be the center of a small village that migrated down the hill toward the river and the mills that popped up and supported most of the town's growth in the early twentieth century. The settlement up on the rise eventually disappeared and is noted only with a couple of old farmhouses and a small flat area that has the remains of an old church, a miscreant cement patch, and a scraggle of weeds that obscures intent.

When she stops by Tara's place to tell her the news Tara is not surprised. "Didn't I tell you. A change of life from an old enemy?" Tara is pleased with herself. "Show me the site!"

"Well, if you look over there," says Tara, checking again to see if her shoes are steady on the hillside terrain. "If you look over there," she says, holding on to a tree and puffing a bit, "you can see the circle. The old green of the town." She looks over at Vivi and hands her the binoculars. "See, here, move them to the right!" Vivi does. "See your house site is directly above the old green. That is so cool."

Tara and Vivi have actually trekked up a hill in the conservation area across the pass from the small valley where Vivi's house will be built.

"I can't believe I actually walked up that hill!" says Tara looking for a log to land on.

"It's good for you, Tara. I think it's great you came for this walk!" Vivi grins at her new friend.

"Where's lunch?" says Tara.

"I think I did better today. Here's a chicken sandwich, and chips. Coke? Apple? Cookies?" Vivi is taking out her picnic and spreading it on a small cloth she has brought along. "A real picnic!"

"Now you're talking." Tara has settled herself on a log overlooking the Valley. "They've found stuff near that old green, you know. Stuff from the old settlement. Be aware when you start digging. Spooks and such may decide to show up."

"I doubt that will be my story, "says Vivi. "Things are always pretty cut and dry for me. I shift from one life to the next and keep marching on."

"Yeah. I get it. But these hills can be pretty crowded. Don't be surprised if you get humbled by what's . . . by who's come before."

"How's your sandwich?" says Vivi, changing the subject.

"Good. Next time more mayo. And pickles are always a plus."

The flat portion of Vivi's land looks out and over past the church. She decides she will orient her view to include its shabby steeple and the hope of ghost dances in the old square. Maybe Tara is right. Maybe Jake can find a new ghost girlfriend and leave her be. A foolish notion but she's somehow comfortable with looking at these past scenarios, despite all her efforts at new beginnings.

"I like the idea of having some company. Even old dreams," she says to Theodore Stillman, the architect she has chosen after a walk around her town's central green. He is the only guy in town and she is not going to torture herself with abundant research. He lives here, he knows the area, he hasn't been sued and she can control the design herself. As long as he is willing to keep her from full bankruptcy she wants to hire him.

"Most people would prefer to look the other way, down the hill toward the river." Ted says as he sizes her up. It seems he has specific standards for siting a house. "It needs to be square to the road. Otherwise it is lost in the foliage."

"Oh, I like that idea!" Vivi says with a smile. "Besides, I like the view."

"No accounting for taste, "says Ted. "And you want a garden."

"Yes."

"And you . . . you want a box?"

Vivi laughs as she walks the perimeter of the proposed house with Ted. She likes him. He listens to her and his price is right. Sheila, his wife, does interiors. She is on a job or a hiatus in New York at the moment, he explains. He is eager to mention her at every turn.

"I want a loft on one floor. One big room. Lots of windows and French doors to the outside. A patio. A place for a hot tub. A fireplace. Wooden floors. No laminate."

"Sounds like Los Angeles. Sliding doors are a good idea. And laminate will keep your budget down."

"French doors and hardwood. And a stone fireplace."

"And a garden . . . how bout a courtyard?"

"Sold," she says.

"Done," says Ted.

And Vivi can see her Blue Willow china on the open kitchen shelves right then and there.

Chapter 18

Anandamaia

The call came off the floor and Vivi hated answering those persistent rings.

"Vivi. Garden. How can I help?"

"Vivian? Hello. Is this Vivian?" The voice is forced, like its owner is listening to its sound too intently to actually connect with the person she is calling.

"Vivi. How can I help?" Vivi continues to mark up her plant delivery list as she listens.

The voice on the other end of the line startles and clears. Then, organizes itself. The tone is from a woman's voice. A studied mellifluousness. Pure flowing honey.

"Vivian. This is Carol. Or it was Carol. I am now Anandamaia. I am coming to an ashram near you. I thought perhaps we could meet."

Vivi's head twizzles as she tries to wrap her neurotransmitters around Anandamaia and the woman formerly known as Carol. The one with the sagging, desperate, black ringed eyes. The one with the bony hands grasping at straws, and Vivi's husband. The one who stole the rights to their last project and had an enlightened awakening and now made it possible for Vivi to build her new home and start her new life. That Carol. That Anandamaia.

"Carol." It is all she can summon.

"I apologize for calling you at work."

The silence is so loud. It's such a long and clattering hallway.

"I work til ten tonight. Why not leave me a message on my regular phone."

"I am here to study with a spiritual scholar at the college nearby. I am not sure you know of him but I follow his teachings religiously."

Beat. Beat.

"Good for you."

"I will send you the information. Goodbye."

An impatient matron comes up to the Service Desk. "I am looking for some help here. Anyone working here?"

Vivi turns to her and scans the woman's face, her rounded shoulders, her expensive tee shirt. The woman is sweating and it isn't from exertion. Hot flashes and the smell of the bag of mulch she has hoisted on her shoulder surround her in a potent cloud of exertion.

"Can you help me, please?" She says this with an edge. She is working out her gentlewoman farmer role but clearly is finding it overwhelming.

"Are you sure you want that much mulch? What project are you planning?" The woman's face melts. The bag is too big for her. She hates its smell and the fact that she has to hoist it on a shoulder to carry.

"No. I am not sure I want this goddamn bag of shit. But they say it makes things grow." She looks at Vivi impatiently. "Can you do something, please!?"

"I'm Vivi. Can I help?" says Vivi, as she grabs for the bag and places it on the ground near the counter.

Amanda is in her late sixties, Vivi will learn soon enough. She has just moved to a little house up off Route 6.

It is clear she is doing this project on her own and she has the fierce crankiness of someone who knows they should be able to accomplish this task but is clearly unable to make a dent in what needs to be done without help.

"All I want is some goddamn color. I hate that's its turning gray outside. Everything is turning gray and spindly. I just want some goddamn color."

"A winter garden? You've come to the right place."

Vivi eases Amanda to a small table at the corner of the service desk and she takes the bag of mulch and puts it on the delivery cart.

"I like butterfly bush. And forsythia. You plant them now they'll surprise you in the spring."

"You think I'll be around in the spring?" Amanda looks at her. "The way I'm feeling today, a morphine picnic may be a great option."

Amanda's edge is not asking for help. It's challenging the Gods.

"Well, the bushes will. Be around in the spring, that is. And we can get you some great coleus for the winter and a few orchids. We can surround you with life, if you want it. Before the picnic, if you want it."

"Plants are fine, "says Amanda. "Pack them up and send them out. "Will you come to plant them?"

"I, well, the store doesn't offer that service." Vivi chokes a little. She's not sure why.

"I'll pay you. I have lots of money. Here's my address and phone number. Call me when you get off work and we can set a time."

Vivi is not sure why Amanda disturbs her so.
"I'll write up your order. And we'll see about the rest."

Chapter 19

Amanda's Mansion

When Vivi rounds the corner she sees that Amanda's little house is not far from her own planned site. The house is plain and congested. That is, small windows, a tiny porch, a front door with an aluminum screen and a storm door sealing it tight. And old. Leaning into itself, protecting secrets or, more than likely, adjusting for rotting timbers like a lot of things, and people, she has encountered recently. Amanda isn't home yet. Their appointment was for three o'clock on Tuesday and Vivi is early to take a look at the grounds.

The house is set back from the small private road that leads to Route 6. There are tall pines that cathedral over the roof and the whole place has a hermit's feel. Not someplace she would expect to find such an urban character as Amanda. Especially someone with lots of money.

"I inherited it." The voice floats out from the shed where Amanda must have been lurking. "I can't stand it much but I had to sell in the city for cash to sustain me and this is what was left me from a cousin. He wasn't much of a friend."

Vivi wonders how this woman will do so far out of town, so isolated. But, then she realizes she is doing the same thing. "I'll be your neighbor. Just bought some land up the road." Vivi smiles.

"Well, how cozy for us," quips Amanda. She is so uncomfortable in her skin and knows she has to try a little harder to be human. "So, here's my story so you don't have to puzzle it out with the other neighbors. I mean, if that's your thing. Carl, my husband left me ten years ago. He found a French girl who lived with him most of that time on the idyllic island of Martinique. Henry finally died last year. Marie Boutique, as I call her, fought the will, insisting that she, Marie Boutique, get half his social security check. How's that?"

Vivi wonders if she gives off the same kind of "I dare you to like me" vibe. Probably not her style. Vivi figures she is more the 'panting lap dog' type but she has never had to look at that possibility quite so squarely.

"That's too bad," says Vivi, trying to keep her boat steady. "Let's walk the grounds. Tell me what you envision."

Amanda slings her a look that asks if she is for real, but Vivi ignores it and starts walking toward the back of the property to see if she can engage Amanda in a good idea and disengage her from her shield of thorns. She notices that Amanda drags one foot a bit.

"How about a bench about here?" she asks, coming to an area that has a large felled tree lolling on its side and giving Amanda a chance to lean and catch her breath.

"Only if you can keep the mosquitoes away. I hate the fuckers."

"Screened in porch. Good start."

"I could have used that last year when I was drinking heavily. Gave that up. Unnecessary punishment in the end."

"Maybe you can use it for reading. A reading porch in the woods," Vivi says hopefully.

"You are a chipper one, aren't you? I do read, actually. Historical biography. It's the only thing that can put me to sleep."

They continue to parry back and forth until Vivi is able to get a sense of what Amanda wants and needs.

"I just don't want anything more I have to take care of. I've been throwing everything out. Everything. I even got a dumpster. And a kid just released from the local jail to haul everything out."

"I moved here a couple of years ago. I did the same thing," Vivi says.

Amanda looks at her. It's been at least an hour to wear her down enough to allow her to connect even this much. She wants peace and comfort and as little work as possible.

"I need air and light." Both women finally understand each other.

They settle on a small screened in area that Vivi will fill with a soft fountain and ferns for the summer. Vivid bushes for spring. Forsythia, Butterfly bush, rhododendrons around the main house. She'll plant Morning Glory for instant satisfaction til the wisteria can establish itself and create a safe canopy for all the seasons. No vegetable garden, Amanda insists, unless Vivi is planning on working it herself. Besides there is precious little sun so Vivi does not press that point.

"Want me to take a look inside and see how we can work in some color there?"

"No." says Amanda. "I'll write you a check."

"Bulbs? Daffodils or Iris for spring. They'll cheer you up! And a few birdhouses near the windows? The birds are great around here."

"I don't want to be cheered up and I'm done for now. I'll send you that check."

Amanda turns to leave.

"Amanda?" Vivi isn't sure what she is going to say. "Amanda. Are you sure you want to make this investment? We can wait til spring if you'd prefer. I don't want to push."

Amanda just looks back at her. “I have to go now.” And she turns away and leaves Vivi in the gravel driveway.

Chapter 20

Amanda's Visitor

Amanda does have to go. She has to prepare her small cottage, as she likes to think of it. She is expecting him around three o'clock. She did her nails a few days back, but Amanda is clear that she is hardly the welcoming B and B, gracious "hostess-with-the-most-est" type.

It has been a long time since Amanda has had a guest, let alone a living companion for a whole week. The last three years have been a necrotic march, she affirms to her unconscious, as she deflects any blame or responsibility for despair or relish. Amanda knows she could have been more gracious to Vivi, but attributes her behavior to the deformed nature of her heart. It's just too brittle to embrace anything except her miffed sense of entitlement. There is no maneuvering. The statute of limitations has expired and Amanda is simply a crusty, left, divorcee whose calculation that she would eventually get the money was wrong. So, she had the apartment in which they had lived on Park Avenue. She sold it. She inherited this tiny old cottage from her mother's cousin whom she had never met. There had been no one left on his list of heirs and she took the sloppy seconds, or twenty seconds, and moved to the country.

She does what she can. She has been seen serving Thanksgiving dinner at the church in town. She showed up last Christmas as well. And she has returned to her painting, a skill that calms her though does not distinguish her in any way.

Ridding herself of her "stuff" has been the best tonic. In one day she got rid of her old heavy mahogany dining room set, the Magnalite pots and pans she got for her honeymoon, all the blankets and towels from her Park Avenue townhouse. The embroidered "his and hers" bath robes, the linens from their trip to China, the glassware she had from his mother's mother. She did not list these things on Craigslist. The house had a large braided rug in the living room. It was filthy. She threw that out too.

The debris kept piling up in the dumpster and she still did not feel clean. She got a can of white paint. She painted the wooden cabinets in the kitchen white. Or she started, then hired that kid again and he finished. She washed the one front window that faced the tiny porch. It wasn't enough. She threw out the curtains. She went to her closet. She threw out all her underwear, every dress and sweater. She painted the inside of the bedroom closet white.

In the end, she has a bed with a white recently painted wooden frame. She has two towels and two washcloths. She has a white mug. And a white china tea cup that her mother had given her on her sixteenth birthday. She has a white wooden kitchen chair in the living room and an easel and a large slab of plywood, painted white, resting on three piles of white bricks. In the kitchen, there is a built in corner booth with a table, now white all round.

She decides to sleep on the floor of the living room on a white memory foam mattress. She covers herself with a white sheet in the summer.

And she buys a white down comforter, two of them. She puts one on the bed, which she does not approach. And she spreads the other one over the mattress on the now white painted living room floor.

Her left leg has been numb for about a year. Never mind. She lays down every night careful to stretch it long. No one is there to hear the sighs that come involuntarily as she finally arranges her body down on the pallet for the night. She sleeps naked. She cannot bear to feel the synthetic nightgown fabric against her skin. She feels her belly before she falls asleep and tries to imagine it less of a weight against her. There is no one to see her face as she rolls to one side, and then to all fours looking up and through the window to greet the day from her knees, breasts hanging, belly loose, eyes clearing. She curves her back up like a cat and forces her spine the other way so her eyes find the window and the road beyond. A cat is somewhere left in her.

It is the end of summer. Her house is clean. Her clothing is spare. Her bank account is shrinking and needs red blood beefing up and that's when the email comes from the college asking locals if they might spare a room for rent for upcoming visitors for college events.

Amanda realizes she has no choice. The morning of the email she paces her house. She goes to the easel and finds the tube of yellow primary. She squeezes a line of magenta, then a line of yellow on the canvas. And an angry pile of radish red. She takes off her shirt. She puts her naked breast, sagging and easy, against the canvas and rolls the one against the other. The colors spread. She places the canvas on the easel, takes her cell phone and snaps a picture of the magenta and yellow, now a bruise above her nipple and stands back for a moment to decide which image is the right one.

That day Amanda does the same thing with a canvas and her left foot. Then her cheek. Then her mouth, then the quiet opening between her legs. And that is enough. She has several canvases lined against the wall of the living room. She has company. The company she will keep to the end of this time around. The ongoing exploration of what it is to be in company or alone, the company of her body pushing against space.

That is enough. She has to go back into hiding. She bathes. Finds clothes from before in the corner of the closet. A dress. She has her nails done and goes to Home Center.

When "that woman from Home Center," Vivi, naïve and annoying, finally leaves her house with all her frantic hope, Amanda comes back inside. She makes a pot of soup. Beans and rice and greens. She takes down her bottles of rum and brandy and puts them on the shelf. She checks the bedroom, opening the small window for a breeze. The coleus and ferns she has purchased at the Home Center look fine under the window. The orchids in the shared bathroom perch on the back of the toilet and she finds a candlestick and a half burned candle and puts it there as well. Then, she gets in the car to go get some fresh bread.

Amanda reads her book until nine. It helps her escape rather than puts her to sleep. She just needed to be a pain in the ass to that woman! Then, she goes out into the night. Her leg is too much of an impediment for a walk so she goes to her car, pulls it into the driveway and looks up at the stars. She likes that she lives in a planetarium.

Cheyenne arrives at ten. He is tall and rangy and maybe thirty-five. She sees him knock on her front door and then read the note she has left under the flashlight. It says: "Welcome. Please let yourself in. There is soup on the stove, wine on the table and bread on the counter. Please eat and sleep and don't be concerned when you leave in the morning for the conference that there is a woman sleeping in the middle of the living room. I do that every night."

She watches him to see if he has any reaction to the note, but he just seems to blink his eyes and then enter. She imagines what it must look like to him. Her house in the country. She knows now that she has prepared the house as if for a lover and it makes her so uncertain that she does not move from her car.

In the morning, she feels herself solid under the comforter and the living room ceiling. She cracks her eyes and looks up to the tall, curious face of Cheyenne. His eyes are an indiscriminate hazel. He smiles.

"I was curious," he says. "You look pretty."

Amanda does not have an answer.

He continues on his path to the kitchen with a coffee cup, which he must have brought with him. She can hear him rinse the cup and shake it dry. He passes back through the living room. Then he goes to the bedroom, grabs his backpack and goes to the front door. He says, "I like the art. See you later. I'm walking back so it'll be late." He crinkles his eyes, enjoying her stunned gaze following him around the room. Then he is gone and Amanda slinks back under the comforter. It is only just dawn after all.

Chapter 21

Vikram's Gathering at the Stillness Center

At the college, the attendees, slightly blurry but extremely willing, gather in the outside gazebo near the chapel. Vikram, tall and vibrant, hair flowing and easy with the colossal joke he shares with Buddha, smiles and welcomes them with his presence. He is wearing his robes. Vivi finds them silly, if not pretentious, but she is not one of the faithful. As far as she is concerned, neither is he. But, no matter, she is not there.

Besides Cheyenne, there are about forty others who have come for this weekend of meditation and talks on the "Stillness of the Self in a Hyperactive World." They have paid a modest fee for attendance and a not so modest fee for room and vegetarian board. Some are on scholarship. Like Cheyenne, several are enjoying one part and not the other. Cheyenne is not the youngest young man and he has the look of the range about him. Expansive in the crowd of crouching seekers, one gets the sense he is there for research as much as peace. There are a few beautiful young women wrapped in scarves. Most of them have studied with Vikram here at the college. And there are a few women older and more serious in search of something they will not find here. Two bearded elders, one with a shaved head and one with greasy strands over his bald pate, sit in flannel and jeans, eyes closed and feeling so comfortable that it makes them shake their heads in surprise at the gathering.

There are only a few of the faithful that are new to Vikram and the Stillness Center. The college hired him away from an ashram in India, near the small town where he was born. After finishing his PhD at Berkeley, he longed for a dose of his own culture again. Vivi didn't know much about this time but he wrote Jake a few times. He was struggling with what it was to be an Indian living in America. He was not sure if all this meditating was worth the effort if he couldn't make a living, as he confessed, he never really had a taste for the ascetic. Jake remembered that part of his old roommate. Vikram always chose the best wine. Jake was always sure he eyed his girlfriends and then, there was that night in New Rochelle. Jake never answered his old friend. Instead, he went along his own life, and every now and then would receive an announcement from the Stillness Center in Chennaie, and then an announcement that Vikram had been asked to open an American branch at this small college. It made sense, Jake thought. Now he could have the best of both worlds. And be adored as well. Jake had to admit he never could come to terms with Vikram and what had or had not happened years ago.

Jake didn't tell Vivi about his communication with Vikram, except she saw the announcement on his desk and one of their added irritants was that Jake didn't trust Vivi with the information. She followed her old friends progress as well, and looked forward to getting the Stillness Center newsletters. She would not keep them but she always knew where her old friend was living.

Vikram beckons everyone to the circle and they take their places.

Gisela, the German exchange student on work-study, punches the sound system and the air fills with the twang of sitars. Folks are a little chilly in the late autumn, early morning, breeze.

"Just cuddle with your neighbor as you sit and go deeper. We are all the same anyway, yes?" Vikram smiles as he begins the meditation.

It is Gisela who remains awake and alert, watching the faithful, checking her lists, making sure everyone is in attendance and comfortable enough. She does not smile. That is Vikram's job.

As she is checking the sound level on the console she can hear the swoosh of someone approaching. It's the sound of a cashmere wrap against silk pants A woman with soft blond waves leans down.

"Blessings to you, Gisela," she whispers.

"And to you Anandamaia!" Gisela smiles a little too broadly. "It is so nice to see you here."

"I wouldn't miss it for the world."

"And I hope you know how thankful Vikram is, we all are, for your gift. We couldn't have offered scholarships without it."

Anandamaia nods and places her palms together with a slight bow. "I knew after India that I had to do what I could to support his 'work'."

"Namaste, Anandamaia. You are such an important part of the 'work'."

Anadamaia straightens up and the Carol within smirks to herself, "Damn right, you loser!"

Too bad Anandamaia can't take over inside and out. The jury is still out as to who is the more authentic, Carol or her new alter ego. But it's pretty clear, that this new benefactress is sure to spoil the gathering.

Meanwhile, Vivi waits in the Home Center mall coffee shop. She chose this spot for the meeting with Carol. Why not give Carol the entire picture, allowing her the full satisfaction of saving Vivi from the penurious working class? A local cab finally pulls up. Carol gets out.

Vivi looks up. Carol is better coifed certainly. She is wearing L.A. cashmere, which is beautiful but never warm enough for the East Coast. Carol sees Vivi through the window and takes a moment to prepare. Carol is dragging along her magnanimous new identity but Vivi is smart enough to see where the seams are still evident.

"Hello, stranger," Vivi says, trying to take the initiative.

"It's so good to see you!" Carol gushes. But it clearly is not. Carol is wondering if this meeting is really necessary but Anandamaia comes to the rescue. Vivi says nothing, not sure what the woman wants.

"I thought you were here to study. Aren't you missing the morning sessions?"

"This is so much more important," Anandamaia smiles but Vivi can't help but wonder to whom that woman is speaking and why she is sitting across the table from her.

Carol senses she better get this show on the road. "Ellen tells me you already have chosen a site for a new house. And you are moving ahead."

"Yes. Thanks. I have signed all the papers."

"So, you're working for Home Center? I hear their politics are pretty bad."

Vivi keeps her eyes steady. She resists saying, 'beggars can't be choosers'. Instead she says, "They only abuse the elderly greeters at the door. All day standing on cement and 5 cents a wave."

"Actually, I hear that is true, Vivi. You shouldn't be so flippant. I think there was a docu . . ." Ah, there she is. There is the woman Vivi remembers.

Vivi cuts her off. "Is there really any business we have missed?"

Carol asks, "How's the coffee here?"

"It's not L.A. but it will do."

Carol takes her time to toddle to the self-serve and get a cup, then insist that the janitor, swabbing the floor, go behind the counter and get real milk for her cup.

When she resettles she says, "Yum. I thought Dunkin Donuts had the franchise . . ."

"Carol. My break is almost over."

This is really hard and Carol is not even sure what she wants to say, or how she wants to play it.

"Vivian, I . . ." she starts.

"My name is Vivi and yours is Carol. I mean that's who I am talking to and I'm not sure what you are after, coming to visit here. Would you like me to say, thanks? Because I have no need of that. Would you like me to say, you are forgiven? Because I really am not interested in any of that. I'll leave you to your spiritual studies to give you absolution."

"I didn't think you would still be so hostile, Viv . . . ia . . ." She stops herself from the longer name. Vivi begins to gather her things.

"And how did you manage to find this conference, Anandamaia?" Vivi almost spits the word out, surprising even herself.

"Vikram was a good friend of Jake's." Carol speaks as if butter would not melt in her mouth. Eyes wide at Vivi. Vivi stops dead and turns facing Carol.

"I beg your pardon?"

"Jake. He was a friend of Jake's." Anandamaia speaks these words as if she has been Jake's wife, as if she has the right, not only to the money she stole but to grieving rights as well.

"Are you kidding me?" Vivi is ready to flatten this pompous L.A. blonde. To her credit, she even looks around to see if there is a hidden camera.

"But I suppose you knew that." Carol's admission brings Vivi right back to the hard plastic bench.

"Carol. I'm sorry. I just cannot bear being near this reborn version of yourself. At least when you were desperate there was something to pity." Now, Vivi knows she has to walk away before she hurls a table at the woman. She remembers when she was capable of that. "I have to go now. Don't call me again, okay?"

"I'll tell Vikram you said hello," Vivi hears floating after her.

She turns on her heel and heads back, and into her face she spits, "Never mention my name again. As long as we both shall live!"

She is aware that is bad dialogue from a Movie of the Week and she can't figure out why it comes out of her. But it works. Carol tosses her curls and hurls her coffee to the trash bin and stalks out.

"I know you are teaching and 'in retreat', but I'll be goddamned if I am going to sit back and get patronizing visits from my husband's ex-lover and . . ."

The phone clatters up from its cradle. "Om shanti to you, too."

"Vikram. How do you know Carol?"

"Ah . . . Anandamaia . . ." he says, bemused.

"Are you aware of who she is?" Vivi is not remotely interested in finding cosmic balance at this moment.

"Yes. Vivi. I am aware. She came to India. She's connected to a very rich guy there. Maybe a shah or something. He's funding her film stuff. Met him at some festival in Delhi."

"A shah? In India. How the hell did she find you?"

"A lot of people know my work, Vivi. I actually have quite a good reputation among many."

"Good for you. You are indeed the second coming. I forgot that part."

She came to India, Vivi thinks. *She came to India?*

"She heard of my work. She wanted to give me money for my work. I took the grant. Then I found out who she was."

"How?"

"She told me. We got to talking."

Vivi spends a brief moment imagining casual Carol and casual Vikram casually drinking tea and casually mentioning that they had Jake in common. Then she sees herself in the fantasy with a sledgehammer ready to drop it on both of their heads.

"Keep her well the way away from me," wails Vivi. "If you are a friend. If you have ever been a friend, keep that demon, fake, sad sack of an Anadamaia bullshit woman away from me."

"You are accepting her money as well."

"What did you say?" Vivi is stunned. There is an enormous clash of cymbals in her ears. "What did you say?"

"Oh Vivi. Lighten up. She's giving you money."

"She's giving me *my* money. She stole it from me. She took the rights . . ."

"Are you aware that maybe the reason she decided to return some of that money might have something to do with me? Have you thought about that?"

The cymbals now clatter to the floor.

"You're kidding."

"I met her in India. She took a private session with me. She told me she was newly rich, newly connected to a new relationship with this Indian guy who has nothing but money. She told me she was not sure of next steps and I told her to pay off all her debts."

"Why did she come to you? How did she find you?"

"I think she loved Jake. Why did you come?"

Vivi's head starts to spin. "Vikram, are you saying you and I have no relationship apart from Jake? Have never had?"

"I'm saying she came to me because I knew Jake. Because she wanted to see who Jake might have been if he . . ."

"If he had not married me?"

"Wait a minute. Wait a minute."

"Vikram, guru man, or whoever the hell you are these days, is not the Vikram that is my friend. The man I knew. The man I cared about, who was my friend."

"I am the same person."

"And me? Am I not the friend you knew? Did we play at romance when we were young, when I first came here, because of Jake, no other connection?" She is pacing and furious.

There is a quiet fullness on the phone. Then, Vivi hears him move something metallic. Before she can attack his deflection, he says, "I am just making tea, Vivi." He opens a can and she can hear the tea leaves fall into his mug. Lavender chamomile.

"Vivi, I was not and am not what you ever wanted me to be," he says.

Now, she can hear Vikram strike a match. Light a stick of weed. Take a puff.

Vivi looks out her window, trying to grab hold of herself. In her mind she sees mounds of tumbleweed being driven into the desert. She sees pebbles rocketing down a hill. She sees boulders from a canyon height cascade to rumble and rest, blocking the entrance to a mine. She waits for the dust to settle. Finally, the fury that has driven her relents. She knows she is asking too much.

"I know, I know. I'm sorry. I am not your job," she says.

"Now there's an admission," he says. He takes another long toke. And gives a gentle laugh. He is listening and he has returned from Guru land to the land of Friend. That's something.

"I am proud of you, Vivi. Thank you for your friendship. I love you. I'm sorry for any pain I have caused you. Please forgive me."

"I am the only person you have left in your life who has known you in your different lives."

She can hear Vikram let out a long stream of air. She can hear him grab more air for his lungs. She can hear him choke just a bit.

"Yes," he says finally. "My witness."

"I need a witness protection plan," Vivi says. She laughs lightly, her chest expanding a bit at last.

"Is it that risky to be my friend?" he asks, almost seriously.

They are both quiet. She can hear Vikram take a sip of his tea. Regain his equilibrium. Reinstall the metal detector sheets. And bolt the frame in place. Vivi wants her last line to enter the sanctum sanctorum before the door shuts.

"Good night, dear. I love you." It comes out of her like spun gold and it finds its resting place in Vikram's heart.

"Good night, dear," he says. "I love you."

Chapter 22

Cheyenne

Amanda sees the backpack before the swing of his arms, the lope of his long legs.

She's in her studio when he comes back to the house. He comes in and she watches as a lamp goes on, he moves from room to room, inhabiting her space.

She moves to her car when the first star comes out. She opens her eyes large enough to receive each star as an eye drop. And finally she loses the battle and her eyes close. He is tapping at the window. He is smiling at her. "You afraid to sleep in the house with me?"

"No, not at all." She rubs her eyes and rolls down the window. "I like to look at the stars. And then my eyes close."

"And you get to keep the light inside your head all night long. Right. I get that."

She cracks a little smile at him. He is a handsome kid. As if he hears her thoughts, he puts his hand on hers.

"It'll be nice to see you later. Maybe we can talk."

"Sure. I mean, sure. I'm around."

"Yes. Well, you're around even if you're not actually around. Your house has its own story."

"Yes. Well, thanks, I guess." She looks at him again. He is smiling steadily into her eyes. He is flirting with her. It seems like it.

"I set your bed up. It's all ready for you inside. Sleep well."

"How is it going?" Amanda is there at the table the next night when he comes in. It's past the dying of the light. She's reading the life of Thoreau.

"I like him. Thoreau." he says. "A real pain in the ass. I dig it."

Amanda snorts into her mint tea. "Dig it?" She can't help grinning.

"Dig it," says Cheyenne. He crinkles his eyes. "I'm beat. I'm heading to bed. Nice to see you." And he turns and leaves her and her tea and her book in the kitchen. She is not sure if she is disappointed. She gets up to warm the water. She picks up a piece of chocolate that she left near the teapot. As she unwraps it, she feels a strange chill from her feet through her calves, through her thighs and a warm resting in her lower belly. Dig it.

Cheyenne sticks around after the weekend with Vikram. He lives in Amanda's house and she tells him about Thoreau and Edna St. Vincent Millay. She tells him about certain habits of the rich and privileged in Bronte novels and about Tom Jones, the novel. He listens usually for a couple hours at night after he returns from whatever he does all day long. By the end of the first week, he brings a bottle of wine back with him. She lights candles in the breakfast nook where there is usually warm bread and soup against the approaching winter.

Tonight she has been listening to music. She has found some waltz music on iTunes that could easily have been played at the dance with Mr. Darcy. She has picked up a copy of *Pride and Prejudice* at the library. And now she dips into *Emma*.

Cheyenne comes in and listens to the music in the doorway as he watches Amanda sip wine from a jam jar. He thinks that she seems less thick than she appeared when he first arrived. He thinks, she must be lighter. She is carrying more light.

"I like the music," he says. She looks up and smiles at him.

"It's lovely. Yes."

"Here," he says, putting out his hand. She takes it as naturally as if he is the next beau on her dance card. He pulls her in and out to the living room. He waltzes with her. She smiles and lets her head fall back. The music stops. He pulls her in close and brings his tall head down, to allow his chin to rest on her head. She feels his heart beating in the shadowed living room. She has not danced in a very long time.

They are not moving now, except for Cheyenne shifting his weight from side to side. And Amanda following. She realizes that she bathed earlier in the evening because he was coming home. She shuffles her feet along with his and wonders if she should lift her head. Let him kiss her. Let herself kiss this handsome boy-man.

He won't let her lift her head. He hugs her very tightly. Body to body, they stand in the living room. Then, carefully, he releases her and steps away.

"Good night," he says. "I left the rent on the table this morning. Did you get it?"

"Yes," she says.

"Good," he says, and steps back again. "Good night."

Chapter 23

Babies Again

Vivi has been dreaming of babies again. She doesn't know why. Since she met Amanda her dreams seem to be seeded with images of old women at caves in pools. They are old and odd and angry in her dreams. Above them hang, like bats, the bodies of small babies, cocooned and catalogued, guarded by the crones below. She has not seen Amanda again but she heard from Vikram that Amanda has kept Cheyenne since the weekend workshop.

"She seems to have bewitched the young man," says Vikram. "He got a job at the library half-time and goes home to mama every night."

"Mama?"

"She has to be close to seventy."

"They may actually be friends," says Vivi, strangely defensive.

"Sure. I'm sure they are."

But Vivi is curious what draws Cheyenne back to Amanda's every night. She has yet to be able to bring such a one back to her home or to her bed. But her dreams are rich with women and possibility and choice.

This time the pools steam a cool mist as she watches the old women, who lay like mermaids, combing each other's gray hair. They do not acknowledge

Vivi. They see her and smile slightly to each other with toothy grins. She comes to the end of the cave and looks up to see the babes hanging swaddled from their feet, their eyes quiet, soothed by the cooing of the water and women as they whisper and gently bubble laughter up to the sleeping forms. Vivi looks up and sees a small wrapped form with a slight lace collar peeking out from the swarm of fabric that cushions the child.

"Oh there you are!" cries Vivi. "There you are!"

One of the old crones looks up.

"She's been waiting for you. Where have you been?"

The crone hands Vivi the wrapped form and she gently places the child on the wet stony ground. She gently unwraps the form. She fingers the familiar lace color, it is just a few strings, grabbing at each other. Vivi puts the lace on the palm of her hand and feels its weight and then continues to unwrap the form, and she unwraps and unwraps the swaddling clothes. At the end there is simply a filament of skin. All that is left. Vivi looks at the filament and strokes it gently hoping somehow it knew it was loved.

Chapter 24

Cheyenne Again

He is ubiquitous. He is everywhere. He is in Amanda's dreams now. And in her everyday breath. She is having trouble keeping herself from grabbing at him, sucking his youth and kindness down into her body and replacing her organs with the juice of his heart. He plays it cool, as if he has no idea of how parched she has been and how just his presence is allowing the beef jerky of her fascia to become buoyant again. Since he has come she can walk easily with no numbness in her leg.

Amanda paints every day. She watches the sky. Then finds something that she can swallow whole and allow to come back out through her eyes and hands and paint brush. She starts with pine cones. The obsessive relevance of all those layers nags at her and she is wound into the seeing of this object. She studies them. Then, she does studies of them. And then, she does it again. The wall of her shed is covered with these studies.

He does not see them. And she often hides from him as well, fearing that her presence will smother him. It is enough that he comes, he eats at her table, and he smiles in her direction as she paints in the shed feigning concentration and total absorption in the nature of the thing she sees.

He feels ephemeral to Amanda. He feels like splinters of hope on a tarp and she does not want to disturb them.

Meanwhile, Vivi is impatient to get her house built, her basement dug, her terraces set before the winter. She hires Cheyenne to dig for her. He comes by and takes his instructions from Ted Stillman, who insists, even to Cheyenne, that his wife will be back from the City and will be helpful in completing the design for Vivi's house.

"What's she like?" Cheyenne asks Ted.

"What did you say?" Ted is not sure if Cheyenne is being disingenuous or sincere.

"You have been married a long time, right?"

Ted coughs a little. "We have been married for over twenty-five years."

"What's she like?"

Ted finds it hard to answer the boy. "If you mean, if she's sexy, I guess I can say that. I mean we never had kids but she is damn sexy."

Ted is confused as to how to describe his wife to this boy. Is he supposed to calculate her by diameter of breast and wetness of vagina?

Cheyenne comes to his rescue. "I mean how does it feel to be connected to someone so long?"

Ted is puzzled once again. "Good" is the only thing he can come up with. "I mean, rough sometimes, but good. Worth it." Ted shuffles in place. He can't seem to find his footing.

Cheyenne crinkles his hazel eyes again and looks away. "Vivi says she wants to build a terrace garden."

"She thinks she's living in Pompeii, that one," says Ted, disgruntled. "Hanging gardens and all that."

"I think that was Babylon," says Cheyenne. "Or actually, now they say they may have been in Iraq or somewhere. Lots of waterfalls."

"Well, no waterfalls around here. She actually wants a tree in her living room. It'll just rot."

"A tree in her living room sounds cool."

When Vivi arrives, she has pictures of terraced gardens from Peru and from California. She wants wisteria and grapes, she says, and an amphitheater of perennials.

"Once they're established I won't need to do anything but stare at them!" *Roses will do, she thinks. Roses on trellises. Unless they all get buggy. The sun may not be as strong here as she is used to. Is spraying an option so near a watershed?* And her thoughts roll round and round, swirling and bouncing her happily like in a kids' trampoline house.

Ted loses enthusiasm for her plans.

"Look here. How about this guy rents a Bobcat this weekend and does the mounds for you. I'm going to New York. To see my wife. She has this big job there."

"Sure, Ted. But promise me we can get the foundation in before the snow. Please. I want to be in my new house by spring."

"You think his wife will be there waiting for him in New York?" says Cheyenne to Vivi as they watch Ted move away.

Vivi turns and looks at him. "That's unkind," she says.

"Why? The guy is desperate. He's so lonely he stinks of it and yet he can't even describe the woman he's married to."

"You've been talking with Ted about his marriage?"

"I'm interested. I'm interested what it's like to live with someone for so long."

Vivi takes a moment. "I'm not sure you know that until it's gone."

Cheyenne looks up with interest. She has something that he had not noticed before.

"Are you married?"

"I was. Twenty years. Long time. He died."

"Oh," says Cheyenne. He lets Vivi decide if she wants to say anything else.

"Any kids," he asks?

"No kids," she says. "Unless you want to count coping with adolescent behavior in your partner as parenting."

"I wouldn't know."

Vivi feels badly about what she has just said. It feels like a betrayal to this cocky, overly curious young man.

"We can talk about it more once I get to know you. Rent the Bobcat for Saturday, will you?"

That night, Vivi dreams about Jake for the first time in a long time. He's not present. But he's sitting in a rocker under the arbor in their old house in L.A., moving slowly back and forth. His eyes are closed. He's humming a little tune. Content. He's been watching, floating around, dropping a pebble in the pool every now and then, but he wants Vivi to know he's still there. Maybe he wants some credit for Carol turning back some cash as well.

When she wakes, she still feels the solidity of the door jamb against her hip and thigh, how her bare feet were against the cool linoleum in their old home. She is not sure how she feels about seeing Jake so present in this life she has created. It's odd for Jake to be content in her garden. But if it's the only thing he can do to get her to acknowledge him, let him figure out why he went through that whole life with her, with Vikram, then so be it.

She feels warm and longing. Happy to see him after such a long time. He didn't turn to look at her but she got it. He didn't wear a baseball cap. She always liked his bald head on her shoulder, to feel the pleasure of the soft strands of his hair moving easily through her fingers.

How tenderly he holds that child, Vivi thinks, when she awakes. Yes. He is making progress.

Chapter 25

Bobcat

Cheyenne is pretty dexterous with the small steam shovel. That's what it is. A little steam shovel. In the shop at the Arboretum, they sold boy's toys and there was a little steam shovel there that she always admired.

Vivi keeps herself from going out to the site too early. She wants to let Cheyenne begin the task so she won't distract him from creating this first step in her paradise. She stops at Home Center and uses her employee discount to pick up rebar and metal fencing. She orders railroad ties and pavers and pays for everything up front. What a great feeling!

She pulls up around 11:00. Cheyenne has created a bowl around the front of the house. And the terraces are beginning to appear. There is a rawness to the torn landscape and Vivi almost regrets disturbing the settled earth. It is surprised, the earth. It's ragged open space grabbing at the oxygen it has not felt in so long.

"Don't worry. It's happy to get some air after all this time. I guarantee it." Cheyenne comes up behind her. "Don't worry. It will settle down."

Vivi smiles. "You feel it too, huh?"

"Hard to miss. It's like the ghosts are rolling up in big plumes of fog and dust."

Vivi is not sure what to do.

"I've already called Vikram," says Cheyenne.

"Vikram?"

"He's going to design us a mandala. A labyrinth. Make it a holy spot. What do you think?"

"Well, I've never really . . ."

"Great! I told him I knew you would think it was a great idea!" Cheyenne turns to her with delight. A cheery twinkle. "Gotta get back on the monster," he says. "I'm chanting as I dig so it should be just fine."

"Right," says Vivi. "Sure."

"He says he's chanting as he digs," says Vivi, cradling her cell phone and rubbing lotion into her chapped hands.

"Dig it," says Tara.

"Did you really say that, Tara?" Vivi smiles in spite of herself. Tara laughs a big chuckle.

"I'm sorry I can't be there myself to see what the cat drags in," says Tara. "I told you the land hasn't been disturbed in a while."

"Come over for a picnic before you go?"

"Nah. I'll grab something at Subway. My shuttle comes at one. Off to the airport and Florida styling!" Vivi is surprised that she is already missing this odd friend.

"Hope you enjoy all that sunshine."

"It'll be great. Housesitting the cousin's condo. Yes!" She takes a moment and her voice readjusts. "So, here's my words. Don't be freaked out by old smoke, kid. It's just smoke. Let it waft like incense."

"I hate incense."

"You have no taste. I'll be online every day doing readings from there while I'm housesitting the condo and drinking in the rays. Call me on my cell if you need me. I won't charge you."

Vivi smiles again. "Have a good time." Vivi shuffles off Tara's words even though there is comfort in them. "Don't buy a timeshare," she says. Tara laughs then quiets.

"Look, your hands and feet and elbows and innards and outers all are ready for this new start. You won't have to say goodbye this time, Viv."

"All this saying goodbye, that saying goodbye. It has just about done me in."

"Queen of Swords! Cut away the crap and go forward my pal!"

"Come back soon, Tara. I'll miss you."

Tara chuckles like the contented chicken that she is. Vivi wonders why she is distinctly jumpy in ways she does not recognize.

"I'll be fine," she says into the telephone after Tara has hung up. She is sure someone can hear her.

Chapter 26

Ripped Earth

Cheyenne works most of the afternoon. He moves around in a circle, digging a path several feet wide and dumping the earth beside him to develop a mound in a half circle. Digging and dumping. Digging and dumping. Then he changes the attachment on the back of the Bobcat and drags it across the loose earth creating tracts of lands, plateaus, a map full of anthills and buried dogs. Then he does it again. Then he does it again.

Vivi loves watching the little machine rearrange her life. She loves watching the young man in his baseball cap and glasses chant Sanskrit rhythms with self-conscious gravity and hearing that gravity slide into the twang of a country western ballad. She loves watching the sun move across the sky and imagine how the light will revisit the turned earth and make it live again. It feels so alive and hopeful and blessed. She wishes Tara could be here to witness this new beginning.

Around three o'clock, the other crew arrives with the rest of the supplies. She's hired a group of guys who hang out in front of Home Center looking for day labor. She welcomes them with bottles of water and a quick tour and they ignore her and move directly to the mounds, flattening them, adding rebar to hold the sides and piling the railroad ties. They move their bodies to the task easily except for a skinny white kid who looks like he hasn't seen the sun for months. The county jail is nearby. It's possible he just got out. Antonio heads the crew. Vivi knows him as he often makes deliveries for the store. He grins at Vivi when she looks dubiously at the skinny white kid. He claps a hand on the kid's shoulder and throws him a pair of gloves.

Cheyenne joins them until the sun sets early, and then as one unit, they stretch their backs, lift their faces in surprise to see they have lost the sun. In its descent they see magenta and blue, a line of extraordinarily fresh white cloud, and like diorama cut outs, the men pose against the sky til the sun is gone and rays of light make them glow like radioactive chunks of coal.

The men leave. Cheyenne doesn't even turn to say goodbye. He is hungry and lost in himself. They are all gone and there is no light. There are shadows and a slight breeze. Vivi heads to her car to warm up and turns on the headlights. She settles in behind the wheel so she can have a view of her new garden in its moment of becoming. It is naked and open and she feels protective. Tara told her that it might be rough, this digging up and rearranging but so far, it has made space in her heart. She can breathe from a deeper place. Nevertheless, she feels the need to keep watch.

She reaches over for the small blanket she keeps in the back seat and settles in. The lights in her car go out. She pulls at the knob but it sparks, she moves away from the shock quickly but her head begins to spin.

She does not feel like she will leave her body. Instead, she cannot. She is rooted, looking at the overturned earth. The shifts of the last three years have been buried deep beneath all her moving boxes and job searches and her coping conversations with Jake's family. They stagger forward with no rearview mirror. She cannot believe she will finally have a home again and wonders how she will do it, who she will be, rooted as herself with still so much to shed and swallow.

Her hand hurts. Her head hurts. And she sinks away from consciousness. She does not remember. She is shaken and shifted and slid into a vortex that moves her down, down into the earth. She feels her feet rooting in the soil and her arms stretching up high, moving through clay and debris and New England rock and her hands reach out above her. She is strong and part of this new beginning and swirling in possibility.

Suddenly, she feels a small filament of skin attaching to the palm of her hand. It rolls from side to side and grows in warmth and volume until a small hand manifests and clasps onto hers. The hand is plump and white, it is fused to her skin and the two of them, Vivi and this plump sweet hand travel up from the depths of the earth. Vivi can look over now and she sees blonde white curls falling over the young arm, the sturdy torso, the yoke of the child's nightgown that clings to her emergent body. She sees the dirt beneath the child's fingernails as they move up from the earth. The child's body becomes plump and full, like a small round bear waking from a long nap.

Vivi, eyes wide, can only open her arms as she listens to the sound that comes from her.

Vivi cannot tell where she is, how she is holding this child, hearing her weep, feeling her own body give birth again as the shadow of the bones moves from her belly down her legs and puddles on the floor. She opens her arms again, her mouth as wide as it will go, her eyes bigger than platters, her ears roaring canals with all the water of the universe rushing past her.

Suddenly, Jake's face appears. He watches as this child comes roaring through her. He reaches out to try to grab the child but misses. They both dissolve in a fury of dissolution.

Vivi looks down in the dark and there is a puddle of fluid, there is blood, there are bones. They drop from a height one at a time into the slosh, and then onto the earth, onto her shoes and the rivulets that drag along her body, until every bone, every slice of flesh and nail and hair and fever has entered and left Vivi's body, and Vivi cannot move. She is inside out and melted in the wax of what was and is no more.

In the morning, Cheyenne finds her wrapped in the blanket she keeps in the car, lying at the foot of the terraces. Her face is dirty and there is blood around her mouth. Cheyenne calls Vikram and Vikram takes Vivi home and puts her to bed.

Chapter 27

Painting Pine Cones

"I made some soup," says Amanda as Cheyenne comes through the door. "Oh, look at you! You look beat!"

"I worked hard. Making a garden. Digging terraces. Building a dream castle for that woman." He pushes his hair back from his face but it flops back. "It should be cool. Eventually."

"Yes. It should be," Amanda smiles at him. She moves a stray hair away from his eyes. "Take a shower? Hungry?"

"Sure."

Amanda smiles and listens as he turns and heads to the shower. She is balanced this evening. There is no danger of her overstepping her fantasies and being foolish. She's made some bread. She has the radio playing Chopin. There is a beer for Cheyenne. There is wine for her. And cookies. She made cookies.

Cheyenne comes back, all shiny and wet. He slopes over to the refrigerator and grabs the milk and pours himself a big glass and slugs it down. He comes to the table and Amanda serves the soup.

"You have a nice day, dear?" Cheyenne says.

Amanda snorts into her wine glass. "Ha! Yes, dear. I had a productive day. I painted pine cones."

"Pine cones."

"Pine cones," she says. "I am obsessed."

"Yes?" Cheyenne's eyes are closing. "Jeez, I'm really bushed. Keep talking. I'll just listen with my eyes closed."

Amanda looks at the exhausted young man as he leans back into the corner booth of the kitchen. And she hears his breath deepen and sees his head droop. She walks to the living room to grab her sketchpad. She sits at the table and turns him into curves and line and shadow. She sees behind each surface and draws his eyelids behind his falling glasses.

Then she blows out the candles and brings him a blanket against the chill. Amanda lets herself close her own eyes not far from the sleeping boy. They sleep together for the first time.

Chapter 28

Vikram's Sand

"Come on, Vivi. Come on now. Follow me and drop the sand in your path. You can do it"

Vikram and Vivi are back at the site of her ravished land. He has made her drink strong scented mint and ginger tea. He disappeared while she slept as if drugged. He returned with several large sacks of colored sand. He pulled her large sweatshirt over her head and insisted that she change into work pants. He stood her up, washed her face again roughly with a lavender scented cloth. He would not let her sleep anymore. He put her back in the car. "Wake up now, Vivi."

Now, he quickly gets out of the car and opens her side, shoving her toward the tender earth, gaping and confused. The sun is valiantly holding twilight at bay, squeezing purple into its palette with its effort.

"Get out now." He is not speaking gently. He is urgent.

She looks at him. "Walk, Vivi. Walk and drop the sand. Yes? Don't stop."

Vivi drags her feet but follows Vikram. Her hands are in a bag of yellow sand. She lifts it out as she begins a circuit of the open earth. The sand falls through her fingers.

"Good," says Vikram. "Here. Keep going. Walk the entire circle and do not stop. And don't come back to me on this side until all your sand is gone. Make sure it is clear, the circle. Go Vivi! Keep walking."

Vikram speaks firmly. He has on his pea coat and his hair starts to look gray in the disappearing light. He drips red sand carefully in a square pattern within the circle that Vivi is tracing, her eyes half-closed, half crusted with sebum.

"We place this sand carefully against ripped earth, Vivi. We trace the circle, we trace the square. We drop every bit of sand in a pattern of color. There is sense and nonsense. There is memory and loss. And we let each grain rest against the earth to remind us of the beauty of every day we have lived. We drop blue for sky, red for blood, yellow for light, white for pure strength." His words tumble and cascade.

Vikram moves with purpose across the earth. He turns as he comes up against Vivi's yellow circles. She trudges on. He lets his voice rise.

"Every grain is a child, every grain is a death, every trail is a birth, every sweep is a bird, a flight, a loss, a love, an attachment, a ghost, a grasping, a trudge. We are all sand, Vivi. You and me. We have lived then and now and then again and again and again. We celebrate it now, okay?"

He wants to make sure she hears this, as he is like a crane flapping his wings, preparing for flight.

"I am saying to you that we are imprinting the many times we have loved each other and lost each other and had children and murdered animals, and laughed joyously and died stinking. We are imprinting this with every grain of this sand."

Vikram steps out of his square and Vivi looks up at him at the bottom of her circle.

"Come here, Viv. Take this red bag and trail it in a spiral. Carefully. But do not stop."

"Vikram." Vivi looks up at him. He is possessed and she can barely speak. "I can't walk in circles. I feel like a spinner top. "

"Keep walking, Vivi. Don't stop and just trail sand. Each step take a breath, next step let it out. Keep going. One thing. Next thing. Then thing. That thing." She looks up at him to find a way to him but he won't connect. He chants fiercely as he too drops sand and prays, repeating the words. "Nothing lasts, nothing is finished, nothing is perfect. Nothing lasts, nothing is finished, nothing is perfect."

Vivi drags the bag behind her. She digs her hand deep into the sand and allows the evening wind to twirl her. The sand rushes from her fingers. It is blood in a centrifuge.

They walk in circles and squares now. In a slower rhythm. Like farmers broadcasting seed.

As they settle into a persistent rhythm, the light is only shadow and a gray horizon. Vivi's breath is steam. She takes a step, spreads the red memory, and takes the next. They walk resolutely now. Vikram is desperate that she hears this.

"We are honoring our time on the planet, Viv. We are honoring now and then and the lives we have shared and lives we have not." Vikram carefully steps across the line of sand and takes Vivi's shoulders in his large hands. He speaks tenderly.

"I have known you now and then, dear Vivi. Okay. We loved each other then, another life, another time. We are honoring it all right now. Yes?"

Vivi blinks her eyes in affirmation.

"You can't keep melting back into then and maybe and leaving your body and floating to Jake, and fucking ghosts, and abandoning children in life after life after life."

"Abandoning?"

Vikram shakes his head and her effort at straightening details away. "We can't keep doing this with each other. To each other. As mother, child, father, lover, sister . . ."

"Vikram. Stop. I can't do this."

Vikram catches his breath and watches as she crosses the lines they have laid down. He sees a random glint from the mica in his first square.

"Look, Viv. Look at the light in the sand. Look. There is the spark. Yes? The mandala has come alive."

And the sun disappears and Vikram goes to his car and turns on his headlights so she can see the mandala in its completion. The light strikes one color at a time. It reveals the sand as perfect and crooked, constant and intermittent.

Vikram says, "We make mandalas with respect and love and acknowledgment of every moment. We honor it. See, Vivi. We are honoring everything we have shared."

If Vivi were more aware, if this was a real moment, she would see how desperate Vikram is for her to hear him. If she were in her body, she would recognize that Vikram is desperate to ascend, to somehow think of candy and fly away like Peter Pan, to leave her behind, to run from her and who they were or might have been. But she sees this from a fog. At some point, Vikram kisses her on her forehead and gets back in his car and leaves her there. Breathing in her own steam, settling into the beautiful colors that she has spread with her friend. She notices that he has left a bag of petals by her.

In the surprise that is nature, the large moon rises from the horizon. Vivi can see the patterns. She watches as the wind teases them away. And then Cheyenne shows up to take her home.

Chapter 29

Sand in the Wind

While Vikram and Vivi pace and bless the earth, Jake feels himself pulled back into his old self. He feels himself pulled back into his old skin. He has no real understanding of how this happens. It feels vaguely like a recoil from vomiting he thinks, in his old Jake head, but then he stops and realizes that he can feel an itch against his skin. He can feel the grit of red sand. He can feel the red sands being blown and coming back through him and lodging where his heart had been. He can feel it like the sand an oyster feels to make a pearl. The electricity of his boundaries sizzle back to an imprint as the colors knock against his protoplasm, the red landing where his heart had been. Why has he been summoned to stand in the windstorm? There is so much sand, so much grit that it finds itself attracted to itself and slowly the dance of attraction creates the shape of a human heart.

Then, he can see Vivi trudging in a trance, he can see Vikram struggling to stay in his body and do the right thing, bless this visitation, whatever it is.

Jake knows he needs to pay attention to this sand, he needs to see the healing that is being requested. He needs to sit up, show up, reach out to Vivi, the woman he had chosen, the woman he had run from. This is his chance to reach her, to be part of her healing and so his own. This is momentous, he thinks.

But try as he might to slip in next to her, she is having none of it. Her spirit is elsewhere. It has been dropped somewhere and is vaulting into caverns he is not privy to. Jake somersaults himself through her consciousness to the moment when the child comes screaming through her. He can hear the calls to Anna Elizabeth. Jake tries to formulate himself to hold the child, to catch the woman, to be part of the birthing, the blessing the sloughing but he cannot. He cannot as much as he might try. He is not welcome. He is not here as a dancer. He is here only as an unwelcome witness.

Jake travels back and back and sees a child in a cold human coffin. He knows it is Anna Elizabeth. He can feel her pulse and then its absence. He can see she was once part of Vivi, or Vivi in another time and place. He sees the child alone in lace, and ill, and a man then helping the woman bury the child. The man strokes the woman's head, holding her loss, being her loss. And he does not recognize the man or the woman with his eyes, which he no longer has, but he recognizes the man and the woman as the energies that became Vikram and Vivi.

And he floats and fights and bumps against their grief and he is thrown from that room where the child is in its icy coffin, where the child is conceived in deep love, where the loss of the child is predetermined. He is flung from the consciousness, he is herded elsewhere. These people he had loved so dearly in his life with Vivi do not want him here. This love is not his. This child is not his. This birthing, this healing is not his and he is hollow and whipped and driven to his own statue in the cosmos. And he comes to understand that Vivi was never his, that

Vikram was never his, that it was never his heaven to have to create a child with Vivi.

It was his job to bring them together so that they can face this reckless confluence of lust and love from a timeline that no longer matters. It was his job to create a frame so they could move through their own business of loss. His loss, perhaps his life, was merely an arrow, instructive of what was to come for them.

He can see Vivi writhing over turning earth, Vikram trying to bury his own part with red sands and empty blessings. He knows that Vikram will run now, run from Vivi. He wants to tell her that but she will learn that soon enough. And he becomes a mushroom cloud of pain and helplessness. He recognizes the ultimate uselessness of his own time on the planet with Vivi. He was only the way to Vikram. He always suspected it and now he knows it to be true.

That night, after Vikram makes plans to get on a train and a plane and fly to India, he goes to the stove and makes some fragrant tea. It is full of cinnamon and Indian spice and reminds him of his Auntie and Uncle, and then the parents that he has lost, and the country that expelled him long before he met Jake. Or Vivi. He has had enough of losing and blessing. He is done with the reliving of grief and the constant payment for some karmic debt from which he cannot get free.

Jake throws his breath over the teakettle and the water boils and bubbles over its spout.

Vikram looks up but still does not believe that Jake is really there, watching him plot his escape. Jake sits on Vikram's shoulder and bites him, a spider in his black curls. Vikram slaps at him. Jake slides down

Vikram's body and enters his stomach, he enters his bowels, he dances and rips and Vikram runs to the bathroom to empty what is left of his own body into the toilet.

Unsteady, he comes back to the kitchen to hear the teapot whistle again. Whistle again and again and louder and louder. Jake's rage, the fury he feels at the manipulation of being merely a conduit for those he had tried to love, compels him. He is furious to see how he was used as pipeline but never claimed his own personhood when he was alive. He was always allowing himself to tell someone else's story, to enable someone else's life. Jake's rage howls and buzzes through the teapot, and the steam fills the room and smoke alarms go off, and Vikram's phone rings, and Jake perches on the overhead light and pops the incandescent bulbs one by one, showering the now dimly lit room with shards of small, spiky glass. The glass is caught in Vikram's hair, it just misses his eyes. His eyelashes shield his open eyes that do not blink.

Vikram looks up and catches sight of Jake, finally. He acknowledges Jake's presence. Vikram can do that. And Vikram bellows. And he throws his cup at the smoke alarm and he heads to the sink and lets water run in the dishpan and heaves it on the flame under the teapot that has started to lick the tea towel, tucked by the tea canister.

"Jake!" Vikram bellows. "Jake! Stop it! This has nothing to do with you."

And there is stillness in the room.

And Jake quiets. Seeing how it has always been exactly about him and how he brought these two together to fulfill their own lessons. The karmic messenger man, he thinks. Winged Mercury in high tops.

And Vikram quiets. And flings himself on his Ikea couch. His head is in his hands, he tries to feel his face. And then he rises, and crosses to his meditation mat. He sits cross-legged by the flowers, the picture of his parents, his guru, the picture of Mickey Mantle and Whitey Ford, and the picture of his childhood home. He sits quietly on his mat. He closes his eyes. He folds his hands. He starts to breathe. And he says oh so softly so that only a ghost could hear, "I'm sorry, please forgive me, thank you, I love you."

And Jake hears him. Blessed and distanced. His fury assuaged, he is now complete. He is done with Vivi and Vikram and the life they all lived. He will leave the two of them to finish their own work. His is complete.

And he spins and sips the light that comes through to him. And Jake rises and leaves. Vikram sighs and does not cry. He is the wounded lion. Beware. He better go. He gets up. He calls Cheyenne to remind him. He must take him to the train, to the plane, to India and far away.

Chapter 30

Vikram's Escape

On the ride to the train, Cheyenne is quiet. Vikram begins to speak.

"I met her, Vivi, when Jake, her late husband, and I were roommates. He was a good enough guy. He was hopeful and over-loved by his parents and I was neither of those things. But he was solid and kind, he was kind then."

Cheyenne holds the steering wheel and listens. His eyes open.

"Vivi was lost too. She had no parents by the time I met her. She was gentle and liquid in so many ways that I understood. Jake attracted those of us who preferred to be tethered to the ground by a great big, sweet, Jumbo elephant and in return, we gave him lightness of being and the cache of sensitivity. He recognized that he was caught in his own thickness and that we, Vivi and I, gave him access to something bigger. Light? Maybe. But he didn't call it that.

So, when Vivi agreed to marry him in all her need and her magnificent survival mechanisms, he jumped at the chance. She legitimized him. Made him less of a business chump and more of a nuanced man."

"What did he do?" asks Cheyenne.

"His father made him take over the box business in California and when he finally made enough money, he got out and started writing bad movie scripts. He had waited all those years to practice his idea of enlightenment only to find out that he was too thick, too mediocre really, to be the artist he so desperately wanted to be."

Cheyenne listens to this guru become a plain man.

"I lost touch with them during those years. Vivi got stronger. Jake more caged and in the end. He had had enough."

"What does that mean?" Cheyenne finally gets the question out.

"Jake took his own life. He was broke. And Carol, Anandamaia . . . you remember her from the workshop?"

"Yes."

"She was Jake's writing partner and lover. The script they wrote finally sold to Japanese anime and made a lot of money. And Carol found an Indian film producer who has nothing but money and she moved to Delhi. When I met her at the Indian Center she was looking for forgiveness and I'm the one told her to give half her money from the script to Vivi and that's how she, Vivi, got bankrolled. Vivi's been looking for home for a long time."

"I think maybe you're part of home for her."

"I can't be dragged into all that longing."

Cheyenne knows that if he was in a bar with college buddies there would be a fair amount of smirking and beer swallowing at this point. But he is in the car with his guru turning into a regular guy.

"What happened last night?" Cheyenne is listening.

Vikram looks at Cheyenne with big eyes. He smiles. "I am not sure really. But there is a long dream that seems to recur back and forth from my lives to hers and back again. It has something to do with a child. It has something to do with allowing things to be born and come through us. It has something to do with madness or indulgence or past lives or this life."

"You guys keep trying to rid yourselves of each other."

"Like a bad case of the runs, Cheyenne. Sometimes hocus pocus is a crock of shit."

The two men laugh.

"You know, Vikram—" Cheyenne starts.

"Save it, young man. I am going now." And Vikram gestures for Cheyenne to stop the car. "I am going off to the Stillness Center in Chennaie. Not sure when I will return."

"Have you told her?"

"No. I am not called to find God through Vivi. Or to find Vivi through God."

"What you seek, seeks you," says Cheyenne. "Didn't Rumi or someone say that?"

Vikram says nothing.

"I am seeking India. It is time for me to be gone and for Vivi to pull up her socks."

"Pull up her socks?" Cheyenne, eyes still on the road, as he pulls into the train station lot, smiles in spite of himself.

"Tell her I said so, Cheyenne. The wisdom of a great Indian."

Vikram gets out of Cheyenne's car and gives a wave as he steps up the stairs to the platform. Cheyenne sees him let go of a large steam of air, like he is an overfilled helium balloon trying to get past the valley to the mountaintop, and miscalculation will be fatal. He shakes his hair. Vivi would have seen how handsome he is. Cheyenne sees a halo of red powder fly and then settle on his shoulders like Satan coming out of the hairdresser. He gets out of the car and is gone.

Cheyenne wonders at how this holy guy, this guru that held hope for him, just turns tail and leaves. And how easy it is for Cheyenne to enable him. Cheyenne chews this over as he drives. Maybe shifting sand and painting landscapes aren't all they're cracked up to be. Maybe leaving and staying are kind of the same thing. Cheyenne lets his mind drift up and over a rift of rocky rubble. He has his own beautiful woman, his own lost child, his own flight and cave of refuge. Why the hell can't it stay untouched and etched in creosote?

The country road is easy and foreign, like cracked glass in a cold chamber. He wants to turn the car and plow through the brush like it is a pile of storks, leggy and brittle and in the way. He just keeps driving though, breaking every leg of every bird he can spot in his mind's eye. And not caring at the necessary refuse of his progress. He keeps driving away from this place and back to his other.

Chapter 31

Blessing the Blessing

Vivi comes back to the site, timid and unsure of what actually happened here in the last twenty-four hours. She remembers that she was sparked by the light fuse in the car. She remembers it made her head spin. She remembers that she got bigger than herself and hollow with a birth that she cannot seem to claim. She brings out her camp chair and watches the shower and whirl of color, what is left of the sand, as it rises from the mandala. The sun finds sparks of light as the magic disassembles itself and settles mundane over the gashy earth.

"Wow. What happened here?" Jorge, the day worker from Home Center, arrives with his brother Esteban. "We're here to finish the terracing, but looks like you have been decorating!"

"My friend and I. We made a sand painting last night. He thought it would help the earth, soothe it."

Jorge doesn't pretend to understand what she means. "Yeah. The colors, they are good. Sand will help break up the soil a little. Make it less dense. You'll see."

Vivi smiles, pretending she is having this conversation. "Right. Good."

Esteban glances over and she gets up and folds up her chair, pretending that she is inspecting the site again.

"Just pacing the garden," she calls to Esteban.

She has seen him waiting outside Home Center for the day jobs and she's impressed he came back with his brother to finish this one. Esteban, the younger brother and happier worker, keeps at his job of smoothing and digging and securing the terraces. Jorge stops to chat.

"I love gardens. At my mother's house in Oaxaca I planted a full kitchen garden. I cut down cactus and pickled it for my *abuela*. I ate the flowers of the summer cactus and cooked dinner for all my cousins."

Jorge interrupts himself. "Steban, we finish here by three. Meanwhile, Lady, where's your bedroom? Where's the kitchen gonna be? You know your view?"

"I've been pretty stuck on the garden but . . ." Vivi walks around the first terrace. "Here. Here there will be a big porch overlooking the center area, and then flowers all around. A kitchen garden off this side of the porch, and a . . .

"Hey, you got it all in your head!" says Jorge. "By spring it will be real!" He laughs with a big toothy grin.

Chapter 32

Cheyenne Finds the Sunset

Vivi has not heard from Cheyenne or Amanda in almost a month. She has found her balance again and contacts the storage unit in Los Angeles, asking about shipping costs to the East coast. It is still too early for that. Tara is still in Florida. After work, in the evenings, Vivi finds herself going through her contacts to see who she can call.

"Amanda? Hello. It's Vivi. From the Garden Center."

"Yes. I know who you are."

"I thought I'd connect, see if you need anything. I understand that Cheyenne left town a few weeks ago. So, reaching out. One person to the other."

Amanda holds her peace. "Yes. That piece of shit guru man took off as well, I hear. Here's to the men who stay." There is silence. "And who exactly are they?" Amanda ruminates.

"You okay?" Vivi asks, realizing she is asking herself as much as Amanda.

"I've been around a bit, my dear." Amanda sounds weary, a little too relaxed. Her evening glass of Merlot is working its magic. "Yes. I told him to leave his guitar. That he'd be back. I've already dusted it! Ha!"

Amanda lets out a long laugh. “He told me he’ll be back before spring. Like Schwarzenegger. In that movie. ‘Ah’ll bee bahck’!”

“Sounds heroic.”

“Manipulative as hell.” Vivi can hear Amanda pour herself another wine. “I seem to have been caught by his charms, can you believe it?”

“Where did he go?”

“I think he’s from Hartford. An architect. Broken heart and all that. At least that’s what I can glean. And he left his driver’s license.”

“That might be a problem.”

“His name is Mark. Mark Schaeffer. Cheyenne seems to be the boy in retreat. Mark, the man of the world.”

Vivi listens as Amanda sets her own head straight.

“How silly this fascination with the boy is. He’s caught me somewhere. Somewhere before sex and after Harvey.” Vivi is not really part of this conversation. “I’ll be back before spring.’ He actually said that to me. Like I was . . . his mother or his lover?” She is muttering now.

She wonders if she thinks Amanda is ridiculous. She needs to think about that. And the way the years stretch out before both of them.

“Let’s have dinner next week, Amanda. How about that? Would you be up for that?” Vivi says a tad too cheerfully.

“Sure. Otherwise I’m in the cave for the duration.”

Chapter 33

Winter Quiet, Winter Freeze

Vivi doesn't call. She instead develops a routine of evening television, watching the Boston local news at 6:30 when she returns from her shift, then making dinner, and eating what she has on her plate in front of the national news at seven. That takes her until eight. On good nights, she walks down her stairs and walks to the green and back. She is too tired to do the local yoga class, but she feels the need to reconnect to some part of her body besides the back muscles and foot pads that she is beating every day on the cement floors of Home Center. All the stores are closed by then, except for the 7-Eleven and the gas station. If she feels particularly eager, she wanders there, picks up a People magazine and heads back. That puts her home around nine when a bath and book are possible. She has been reading murder mysteries that evaporate in her brain and sometimes treat her to sleazy dreams. And that's how the time is spent. The cold is coming in and that is a comfort to Vivi. She looks forward to cocooning, if she can just find a way to rest.

By November, the turkey decorations at the store have given way to red Christmas cheer. The poinsettias that are shipped in to the store are hers to sort, tag and place. Joe is still on the night shift so Cheryl gives this task to her.

"They look pretty good this year. Can you get them sorted and out, Viv?"

"It's only the second week in November, Cheryl." Vivi resists this task. Something in the red of the potted creatures. Lascivious and luscious. Out of place in the warehouse. "You know I had a wild poinsettia tree in my garden. They're actually from Mexico." Vivi offers. Cheryl is not impressed.

"Join the Navy and see the world, kid." Sometimes Cheryl has no idea what Vivi means when she talks but she does get the job done. "See if you can keep these babies alive. I'm ordering paper whites for spring."

Vivi spends the day sorting and putting out the poinsettia display. Her head aches from the fluorescents above her. Her back aches from moving them all from one cart to another. Her heart aches for the way they stir and tumble the stitches that she has carefully placed against her memories.

As the weather changes, Amanda feels herself freezing like an old pipe too close to the outside wall. Her leg numbs again, returning to its former state. Before he came. Her hands cripple from her everyday obsession with seeing and imprinting, her desire to prove she is still sight bearing.

In the early mornings, she cannot move her leg without a calculated heave to the left under the covers. Slowly she inches her limb to the side of the bed, beneath the bed covers, praying she will not be impaled with the pain that gnaws at her equanimity.

She tests the limits of her fierceness and moves both legs. She waits, but today she is lucky, she is simply stiff. She feels nothing, but cannot move. Perhaps that is progress. She heaves her naked leg straight up, then carefully she lets it fall left, far left and right, far right and tests the fascia and muscles, the nerves and calcified joints. Surprised and reluctant, they creep to life.

Amanda runs the tub and tosses cups of lavender Epsom salt into the mix. Grabbing the gunwales of the boat, she lowers herself, feeling the strength of her pecs, her shoulders, her arms to the hand. The warm water surrounds the errant mass of rusted tin which is herself and slowly, the heat loosens her, welcomes her back from confinement and allows her to reconnect her body to her spirit, the frozen fascia to some kind of life.

Chapter 34

The Day After Thanksgiving

Vivi works Thanksgiving, and Cheryl invites her over for turkey sandwiches and a replay of the Macy's parade on her widescreen after her shift. Joe is there, and some of Cheryl's cousins. It is a noisy bunch and they are all on their second round of food having had the real feast earlier in the day. Cheryl sits back and lets one of the kids serve them, the two working stiffs, at the dinner table. Someone lumpy sleeps on the couch, the television blares and the youngest cousin fights with her drunken mother for the keys to the car. Cheryl sends Vivi home with the bones for a turkey soup and Vivi falls into bed.

She does not dream and, as always, her body is wary in that state. Deep sleep has not been kind to Vivi. It's there that the demons scream at her, forcing her to dance with them. She tries, but like the wearer of the Red Shoes, she can never stop dancing. She is whirled and whipped by the various furies but tonight it is different. It is quiet and dark. There is a freshness that is unfamiliar.

Maybe it's the tryptophane or maybe the drain has opened and the demons and ghosts have circled and slid somewhere else. Vivi dares to move more deeply to rest. She breathes out. Then in. Then out.

Jake does not return. He is gone, there is no spark of him. There are no pruney women with jagged breasts offering her babies hung like bats. There are no gardens that weep for her, or kitchens that resent her absence. Vivi sleeps and it gives her strength.

The next morning, she calls Amanda.

"How was your holiday?"

"Oh, hello."

"I have time off this week. Would you like to come for dinner? I'm making turkey soup."

The women have a good time. The wine helps. Vivi finds some sage and makes great muffins. She is pleased and happy. The deep sleep of the last few days has pushed her through a rabbit hole. There's more room for someone else.

"I knew the jig was up when after twenty-seven years of never looking me straight in the eye, he sat down to dinner and told me, 'I know your eyes are brown. I always have, you know.'" Amanda is holding forth.

"Were you surprised?"

"Well, I tried to picture him thinner and sexier, you know? Like the man that I married. But I couldn't see him so it was okay. Kind of a relief. He told me he was going to Martinique with the secretary." This strikes Amanda as very funny and she starts to guffaw. "Harvey says to me, 'Amanda. I don't want a scene but I am moving to Martinique with Candy Vega.'"

"Candy Vega?"

"That's her name. It was okay. She probably still likes him."

"Did you ever like him?"

Amanda smiles. "I really liked him the night he came in from work and said, 'Paint more pictures because we're gonna buy a HUGE apartment and the walls need to be filled. You've gotta class up our act, Mandy!'"

Vivi smiles. "Mandy, huh?"

"I think that was the last time he called me that."

"Jake came up with Vivi. I was Vivian before that."

"He didn't get it wrong. You're kind of a Vivi."

"Is that a compliment?"

"Sure. I'm drunk enough." Amanda looks around Vivi's spare little room and starts to feel the walls move toward her. "I gotta go home. Thanks for dinner."

Vivi looks out the window to the night now turning white. "Look, Amanda. It's snowing. First snow of the year."

"I better get back to the cave."

"Hope to see you again before spring."

"Yeah, it may be possible. Thanks."

Amanda has had a lot to drink. She doesn't want Vivi to drive her home. Instead Vivi watches from her front window as Amanda navigates the slippery stairs and unsteadily gets into her car.

"Call when you get home?' she says.

Amanda smiles at her. "Sure. Thanks. Why not?"

The women part.

When Amanda leaves, Vivi gets out her winter coat and boots and goes out into the quiet. She loves how the sky is white again, cleaned out by a new season. She walks to the green, hearing her boots in the snow. She sits on the bench next to the wishing well and hears a couple of kids yelling with delight as they slip and slide down an unseen hill. She wonders if the snow will pile up on her if she doesn't move. If she will eventually become the Tin Man like in Wizard of Oz and in spring, someone will oil her back to life. She sits there for a long time, until she can see that leaving her spot will make a difference in the way the snow piles and how it will be discovered the next day. Then, she goes home and sleeps again. Simply and easily.

Amanda goes home and gets into the bathtub. She thinks about Harvey. She thinks about Cheyenne. Her fingertips are wrinkled and thin, like bulrushes, she thinks. She thinks of Moses being found cast out on the river, slowed by the rustle of those thin spikes that steer him to his remarkable life. She wonders how it would be to slip down the river and be found. The rush of the water from the tap catches her and allows her to give over to the rhythm within and without. Her body convulses beautifully and she is deeply satisfied.

A white fluffy towel sits on the toilet waiting for her. She is so pleased to move it along her skin and imagine herself young and beautiful and having married the other guy at the mixer, the art major who didn't have enough money to buy himself a beer, let alone take her out for one. She wonders if she'd be here now, thinking of Harvey in Martinique, if that had happened.

Her dinner with Vivi has cheered her. She feels like she can make it another day. Maybe another season. Even though she regularly looks back, like Lot's wife, she doesn't necessarily have to turn to salt, does she? She knows there is much poison flowing through her since the divorce. She feels it seeping in her bones, her leg for one place, certainly. She is wary and defensive around her desire to survive. Still, she isn't truly

Lot's wife. She sighs and catches sight of her face in the mirror. It is steady. It is thickening. She can handle that tonight.

She wipes herself between her legs and there is blood on the towel, but she doesn't see it until washday.

Chapter 35

Slush

Winter moves through the two women in the town. It does not bring them closer but it allows them each time to marinate, ruminate in the rush of change that has embraced them both. For Vivi, it is a shedding of old memories, grinning like prom gowns too tight in the closet. For Amanda, the weight of this sweep of desire wipes clean old slates and the emotional dermabrasion is forcing her forward. Neither of the women know if they can charge through their respective doors, but each of them feel them buffed and rubbed, time demanding change.

Vivi is restless to get out of her little apartment and can barely stay put through the snow and ice whipped ice sculptures all around her. Every night she churns in her dreams, gnaws at the ties that bind, dreams herself into spring.

Amanda rattles around her house. She avoids the room where Cheyenne slept. She does not even acknowledge the guitar in Cheyenne's room. But sometimes, maybe when she is asleep, she is drawn there. She picks up the guitar in the dark, strums it, lets it rest next to her white flannel nightgown and feels the way it vibrates against her body and through her empty house.

Cheyenne has returned to his mother's house in suburban Hartford.

It's empty too. His mother left a note. "I'm a snowbird again. If you show up, you can call me. Aunt Margaret has the number. But then, I can't be sure." He goes back to work at the local architecture office and draws some plans for suburban houses. He looks for his old girlfriend who is not there and not coming back. He drinks a lot and keeps his radio tuned to a scratchy R&B station all day and night, even when he's not home.

The land is resolute in its retreat. Creatures are either buried or scraped by its icy edge.

The miracle of the gray bearded trees eventually shatters with minimalist hubris. Sloppy spring smothers its austerity. Vivi can't help but burst from her cell.

"There you are!" she can hear him running water in a sink. He must be in some kitchen.

"I've been tracking you down."

"Who is this?" says Mark.

"Oh. Sorry. It's Vivi."

"Oh, Vivi," says Mark, feeling the distance between here and there. "Right. How are you? How did you find my number?" He finishes pouring his coffee. Vivi, he thinks.

"You left a bunch of ID at Amanda's. She gave me your number."

"Oh."

"How are you?" says Vivi, realizing that he may not have any interest in renewing a connection that she never thought was broken.

"I'm fine."

"I've been looking for you," she says.

Mark is not sure he wants to be found but he listens. "Oh. Really?"

"I need someone to do the finish work on the house. It's framed, it's mostly dry walled. Kitchen is in, almost. Bathroom's in mostly. Just some painting. Maybe hanging a few pictures." Whether these details are true makes no difference to Vivi. The house is complete in her mind's eye.

"I'm not sure when I'll be back." Vivi lets him hear himself. "I mean, I have a job here til June and probably not free. Til, you know, June." No one is at the house and he can do what he wants. He thinks, "I have my freedom," but realizes no one really cares what he has or doesn't have.

"Well, I thought I'd try. I mean, I have been going stir crazy waiting for spring. And I practically dragged the crew to the site before the snow melted!"

"Oh. Yeah. I get it." Another pause.

"I wanted to tell you that Amanda is sick. I ran into her last week." Vivi's voice comes back at him, she's coming closer.

"What's wrong with her?"

"She won't tell me everything but I think it's cancer. She had an operation, had a round of chemo and who knows? She looks like hell. Could probably use some financial help, I mean if you came back, and rented from her, it would probably be a good thing."

Mark thinks, *I don't owe her anything, do I?* Cheyenne says, "Yes. That would be a good thing. I'll see what I can do."

"And there's the labyrinth. Remember. You promised me you'd put in a labyrinth." They both leave the space for visions of Vivi being packed up from the weeping mandala to float back to them. It sobers both of them. Jogs Cheyenne's memory and Cheyenne pokes at Mark.

"Right. Yes." Cheyenne starts to locate himself once again in terms of Vivi. "Vikram back? Coming back?"

"No idea."

"Got it. I'll let you know what I can do." The Mark part of him answers. It's like he has to discuss what's best with Cheyenne and he's not sure Cheyenne needs to resurface right about now.

"Okay, Cheyenne," says Vivi. "You're missed in these parts. The winter has been long and not great for us bears. The ones who can't find the right cave to sleep in." Cheyenne smiles.

"Yes. I've been having cave location problems myself," he says.

"See you in the spring, then?" Vivi sparks to the idea. She wants to show him how her garden has healed the earth and how she has a new beginning to share.

"Sure. See you in the spring," he says, feeling the scent of her enthusiasm.

"I hope it was okay to call."

"Sure. Of course. Nice to hear from you."

"Sure. Yes. Well, whatever. Nice to hear your voice."

"Yeah. You too."

The conversation ends and sits in the air between them. The best that can be said of it is that it happened.

Chapter 36

Coming and Going

It's May. Vivi is in her new house. The large front room looks out over the terraces, which she has lined with flagstone. The three levels have been planted with forsythia, lilac and butterfly bush and spring is starting at the bottom and will move up to stay through the summer.

In March, the foundation was dug and poured. And wood arrived, already sliced. It opened itself to the violence of nail guns and table saws and settled into its role as shelter. Whatever protests the wood may have had at being ripped from its roots, refashioned into someone else's dream, it kept to itself in creaky settling heard only by an overhead hawk and a family of mice scoping out a new home for themselves.

In April, Vivi paid the crew extra to start the project. She told her landlord she was out May 1 and she moved in, with half a kitchen and only a toilet and washbasin, but she is in, sleeping in the middle of the room and happier than she has been in a long while.

Now, she sits in the middle of the room, sun shining in, an easy breeze from the porch. Her boxes from L.A. arrived last week and she has been stepping around them all week, deciding whether to open them one by one or maybe just throw them all away.

She starts with the box that's marked "kitchen." After the sweep of the cutter across its dusty top, the box gives up bubble wrap, styrofoam peanuts and finally, her Blue Willow plates. They appear one by one. She slips them from the packing paper and washes each one carefully. They are mostly clean, but she finds she has packed one that still has a bit of toast, or shiva pastrami stuck onto it and wonders what it must have felt like, mummified in a box for almost four years, preserving dinner in L.A. to be rediscovered and washed down the sink here in her new home.

The boxes are not as badly organized as Vivi had feared. She finds her bright rag rugs right next to her big, thick bath sheets. She drops the wonderful yellow and red and bright blue circles on her clean wooden floors. They remind her of the freedom that California engenders. There is more color in the West and people are not afraid to fight with the sun for attention. Things are more muted on the East coast. No need for trumpeting in this landscape, but "a woman like Vivi needs color," she thinks, even in the rooted and etched landscape of New England. She smiles, recognizes that California changed her in a way that she enjoys. This is a good thing. She can value her time there in the little ways in which the rugs remind her.

More dishes, silverware, kitchen towels. Her teapot. She takes the top off to see if she can still smell the mint that she plucked from the garden. No. It is gone. The duvet cover. The afghan she threw over the back of the green sofa which is somewhere in someone else's house now. The pillows from their bedroom. The pillows from their bed.

She had slid her hand under his pillow when she went to see if he would wake. His head was like a rock on the pillow and she could not feel it spring and smooth itself back into the cradle of her hand The head was dead as was the rest of the attached body.

Vivi shakes that thought off and takes the pillows to the deck to get the scent of the garden into them. She moves the linens to their shelf in her new bathroom. There is a window that looks out over the garden, and stone floors that are heated in winter. Sun is streaming in and she admires the terraces of hope, full of beautiful greenery and lilacs soon to burst forth. The towels will change, and shake their memories. The pillows will heal in the sunlight. She is sure of it.

She decides to open one more box. She slits the top and sees that fur coat that Jake's mom sent her. Vivi had explained to Shelley there was no need for fur in California. Aside from the obvious issue with heat, anyone seen wearing fur within 50 miles of Beverly Hills would be paint-bombed by PETA, that vigilante pet friendly lobby that always confused Vivi. She is not sure if she should risk returning it to Shelley now. But she did promise she would return family heirlooms when they met last year. If she finds Shelley's mother's pitcher, that will tip the scales toward a visit, she promises herself.

There is also a small zipper case of Chinese fabric at the bottom of the box. Vivi reaches down for it and then sees packets of papers in an open manila envelope she had thrown in at the last moment.

The envelope is first. She slips out a small pile of green and gray documents. Death certificates. At least ten of them. She remembers how disgusted she was that she had to prove that Jake was dead with every official duty there was to perform after his death. The insurance company, the telephone company, electric bills, banks, investment accounts—even though both of the bank and investment accounts were dry and empty like the California desert.

She remembers opening the Safe Deposit box at that small branch on La Brea with the blue tile roof. She had had to present the death certificate, and the keys and then go to a tiny room where the curious

Latina tellers and Asian bank officers pretended she was unobserved. The gasp she let out when she saw that every one of their stock certificates had been removed was audible all the way to the Hollywood Bowl. Her mother's pearls were gone and the diamond cocktail ring that Shelley had sent to her and told her to keep for a rainy day. In the box was a note left by Jake, "Sorry Vivi. It will be worth it one day, you'll see."

Vivi wonders if she will need these any more. The death certificates. They cost ten dollars apiece, she remembers, and so decides she'll keep them somewhere. Not sure where. Maybe near the stove so they can burn themselves up!

Now her attention turns to the Chinese zipper case. She slides it open and inside she sees two small figurines. Lahkshmi and Vishnu. The small statues that Vikram gave to them when she and Jake announced their engagement stare back at her, smiling mysteriously. There was a beautiful story that he told them then, she remembers.

The last item is wrapped in tissue paper. It is old and looks like some kind of pointer. "Oh. It is the antique Vajra!" This is the gift she gave to Jake for his birthday in New Rochelle that night. The gift symbolizing wisdom and equality and mirroring and all good blessings for their marriage. She must have chosen it to impress Vikram. How could she not have done so?

How clueless she was. She remembers how Jake kept the kitty in his arms all night after that gift so she sneezed uncontrollably and was forced out of the room, into Vikram's arms. It had been the last big fight that Jake and Vivi had before they married and it was so full of fire that it soldered the two of them together for the duration. She had Vikram to thank for that, too.

Chapter 37

Disintegration

Amanda feels like she is turning to ash. She is terrified most of the time and pretending she is a painter doesn't help. She thinks that it was smashing the canvas and paint against her openings that gave her cervical and then uterine cancer. She thinks she can control it all. She knows she is riding a rodeo car that will smash the railing at any moment. There is not much to do but paint when she doesn't have chemo brain, and drive around when she feels better or when she feels bad enough that she wouldn't mind being in a car crash and checking out sooner. She hates every part of this. And feels like shit.

When Vivi shows up to propose a spring garden, she vomits in the kitchen sink in front of her. Maybe just to push herself to the limits of disgust. No one could have more disgust than Amanda does for herself so it does little to impress Vivi.

"When I went to the doctor's office there was another woman there," she tells Vivi. "She was over sixty, like me, so no one really was sympathetic about her illness. I mean she had lost her juju anyway so why worry about it now. I think she was Israeli. Something about the way she dressed, or flattened her t's. Anyway, she had a loose t-shirt on. She and I were all alone in the waiting room and she was frantic. Frantic. She got up to get a cup of tea and stopped all agitated in front of me. 'Can you believe it, she says to me?' And she grabs my hand right then and there and makes it feel the large lump at the front of her breast right near her nipple. 'Maybe they cut it out, she says, but then where will my Izzy suck?'"

Vivi doesn't really know what to say but she manages, "Jesus. I'm sorry."

"Yes, me too." Amanda concludes that these stories, meant to shock, are worthless to waste on Vivi. She does not disgust easily, and seems so willing to get to the next thing. Amanda asks her, "Why are you here again?"

"I want to plant a garden for you. Flowers, some vegetables. Mint, chamomile, asters."

"Why?"

"It's what I can do." Vivi looks at Amanda, tough and pissed, and Vivi feels herself, steel herself. She is grateful that somehow her own pain has not morphed into morbid self-destruction at this point. That it is not conspiring to confound her suffering with even more of the same. At least not yet. Mostly, she wants to get away from Amanda and her cancer and her pain. She doesn't want to catch it. After all this time, she is finally finding air again and she simply wants to turn around and abandon this woman who has no one and most assuredly would abandon her if the tables were turned. But instead, she feels herself sprouting roots and standing her ground. She needs the job. She needs to start growing things again. She needs to show up for someone else.

"I'm not dead yet." Amanda somehow follows the whole line of thought that Vivi silently processes in front of her. Amanda realizes that this Vivi person is on a mission. "What the hell," says Amanda. "Plant the flowers and as long as they bloom I'll be full of life, right? Like that O. Henry story, The Last Leaf."

"I don't know it." Vivi looks past Amanda's effort to be gracious and goes to images of full grown plantings, strong, lush and possible. They sustain her.

"Great story. I used to read and paint all the time." Amanda is looking for common ground.

"Sounds great." Vivi smiles but she is not prepared to bond with Amanda. Only plant her garden.

Amanda goes on. "That's all I did before I married and I knew all the stories and all the paintings that went with them. A girl is sick. She lay in bed waiting to die but somehow sees a leaf holding on the brick outside her window. She figures that as long as that leaf can hang on, so can she."

"And does she?"

"For a while," Amanda sits down and takes a breath. "But we only have so much control. She dies eventually, despite all her wishes and wailing. And then we discover that a friendly artist who loved her somehow had painted the leaf so she could see it. He painted her hope."

"A nice story."

"He needed her as much as she needed him. A nice combination." Amanda smiles and Vivi responds with a noncommittal smile.

"Have you heard from Cheyenne?" Vivi asks.

Amanda goes dark. "Why should I hear from him?"

"I thought he might be in touch, I thought he might sail back around. Seems like the type of young man who can sense these kinds of things."

"What kind of things," barks Amanda.

"Just . . . when folks could use some support, some help . . . he seems the kind of . . ."

"He's a willful overly romantic kid, Vivian. Licking his wounds from something or other. He was nice to look at for a while." Amanda looks to see if Vivi has fallen under Cheyenne's spell as well. But, Vivi has yet to encounter that part of him. "We're too stocky, too thick of life for him," Amanda warns. "He's curious what we got, but he's got no grown up guts, really."

"I never thought about him like that," Vivi responds.

"Oh," says Amanda. "Okay then. Plant the asters. They're worth it. I'm going to go lie down."

Chapter 38

The Desperate Gardener

Vivi works hard on the garden. She even researches bulbs that may have missed their planting time. No matter, she wants to paint a palette for Amanda. Maybe for herself. She consults the *Sunset* garden book to make sure she gets the right plants for this part of the country. All her favorites are there, asters, coneflowers, daisies. She can scatter them in the sunny area beside Amanda's workshop and there will be color all summer.

She hasn't been back to Home Center since she quit her job in March. The payment from the anime project comes in steadily and now word is that the characters are being licensed worldwide. That news was enough to trust that she could leave Home Center for now. Cheryl told her she was always welcome when she got bored.

She needed that job to get her through the winter, before the house took shape. Even the waxy philodendrons and the coleus in the green house kept her going. And it was warm and sweaty in there. The bone cold of the winter released its grip in what she came to see as her own personal oxygen tent. She planted bulbs for the floor whenever she could hide from her boss, Cheryl. She needed to get her hands in dirt, to smell the promise of the amaryllis and paperwhite bulbs that would sell for the holidays.

When she did go out to the floor, she managed to stand in the middle of the poinsettia display, insisting the red color and consistent show of faith moved up her legs like poison ivy, giving her strength, making her itch into a new beginning and helping her shed her old skin. Ever since she was washed and rewashed, rebirthing her Anna Elizabeth, that mystery child she has carried in dreams for too long, she has needed to find a way to shed that skin. Like an afterbirth, she thinks. If I can leave the afterbirth in the earth even in a shitty Home Center green house, it might compost and mulch and be spread to the other unconscious gardens in the Valley.

Those baby dreams have stopped for now. When she thinks of that child from her dreams, when she thinks of how Vikram understood and pulled that child from her, how he made her drop water paste and sand over the earth to seal the birth, she experiences humility. It is not insufficiency she feels. On the contrary, she is full of her accomplishment, of motherhood. Of what it means to let another into and out of herself. She used to be scared of a sense of release so enormous, but somehow, the rebirthing has left her humbled and grateful. Even if it is all in her imagination and even if Vikram had to run away to prevent that spirit child from looming once again.

Now it is spring and Vivi walks back into Home Center as a customer and finds the wildflower seeds and the hopeful eight packs of herbs and tender shoots of soon to be wild vegetation. She finds a small drum of regional wildflower seeds, and grabs gloves and a new spade and hoe. She finds iris bulbs and even a flat of tomato sprouts and basil that she will keep in her kitchen.

This trip was for Amanda's job but she can't keep herself from the marigolds and the beans, the peppers and cukes, the lavender and chives.

At the end of the aisle she sees that they have gotten a shipment of arugula and endive. She had been rooting for those items for at least a year and she's glad that Cheryl finally gave in to some more exotic fare.

Vivi thinks about the gardens that have changed her. There was that trip to France where she fell in love with the yellow and blue tile kitchen just off Monet's sacred pools of 'lillipondi'—water lilies. She remembers sitting under a willow and missing the last train back to Paris because she wanted to see twilight through its leaves. And in Hawaii, above volcanic ash, Jake was cranky when they walked there and smelled the fragrant delicacy of frangipani. And, the New York Botanical Garden where she and Jake strolled during their courtship. And Descanso Gardens, on the other side of the freeway in L.A., where the roses bloom fiercely in all that California sun. She still admires the fact that they make themselves beautiful in all that heat. She has never managed to look good above sixty-nine degrees Fahrenheit. The memory of the cactus and drought tolerant plantings of the Theodore Payne Foundation and Joshua Tree National Park still stun and prickle her with their boulders and spikes of leathery domination.

The most important garden for Vivi was in the Massif Central. In France again. Vivi fell in love with the mischief of Claudine in the early books of Colette Willy and she and the writer became fast friends in the ethers. She read everything Colette wrote. Vivi loved that Colette escaped from that bastard who took credit for all her work and didn't approve of her when she became an acrobat. She loved that she eventually had a makeup line that she sold to aging women. Vivi's favorite book, *Cherie and the Last of Cherie*, stunned Vivi with the forlorn loss of love and the stubborn gleeful revenge of age as the heroine presented her older self to her younger lover. He came needing her to rescue him with her need, but when he showed up she was no longer needy and more beautiful to herself than anyone else. All of these tales felt approachable to Vivi, a Midwestern girl at heart, with not enough mischief in her own life. They felt approachable because Colette loved gardens. Colette loved her mother, Sido, but was never quite sure if her mother fully understood her. Like Vivi and her mom. But Sido loved gardens and that is where Colette and her mother met. Colette wrote a whole book about her mother and the way she swatted the bees, and tended the weeds and ignored the beauty and drank in the pathways and labor of her own beautiful garden. Vivi never had the chance to walk a garden path with her mom, except for the Palmer Park excursions to feed the ducks when she was little, but that was enough of a connection for Vivi.

In Detroit, at her Aunt Shirley's house in Palmer Park, there was a backyard. Aunt Shirley would call the Salvation Army every Memorial Day and ask for a guy to come and plant exactly twenty-four geraniums in a straight row against the backyard hurricane fence. That was the garden. The guy would always show up with a hand spade and a bottle of whiskey in the inside pocket of his jacket. He would fight with the hardened dirt, pull out last years calcified remnants of plant and then stick the new one in the same hole. He never would comb the area around the hole. He left the stones and the gum wrappers and whatever other winter debris had floated in from the back alley. Then he would trickle water over these plants, proudly purchased from Frank's Nursery. Vivi remembered it always looked like he was peeing on the plants from her upstairs bedroom window. She wondered if the guy ever played in the dirt when he was kid because he sure didn't know how to do it when he stuck those doomed, hearty annuals in his aunt's backyard.

Vivi knew she had no real skills. But she knew she loved the earth. She knew she admired physical work and delighted in the investment and hope of a living place that would grow and yield treasure. Gardens are vulnerable to the weather, to poison, to neglect. But most gardens create themselves when they are encouraged to grow. What she discovered in California, was that sometimes beauty can even be self-sufficient. Water helps everything but she remembers her first garden in L.A. growing in full sun, with no shade, and only a perfunctory spray of the hose.

Later, she came to understand the lore of gardens and how there are documented fairy sightings and slug battles and snail drunks near beer deposits that are supposed to kill them, but just make them sing louder. Every now and then when she took a toke of some weed that Jake left around, she could hear the snails singing and she didn't think it odd at all. They were probably all engaged in mischief of some form or the other.

It is hard to keep things from growing in California, but it's hard to know the rules. And the gardens, like the people, prefer to be showy. Beauty can grow no matter the heat or the water, the temperature or the shade. L.A. believes in sun and how everything deserves a place in it. Sometimes that works for humans, too, but not always—as Jake discovered. It is what he always hoped for. That all that sun and positive thinking would yield fruit. But in the end, Vivi thought, it just addled his brain.

Vivi has not created a new garden for someone else yet in this new life of hers. She has not created a place where things will grow again on their own, not egged on by daily concern and steady encouragement. And not in this East coast climate of lush green foliage and rocky terrain.

Her own terraces, that she visited through the winter months, that she nudged forward by tucking burlap blankets around their tender trunks, that she walked and talked with when the snow fell, have returned strong with spring and ready to be part of the family. She is delighted and strengthened by every new bloom and sprout.

She knows that Amanda will judge her health on the growing of the blooms outside her windows. She knows that Amanda will hate them if they flourish or weep if they crumble and die, as she is doing. Vivi knows that about Amanda and knows that Amanda's fire and poison can be cooled and softened while she decides if she will recover or if she will give up to the cancer and call it a life.

Chapter 39

The Force that Through the Green Fuse Drives

"So, I brought a bunch of stuff. Want vegetables? How about a vegetable garden?" Vivi is excited to bring her box of life to Amanda's cottage. She places the cardboard trays and Home Center plastic bags on the kitchen table so Amanda can see them.

"Are you crazy?" says Amanda. "Who's going to take care of all this?"

"It won't be difficult. I can broadcast the wild flowers and they will grow on their own. As for the rest, I can come by and check on everything. Check on you."

"I don't need you to check on me. I'd prefer it if you'd leave me alone." Vivi looks up.

"No, you wouldn't Amanda. That much I do know. I know you wouldn't prefer that."

"Hate to disappoint you, Vivi. But I hardly know you and you are trying to take over life."

Vivi stops and looks up at her. "Am I? Maybe that's good."

Amanda looks out the window. She sips her tea. Vivi notices pills on her table.

"Jeez, that's a ton of shit right there. You take all that?"

Amanda smiles. "Well, that was sensitively said."

"Oops, sorry," says Vivi. Vivi remembers what it is to deal with cranky, sad and sick people. She thinks, *Here's a use for that skill. The one I learned so well being married to Jake!*

"No, you're not sorry. You're provoking me." Amanda says. "But that's okay. I'd prefer a morphine picnic, really."

"What does that mean?"

"A morphine picnic. A bottle of wine, a loaf of bread and a jug of morphine to drip happily on my tongue. Sleep myself to the other side."

Vivi looks at her cross wise. "I thought they told you that you could make it."

"Did I say that? Is that true?" Amanda is casual and even cruel.

"The last time I was here, that is what you told me."

Amanda looks out the window. "Perhaps. Perhaps."

Vivi feels a gusher coming from her gut.

"What are you playing with here? What exactly are you playing with?"

"Vivi, leave me alone will you? You are really a pain in the ass. If I choose to indulgently contemplate my own end, it is no goddamn business of yours."

"Well, I certainly don't want to show up one day and find your inert body snugly tucked in the bedclothes!"

"I'm not sure you're the one who I'd want to find me."

Vivi reaches out with her right hand and slaps Amanda's face. It startles Amanda and paralyzes Vivi.

"Oh my God," Vivi says. "I have no idea where that came from? I am so very sorry. I . . ."

Amanda looks at her with hollow eyes. "What the fuck is that, Vivi? Just what exactly the fuck is that?"

Vivi begins to gather her things and heave them into the bag.

"I have no idea. I guess suicide is not something I take lightly." She stands to face Amanda. "It doesn't engender sympathy in me. I guess it makes me furious! Like I'd rather kill someone myself then let them, lonely and ferocious, slit their own throat."

"That so," says Amanda.

The women stare at each other and are surprised at the stand-off.

A car pulls up in the drive and again, both women are surprised.

"You expecting someone?"

Amanda looks out the window. It is Cheyenne. It is Cheyenne out the window. Tall and lanky and with a backpack and a bunch of flowers that he must have brought all the way from Hartford. Cheyenne is back.

He walks through the door and the women hear, "Honey, I'm home."

Amanda heads to the sink and vomits. Vivi looks up and her eyes, like mad missiles, fly for protection behind his open pools.

"Bad time?" he asks.

Vivi moves quickly out the door. Amanda breathes heavily at the sink. The smell of vomit fills the air.

Cheyenne says, "First thing, I'll open a window."

Chapter 40

Setting Up a Plan

Vivi rolls over into the May morning, groggy.

"Viv? Vivi? Can I come in?" His voice is strong and surprising. Vivi grabs a long tee shirt and rolls from under the covers.

"I'm in bed. It's early. What do you want?"

"Welcome me back!" She can hear the smile in his voice and she smiles right back.

She is surprised that she has missed him. She can hear Cheyenne in the living room.

"God. The view is great from here!" He must be looking out the window at the terraces. "The bushes actually look like they flowered. Wow!"

"The forsythia went crazy about a month ago," she calls from the bedroom. "I'll be right out."

"That's okay. The place looks great."

She can hear him go into the kitchen area. "I want some coffee. Can I make some coffee?"

"Sure. Sure, make coffee."

Vivi arrives in the kitchen to see Cheyenne struggling with the small cappuccino machine. "Here," she says, "Let me."

And just like that they take up their domestic tasks, and start making lists like the partners they seem to be.

"I'm renting again from Amanda. Like you said. She needs the money"

"Good," Vivi gives him a sideways glance. "You staying?"

He gets milk from the fridge and sits down with a bowl of granola. "I'm staying."

The two of them refresh their to-do lists. Get Amanda to the doctor in Boston one more time. See if there is anyone left for Amanda, her husband, Harvey in Martinique? Or did he die? And is there a daughter? Was there a friend? Why do they think there was a friend?

Cheyenne looks up at Vivi. No make-up, but fresh, even rumpled and slipped from a dream.

"You look good, Vivi. Better than the last time I saw you."

Vivi smiles. "Yes, well thanks for that." Vivi does have an open ease and a sheen to her hair in the morning sun. Maybe because she is not hemmed in by the Home Center regalia. Maybe something about her smooth skin and the way she smells like the outside.

"The bushes are growing. The views really work. Even looks like the magic circle at the foot of the terraces, there, even that looks fresh." Cheyenne is referring to a soft fur green that has come up over the magic circle at the root of the terraces. That place where the spirit of her child, that child, came and reentered and then went free. That place.

For his part, Vivi sees something new in Cheyenne. Something is settled in him. Settled behind his eyes. It's the beginning of wisdom about something. Maybe it's a scar.

"It was madness, really. All that happened before you left. I don't know . . . well, you have any idea what really happened?" Vivi is staying busy with making coffee, but she has been waiting to ask this question of Cheyenne. She has never really understood what happened before he left and before Vikram left, and before her new home began to grow.

Cheyenne looks at her. "Well, it seems that something came out of the earth, through you and left you with a hell of an open channel. Very science fiction but it sure made for some windy action!"

Vivi looks away. "Yes. Something like that. You think that's weird? You think I'm imagining the whole damn thing?"

Cheyenne laughs. "We got to release and conjure ancient spirits? Right? That sure was a tribal brain fuck. I was blasted away, just like Vikram, but then, he kept going." He stops and considers. "I guess that was cool."

"He ran away. Cool?"

"Understandable. He's a guy."

"Oh, that's how it's okay. He's a guy. Not a guru. Yeah, I'll buy that."

Cheyenne takes another slug of coffee. "All's well that ends well."

"Sure," says Vivi. *Another cowardly fuck*, she thinks. Then she says, "All's well that ends well. But I'm not exactly sure we're there yet."

Chapter 41

Boston Chemo

Cheyenne drives Amanda to Boston for another round of chemo. They are in town for a few days. They are staying at the Newbury Guest House. At least, Cheyenne is. Amanda gets a room at the hospital for out of towners. She gives him a name and phone number.

"So, this person knew me when. I mean, she knew me. She might want to know me. I mean, she might be able to help. I mean, if I need help. Though I don't know. Not like she was rushing to my side when Harvey took a powder."

Cheyenne looks at Amanda mystified. The left side of her face is slightly drooping and her wig is sliding to one side.

"Took a powder." She realizes he is scrutinizing her. He notices how she has morphed into someone she must have been before she reinvented herself in that white house with those pussy paintings.

"So, Harvey was a lawyer?"

She straightens her wig and looks into the pull down mirror on the passenger side of his station wagon. "He was a lawyer. He was an ambulance chaser! That's what my Uncle Harold called him!"

Amanda lets her lips come back like a chimp and grins. "He was a crook, But, he was okay. And he worked hard. And we kind of lived our separate lives, alone together, kind of."

"That sounds like a good marriage."

Amanda snorts. "You think? Remind me to get a couple of big scarves. I feel like I am being gagged by spiders." Amanda is having little luck taming the synthetic wisps of her wig.

Cheyenne pulls up to the hospital parking lot. "You want me to take you in?"

"Where?"

"To the infusion center. You want me to take you in."

Amanda looks at him from under the spider legs. "No. I can do it. Thanks."

"I'll call you later, maybe?"

"It won't get bad for a day. They just want to keep me here til I get through the round. I mean, I know I could have taken the train."

"I don't have to stay, Amanda. I can come back and get you. I mean you won't have to pay for the guest house."

"I'd rather," she says. "I paid the bill."

Next day when Cheyenne comes by her room, she looks pale. "Damn everything but the circus," Amanda says.

"Beg your pardon?"

"To understand is to stand under, which is to look up, which is to believe in God."

"You writing poetry now, Amanda?"

"I had a friend here. She worked the desk in the gallery where this nun showed her work. The nun got sick and then got better and then got sick and then got better and then got sick. She just got tired and she had done her work. And then she died."

"Is that the friend you told me . . ."

Amanda shifts on the hospital bed in the hospitality room where she is tucked in, now grey and perky.

"My friend worked the desk. She was just a regular girl. I think she loved me. She wore plaid skirts and had braids." Amanda takes a breath. Closes her eyes. "No. She loved me," she says.

"That's nice. That's lucky."

"She was all freckly. All over herself, like someone spilled the bottle of jimmies from Brigham's and never cleaned it up."

Cheyenne knows she has some deep fire rumbling in her bowels but he has never really contemplated her in love with someone, neither her injury lawyer husband nor this girl in plaid skirts from lots of years ago. Amanda sees this in his face. The burn of her obsession with him is another humiliation.

"I just wanted to smoke dope and I liked kissing her." Amanda looks quickly at Cheyenne. "That probably sounds disgusting. I know I always thought that the idea of old fat women making love, even when they were young, I always thought that was disgusting, oozy and unattractive. I'll shut up now."

Amanda closes her eyes and allows the drugs to take effect. "You go to your appointment yet?" she says.

But she is asleep before she gets an answer.

Cheyenne leaves Amanda and heads to the address that Dustin, the architect he worked for in Hartford, gave him.

Jim Ennis Design is in an expensively casual storefront off Newbury

Street. Dustin thinks Jim will like Mark's work, and Mark needs money if he is going to make his retreat life a viable option. And they settle on Mark doing drafting jobs for the firm. They sign no contract while Pilar, the exotic girl from Spain who sits in the back of the studio, pretends not to see his pasty white face, while Mark wishes his beard would make him look more sexy than ascetic, as he moves to make sure she sees his slim and strong body extending a handshake to Ennis, striding forcefully out the door and easing around the corner out of sight. They see each other like an image set in old fashioned chemical quicksilver. Then he leaves, making arrangements to pick up his drafting supplies from a shop across the river in Cambridge.

Amanda sleeps all the way back home. He puts her into his bed and moves his things to the living room. She is too tired to protest. She will sleep in his bed and have the pleasure of the skylight, the muted table lamp and direct breeze from the window. He takes his drafting materials to her studio, now sinking under her pine cone sketches, and clears a clear and simple space. He will work here and take the place as his. There is a goodness to this that surprises him.

Chapter 42

Sucking Popsicles

In a few months, Amanda is sucking mostly popsicles. Cheyenne is given the bottle of morphine from the doctor and he drips a few drops under her tongue according to the schedule of the hospice nurse.

When Amanda agrees to go into hospice care, Vivi doubles her efforts at planting. She makes sure that the morning glory is twining under the bedroom window so Amanda can wake to the beautiful blue flowers. There is a bee or two that finds its way to the window. One is a honey bee, greedy for nectar and the other is a large black borer bee who burrows hungrily into the old wood around the window frame. He keeps a constant hum up with his attack on what's left of the old house.

"It feels like he is trying to drill her out," Vivi says around five one afternoon when Cheyenne comes in from his studio and Vivi is washing her hands in Amanda's kitchen sink. She scrubs at the dirt under her nails but doesn't try hard to remove it.

It is late July now and they have been keeping this rhythm for two months. Vivi fighting to plant life, Amanda trying to slip away with no pain and Cheyenne balancing the two women in their various dodges. Cheyenne has purchased a television and set it up in the kitchen. It's metallic light and cruel laugh tracks keep the night nurse content but

Vivi always leaves before the nurse arrives and the cans of soup are opened and the plastic music rolls out like a ticker tape, coating the house in a thick mediocrity.

"It's not right, you know," she says to Cheyenne. "It's like wrapping the dead in styrofoam."

"It keeps Matilda happy and if Matilda is happy and her large family of Dominican children are happy, then I am happy," says Mark. He has become more Mark since the hospice process has begun and he has revealed himself to be a man who works, and thinks about money and earning enough to go elsewhere and be someone different. Vivi recognizes this in him. It is a process she recognizes from when she lost Jake to his father's bank account.

"I suppose it is inevitable," she says to Mark one night when he comes over for a meal, escaping Matilda and her cans of Campbell's soup and saltines. "It is nothing to be ashamed of."

"I don't think I said I was ashamed," says Mark. "I can't stay here forever. I have to figure out something to do with my life."

Vivi smiles slightly at him. "Have some wine. It will help."

She pours him some crisp white, still cold from the fridge. He grabs some almonds. A few grapes. He drinks the wine. They take their glasses to her terrace as they do most nights. They are both tired after their days. Mark is working on a big building for Jim Ennis and it keeps him busy. Vivi has several gardening clients now, and she and Esteban and Jorge have a small business. She designs a concept and then they put in the hardscape, sometimes dig a pond and then plant the water lilies or the cat tails, trying to fool the home owner into believing that they live in a quieter time and place.

Vivi is looking good and strong. She is fit and easy in her body and has hit her stride again. Though she is losing her periods she still feels vital and full and unburdened by the change inside of her. She is tan from her garden work and tired in a good way every day.

Vivi looks over at her friend. "You, my dear, are pale and frail. I dare say, you have husband's disease with no wife. Working too hard for no reward except our dying friend and a glass of wine with me in the evening."

"Husband's disease. Now there is a compliment." He smiles, a little softer with the setting sun.

"Yes, actually. It can be very appealing. Very steadfast and comforting."

"Glad to be of service." Mark settles at the sound of her voice. It is an easier feeling than he has had in a while.

"I spoke with Jim Ennis today." Vivi smiles quietly.

"You did?"

"I did," her eyes twinkle despite her attempt at cool. "He liked my design for the Longman's house. He said he'd 'keep me in mind' for his next project!"

"Well, that's good . . ."

"Yes, to be kept in mind. It is forward progress."

Mark takes a swig of his wine.

"Yes." Vivi looks at Mark and cannot find the idealistic young Cheyenne.

"Mark," she says.

"Yes." His eyes are closing from the day, the wine, and the relaxation.

"Take a bath. Come stay here tonight. Stay in my bed. We will both sleep well and you can go back to your savior role tomorrow. Matilda is on until 6:00 a.m., yes?"

"Umm, yes."

"Go. The tub is there. The towels are there. And my sheets are clean."

Mark rises sleepily without a thought. "Yes," he says. She smiles and starts the tub for him, keeps the lights low. He takes off his clothes without a thought. And sinks into the tub.

When he gets out his eyes are half closed and he falls onto Vivi's side of the bed. When she comes in, having done the same, she rolls him over to the other side, by the window, and claims her own spot. They crawl into bed. They begin to slip away, and his arm comes round her and holds her breast and they breathe and sleep with the blessing of no dreams. When they wake, they smile, rise, and part quickly to start their days.

Chapter 43

We are Here and She is Not

It has taken a long time for Pegg to respond. When Cheyenne gave the information to Vivi about Amanda's old friend in Boston, she wasn't sure how to follow up or follow through. But then she realized she had no contact information for Harvey or the cousin or anyone from Amanda's former life and someone might want to pay tribute, say goodbye.

Pegg wanted the artwork. That's what she said over the phone. She is married to a Douglas Fineman of the Fineman Gallery and they live in Newton. Dougie, as she calls him, is well into his eighties and doesn't get out much, but she will drive down and see Amanda. That is, if Amanda is up for a visit.

"She's in and out at this point and likes her morphine dose, but she thought, I mean before she entered hospice, she thought maybe you might want to know that she was sick."

There is silence on the phone and Vivi is waiting respectfully for the news to sink into Pegg's head. Instead of deep pulsing grief, however, she can hear Pegg shoving some chairs around.

"Watch out," she says to someone on her end of the line. "Watch, yeah, okay. I swear you're gonna kill us all with that goddamn walker."

"I beg your pardon?" Vivi tries to lasso the attention back to the subject at hand.

"Oh, it's Dougie. He's a killer with his devices."

"Ah," says Vivi, not at all sure what the correct response might be.

"I can come down next week. Can take a look at what she's got left."

"Pegg. Do you have contact information for her husband, Harvey? Somewhere in Martinique? Or the cousin who owns the house?"

"Harvey died. Maybe over a year ago. She sent me a note about it. Like she did when she lost the apartment, and moved to the country, and needed some money."

"Oh."

"The county will have ownership information on the house."

"Oh."

"Yeah, oh is right."

"I can come and value the paintings, whatever is left, and try to put them in the gallery, see if they sell, but that's really all I have to offer."

"I wasn't sure. I mean I didn't know how close you two were."

"Amanda and I were close years ago. She went back to Harvey and her cushy life and I got over it, found rich ol' Dougie who bought me my gallery and have been just fine thank you. That's about it."

Before Vivi hangs up the phone and wraps the whole idea of a happy ending into something like an air sickness bag in her head, Pegg says "And no need to send me the ashes or anything. I opted out of being her witness a few heartbreaks ago."

The shake of Vivi's head does not dispel the enormous feeling of waste and witnessing of a passing fancy.

"It's like Amanda's life, the chances she took or didn't are a pale wash against the sky. Like she was somebody's idea of interesting, but she never bought into the idea herself, and in the end she will fade away, and her paintings will go to the Salvation Army and that will be that."

Mark and Vivi are sitting on her porch again, drinking in the purple of the sunset. Pegg's sang froid is the topic of their conversation.

"Amanda was pretty passionate. I mean, her secrets. I think that's why I stayed with her. Her heat, her containment made her prowl like a cat around me. I confess I found her heat astonishing, and toxic. She would sketch me sometimes, while I closed my eyes at the table and I felt like she was scraping my skin, wanting me so much."

Vivi looks over at her friend. "She wanted you that much?"

Mark grins. "Yep!"

Vivi grins too. "Wow. I don't think I have ever experienced that."

Mark smiles slightly at the sunset. "It's because you're too available, Vivi. You are exactly what you are. Your secrets are pretty transparent."

Vivi says, "I don't think I have any."

"You give them away. Secret them in the bellies of those you value. And those of us who carry your secrets are bound to you, even though you don't believe that."

"Wow. What does that mean?

"No idea," says Mark. "And just for the record. You don't get how attractive you are. I mean really."

Vivi smiles. "And what does that mean?"

Mark takes a chance and winks at her. And Vivi dissolves into laughter. He laughs too.

"Pretty suave for a kid," he says.

"Some kid," she says. "Careful what you wish for, kid. It ain't over til it's over."

"That's great to hear!" Mark gets up and pulls Vivi to her feet. He hugs her really tightly and lifts her from the ground. She can sense a small swell in his pants.

"Well," she says. "I'm honored," she says with a smile.

"It ain't over til it's over. You said it! Let's have dinner. I think we should plan to be at Amanda's the next day or two. Hospice nurse says it's close now."

Vivi absorbs the warmth of their banter and his hug. She feels very grateful and her heart opens as she turns to Mark.

"But, there is no one for her! Just us. I mean how can she pass with no witness? No weeping? No tick against the landscape? God. It gives me the chills."

"Vikram would have an answer for that one. But not me."

That night, Mark turns to Vivi in bed. "Will you make love with me?"

Vivi turns to him. She reaches up and moves his hair from his forehead.

"That's a nice offer." she says.

"Will you?"

"Um, why?"

She can feel Mark smile as much as see him.

"Well, I want you to hold my secret for me. I want to see what it feels like. I want to crawl inside your heart and give you as much room as you may need to believe that there is some kind of sense for me being here and Vikram being gone and Amanda dying and . . ." Vivi blinks her eyes at him. "And I think we fit in an odd jerky way. And I really want to be right inside your wonderful body and soul. How's that?"

"That's impressive. Are you a good kisser?"

"For a kid, I think so."

"Oh! Bad move. Age related comments will not help."

Cheyenne reaches for her. He pulls her very close so that her face is crushed into his neck. "Please, Vivi." He kisses her.

"That was good," she says. And she kisses back and they do that for awhile until they decide to take off their tee-shirts and sweat pants and lay naked on top of the sheet. Vivi presents herself in all her soft and hard landscape.

"This is it, Mark. This is okay with you."

"You're beautiful," he says. She smiles and looks right in his eyes. She puts his hand on her breast and her full belly. He smiles.

"Yum," he says."

"Okay," she says. "No regrets!"

He pulls her down and sings Piaf at the top of his lungs. "*Rien, je regrette rien*," and he throws a pillow at her and they roll and they roll and she opens fully to him and he slips in and rests and breathes and grows stronger and explodes. Her whole body opens to him. Her whole self swallows and is swallowed and they stay locked in each other all through the night. It is remarkable and outside the window the trees sway and sweep, reaching for the new breath that they can feel in the crook of their branches and beneath the green dermis that is metabolizing into life.

Chapter 44

Honoring Departure

Vivi is outside Amanda's window digging in plants and Cheyenne has walked inside to see how Amanda is doing. Amanda's breathing has been labored and rattling for a few hours. The hospice nurse has been here since the morning.

"I'll stay a few hours," Sandy says to Vivi and Cheyenne. "It shouldn't be long now."

When Sandy heads to the kitchen and Cheyenne is in his studio sorting out what his lines on paper might have to do with Amanda's, Vivi comes in and sits quietly next to Amanda's bed.

"Amanda. It's Vivi here. I'm just sitting here. I thought I would sit with you for a while."

There is no movement, no change in the rasp. Vivi thinks it sounds like Amanda is heaving into her watering can. The echo is against tin. Could Amanda be mineralizing already?

"I want to apologize to you." Vivi sits up to speak rather than stay with the idea of tin and bone. "I mean, about slapping you a few months back. About being righteous and insisting you stick around to slip away on my terms . . . or someone else's terms. I don't know what's right. I don't know if suffering needs to be a part of saying goodbye and becoming something else. I hope you haven't suffered too terribly. I know you always said you loved drugs! And the morphine is certainly flowing freely." Vivi listens to the drivel coming out of her mouth. "Oh god. I can't seem to get words to bend to this moment. I guess it has been a gift to me that you are taking your time in making your way to the other side. Selfish. Watching you go. It helps me figure out my own balance sheet. Not that this is your job. Oh god. Sorry. Sorry. Sorry." Vivi listens to a few more rasps. Her mind cannot keep her from comparison and the image of a whooshing iron lung lunges onto her mind's movie screen. These images are not helpful in getting herself to speak coherently. "This—being with you now—somehow helps me time things. Catch up with time lost, opportunities spent. With Jake I mean. I mean, once when Jake was sick, a few months before he died, I asked the doctor how I was supposed to help him. Make him comfortable if he was in distress. The doctor gave me a bottle of liquid morphine. He told me I could put a few drops under his tongue if things got bad. I mean, I think the doctor was giving me permission to help Jake leave if I wanted to, if he wanted to do that. There was some righteous indignation on my part and then I heaved the bottle into the canyon because I was afraid maybe it would be too easy, too easy to help him out. Too easy for him to leave. Too easy for me to be rid of him, and he of me, and I was frightened because I did not know what was right or wrong. So, I pretended I was offended and that life is sacred and all that. But really, I didn't want the power of determining his path, my own path, I just didn't want it."

Vivi is not sure if she is talking out loud. But she continues anyway.

"So, I guess what I want to say is that I admire your own strength. Your willingness to make your own decision even though I slugged you for voicing it. And I hope next time around, I mean if you come back and believe in all of that, I hope it's easier or more challenging or whatever it is that will . . . be better, you know?"

Cheyenne comes into the room. He has been listening at the doorway. Vivi's low mumble, Amanda's rasping and occasional rattle. The nurse comes in.

"Amanda. Amanda. I am going to wash you now. I have some very warm water and lovely soap. Your friends tell me you love this soap." Sandy, the nurse looks over at the pair of them. "You want to help?" Cheyenne looks at Vivi.

"I think it's okay, Mark. Cheyenne. I think it's okay if you want to help."

Cheyenne moves to the bed not sure what his job will be. "Here we go," he says and stands ready.

The three of them pull back the bed covers and reveal Amanda shrunken in the white nightgown Vivi had purchased for her. She couldn't find any pajamas when Amanda came back from the hospital.

"I don't like pajamas," Amanda had said. "I like the feel of cool sheets against my skin."

Vivi had no problem with that but she bought a couple of white cotton gowns and had them in the drawer in case Amanda was to be overruled. Vivi thinks it was Matilda, the night nurse who swaddled Amanda every night. First in the night gown, then in the cool white sheet. Matilda would take a wash cloth and move it upward across Amanda's sweaty face, pushing away the lines and leaving her with a slight damp ridge on her hairline.

As Sandy moves out to get the wash basin from the bath room, Vivi smiles across Amanda's body. "It will be okay," she says to a slightly shaky Cheyenne. "It will be okay."

And Cheyenne nods.

"I'll do it." A husky voice from the living room floats to them. "I been washing her every night. I came early today 'cause I figured it was a special day, special time. I'll wash that woman. We know each other."

Matilda sweeps back into the bedroom with two large white towels and soap, hairbrush, tooth brush. Cheyenne and Vivi step back.

"What you two looking at?" Matilda snorts. "We are getting Ms. Amanda beautiful to meet her Maker."

Matilda gives Cheyenne the basin and motions for him to go fill it. Meanwhile, Vivi and Matilda pull up the white cotton gown. Her body is smaller but it is not vacant yet. There is a resilience around her breasts and her stomach. A soft movement as her lungs labor above and below these parts that were, for Amanda, so defining of her time on the planet. Cheyenne returns with the basin. The water is warm and has a sweet smell of lavender.

"Good" says Matilda. "Now, you step out, young man. We'll call you for brushing her hair. That okay with you, Ms. Amanda? That okay?"

Amanda makes a small shift of her head. Matilda works swiftly with a soft sponge and a white wash cloth. She washes Amanda's legs and feet. She moves to her belly and caresses what is left of her breasts. "Here, Ms. Amanda. We're gonna cover you with this big white towel, make sure you're not too chilly." Vivi arranges the towel over Amanda and watches the ease and strength of Matilda as she handles Amanda's arms, massages her fingers and palms, wipes and wraps everything down with the thick white towels.

She moves to Amanda's face and dips the wash cloth in the warm water. "Here we go, let's wash that face." Amanda brings her face around like a moon to the magnificent black woman who is cradling her like a child. Vivi thinks she sees a smile. Matilda allows the cloth to wash around the crust of Amanda's dry lips, she washes under her nose and allows the cloth to move up across her forehead. Matilda lets the cloth rest there for a moment. "Oh, good thing we washed your hair yesterday so you are fresh and clean, yes?"

Vivi gets the glass of cool water and the toothbrush that Matilda has brought in with her. She holds it while Matilda dips the brush and gently eases it into Amanda's mouth. "Here you go. I know how you like to feel fresh. Let me brush those teeth a little." She swishes the brush in Amanda's mouth and brings the glass over for Amanda to spit out whatever is left.

"Boy! Mark! Come lift this woman so we can change the sheets."

Cheyenne appears in the doorway and moves to the bed. Amanda is swaddled in large white bath sheets. "Here, lift her in your arms. Go ahead."

Cheyenne bends down and Amanda takes a breath. A long one. For a moment, she opens one eye and looks into Cheyenne's face

"She's awake. You're awake, Amanda. You look beautiful," Cheyenne says softly.

Amanda opens her eyes and feels the strength of Cheyenne's arms around her.

Vivi and Matilda rip the sheet off the bed and billow a fresh one up, a welcoming tent. They look over at Cheyenne holding Amanda as the sheet settles.

"You're so light," he says to her. "Beautiful and clean and light." he says.

She takes a big breath and her eyes fix on him. Her body settles in his arms. And then she puffs out air. One puff. And she is gone.

Cheyenne holds her bones. Vivi looks over at this tender young man holding such beautiful death.

"Amanda?" Cheyenne doesn't know what to do, but he looks up to see if he can make contact before she is gone. "Amanda? Thank you. Thank you, Amanda."

And she is gone. Matilda touches his arm. "Put that woman right here. Put her down now. She's ready to rest." Carefully, Cheyenne lowers Amanda's body onto the bed.

"Goodbye, lovely Ms. Amanda. It was a pleasure to serve you." Matilda shuffles out of the room. "Sandy? Sandy? You still here. Best to call the folks now."

Vivi and Cheyenne sit down next to the bed and next to each other. The shadows will be coming in soon and Vivi reaches to turn on the lamp. Vivi and Cheyenne touch each other's hands.

"So, the ambulance will be here in maybe an hour or two. You two okay sitting with her til then?" Matilda has her glasses on, with papers and a pen in her hands. She is taking care of business.

Vivi looks up. "Yes, well, yes? Are you leaving now?"

"I'll be around but it's good to sit with her."

A car pulls into the driveway. And Vivi looks out to see who could possibly show up now. A woman about her own age, maybe a little younger gets out of a Toyota RAV4. She has on Eddie Bauer from head to toe. Horn rimmed glasses, a blond bob easing to grey and freckles, lots of freckles.

Vivi can hear Matilda in the front greet her. "Who are you. please?"

"I'm here to see my old friend."

Vivi gets up and walks to the door. "Pegg? Is that you? I'm Vivi. Pegg, Amanda just passed."

Pegg shows more frustration than sadness. "Damn. Dougie took forever to get settled in after his appointment. Let me go in and say goodbye."

Pegg heads to Amanda's bedroom. Cheyenne looks up. He moves to leave her a spot.

"Hello dear," Pegg speaks cautiously to the corpse. "A day late and a dollar short." She takes Amanda's hand and sits with her. There is a long thick silence. "I did love you, dear. Damn everything but the circus."

Cheyenne is up and away. Vivi stays in the living room. Pegg sits next to Amanda's body. She moves to sit on the bed and places her hand on Amanda's forehead. "Still warm. Still warm." Pegg stretches out next to her friend and lover. She holds her hand, she rests her forehead on the chest, now still and becoming stiller. Pegg closes her eyes, breathes in what's left of Amanda and falls asleep.

"Goodbye, dear. Until we meet again," her body sighs.

Chapter 45

Painting Pine Cones

"I think they will sell. The pine cones, I think they will sell. They're very good really. Deep and detailed. Good work."

Pegg has gathered all the pine cone sketches from corners of the studio. She has found a cache of small acrylic paintings as well. And then some hands. "Whose hands?" Pegg shoves the question at him. "Yours?"

Mark looks down at his hands. "Maybe." he says.

"They're soft. Softer than now."

"I've been torturing lines. Doing drafting for a Boston firm."

"Oh. That'll get you in the end," she says.

"Thanks for the thought."

"No matter." Pegg waves a hand. "Were you her lover? Really?"

Mark is taken aback but happy to answer. "No. We were friends. I rented a room from her."

"I bet she liked you. She coveted tall men. Harvey was short and squat, and then I was always hiding under a rock. She longed for tall trees and strong stock."

"Lots of tall trees here."

"Yes. In her last exile I can see that. And lots of flowers. Amanda was not one for flowers."

"Vivi's gift. She's a gardener. Does landscape design."

"Pretty, but not Amanda. Amanda was an outline person."

"I guess I never noticed."

Pegg looks over at him wondering if he is rude or clueless.

"I guess I didn't really know her very well."

Pegg looks over at him. "Licking your own wounds, were you?"

"I don't know if you need say that."

"I don't. I don't need to say that. It's none of my business what the hell you are doing in this tiny hamlet, drawing lines under tall trees and fascinating the old folk." Pegg had a smug smirk that Mark hadn't seen in a while. "You going back to civilization now that your mama tit is gone?"

"You're a fucking piece of work, Pegg. Excuse me while I go meditate on your wisdom."

"I'll call Vivi with a list of paintings. What I think they will sell for. Not that either of you get the stuff. It's mine, I guess. Her only kin of some kind, I guess," she calls after him

Mark walks out of the studio, letting her voice fall on the gravel path. He heads to the kitchen for coffee, smarting at Pegg's psychological wrap up. As he goes to grab milk in the fridge he catches sight of that orange sketchbook Amanda was always carrying, always kept on the book shelf. He ruffles the pages and his face stares back at him. Sleeping, standing, naked, draped. Eyes, hands, shoulder blades, lip.

She was watching him always. She recorded him always. She caught his shadow and held it for all those months when he thought he was a cipher, a romantic cowboy in exile from the ranch. She was obsessed but she held him, got him, preserved him so he can now study who he was all last year. He hasn't lost a year. She recorded every shade and shift of it. And now he will have to hold himself to account.

There was so little in the house really. Vivi let Mark deal with the studio and she folded everything and packed up what dishes were in the house, Amanda's clothes and the 'pussy paintings'. Vivi wonders if Pegg saw them. Maybe Mark will put them in the car and drop them in Boston next time he goes up for business.

The realtor that contacts Vivi says the cousin wants to put the house on the market as soon as possible. Jordon Kale is his name. He is local, but reluctantly so. Jordan is a town kid who went off to college and after a few years trying to find a job in the city where he studied, he came back to sell real estate in his father's firm.

"The house looks better than it has for years. We used to rent it to summer folks. But I don't remember the gardens. And it's good with all that white paint inside.'

"Yes, Amanda was an artist so she liked a simple space. I planted the place, especially when she got sick. I thought it might cheer her up."

"It looks great. Thanks."

"Sure." Vivi reaches into her pocket and pulls out her new cards. "I do landscape design. Ever need me, please feel free to give me a call."

Vivi's encounter with sex and love again has given her different dimensions. She is smooth where she had let herself be rugged, a survivalist. She is stronger knowing that certain parts of her are not vulnerable to her young lover's touch. And, delighted that she can be present for their encounter without the crushing need to be filled up and saved. She feels proud somehow that she is turning into the next version of herself but there are still traces of the old Vivi, the unsure one, the one letting things happen to her instead of making things happen for herself.

A young realtor stands before her. He can give her work. She wants work. She is not sure that her usual way of operating will suffice here. Usually, she lets her work speak for herself. But if she is going to be a woman with a handsome young lover, on whom she does not want to depend, then she has to figure out who she is as a business person. She gives Jason an extra smile as she hands him another card. "Call me," she says, vaguely aware that that comment may have come out all wrong.

Jason looks at her for a moment and dismisses the idea that she is coming on to him. Still, he is not sure and his discomfort comes from somewhere he has not visited since he was a testes driven football player. "Wow. Landscape design. Will do." He smiles awkwardly, defensive.

"Hardscape, soft scape, drought tolerant." Vivi pushes ahead. She is not sure what she is feeling about this encounter but it is a new feeling so she trusts the fact that she cannot identify what transaction she is promoting.

"Drought tolerant. Sounds like you have California in your veins."

"Does it show?" She smiles again.

"In the most complimentary way, Ma'am."

Vivi smiles at him, looking for center. She clears her throat. "Jorge and Esteban Nunez work with me. They're great maintenance gardeners. And they'll plow in winter." Close the deal, she thinks. Is that something that Jake used to say?

"Okay. Okay, I have your card," says Jordan, not sure how to identify the buzz he is receiving from her.

"Right, you do," she says, almost coy. She knows she is definitely in uncharted territory. *So what?* she thinks! Be bold! Be beautiful! Maybe she has just slurped too much caffeine this morning.

"It'll take a while to sell the place. Never good to put something on late August or September but we'll do our best."

"Oh, of course," she says, and touches the sleeve of his jacket.

He has to put an end to this somehow. "Meantime, if your son wants to keep his studio there, it's good to have someone around the place."

"My son." Vivi stops at that one. Really? Her son?

"Right. I mean you guys live at your place, right?"

"Well, he was Amanda's renter, really, and . . ."

"Sure. Well, whatever." He has done his work. "Sorry."

"No. No. No problem. Thanks. See you."

"Right," he says, looking past her.

"I'll let him know." Vivi calls after him as Jordan turns and goes.

Vivi watches him walk away, slightly dazed. She did not play this encounter correctly. She knows that. She is willing to own up to that. But, that was an unkind cut from that college frat boy. Her son? Really?

"Oh my God," she thinks. "I have to go drown myself."

And she heads home, locks herself in the bathroom with Oreo's and grape juice, and sinks into the tub. She even pulls the shower curtain around her for extra protection. "Oh, boy. Oh, boy. What just happened?"

Vivi has not really considered the age difference between she and Mark. And of course, their arrangement is a friendship, not a forever life. But, sitting there, licking the white cream off the open Oreos, she is surprised that the reminder of their impermanence distresses her. The comfort of their friendship is all the better for its lack of urgent need. All the better because it has a rationale to it that she feels protects her in some way. She has allowed herself to soften to their rhythms, open completely to their careful, deepening lovemaking. It is surprising for her to realize that she is comfortable losing scales and enjoying her newly supple skin.

Vivi hears thunder out the window and a rainstorm comes up and surrounds the house this late afternoon. She stays in the tub and feels the raindrops hit her cold shoulders through the open window.

When Vivi was little, very little, before there was loss, when there was only the crinoline of her new white dress, and her small white gloves with ketchup stains on the finger tips, then, at that time Vivi did not dream of being saved. Or of being joined. Of being a princess or a queen of the cinema.

She looked at the world with wide eyes that stood alone. The eyes watched her father depart, her mother's eyes grow narrow with worry, her Aunt and Uncle sing too loud and squeeze her too hard when she and her mom came to live with them. Now, at this time, when she is starting her life again, she knows that she must make a choice. She knows that has to be a choice that will sustain her. She knows that life can fade away, like Amanda's. She knows people can get eaten by acid and defeat, like Jake. She knows that. But she is not in the habit of wanting and receiving what she wants. Instead, she has chosen what will work. Jake "worked" for her and he was happy to make her happy, if he ever could. Vikram was her spiritual savior, heart love, but he tired of that role though it surprised him to recognize himself in another. Cheyenne shares the same open moment she lives in. He takes what comes to him and it morphs into something he thinks he can trust. This is how Vivi lives.

Today, she is not sure if that is enough. She is not sure why she is nauseous and feeling bloated after all that work in the sun. Maybe that is why she acted so oddly with that young man.

Visits to Jake's family sink her. They have no loft left in them. Shelley has lost all buoyancy and is living now barricaded behind piles of old paperbacks and unopened mail. Vivi feels the compression of Shelley's choices. She is grateful. Her work, the grace of new life planted and raised in the sun gives her a thin line of continuum to hold onto. She never yearned for a child, or the dream of a child loved and lost some other where on a time line she does not understand. She does not hold on to memory. She does not hold on to goals or the people who promise and cannot deliver. She holds on to life as it recreates itself but today it is raining and she is not sure if it is enough to admire life if she cannot find a way to live it on her own, being her own energy source. She can plant a garden but there is a selfish desire to imprint herself that she recognizes with every seed she casts, and every bush she wills into bloom. That used to feel right, or enough, but she is just not sure these days.

She gets out of the tub and counts the number of lines that have formed on her withered fingertips. Out the window, the gray is still gathered. She needs to put on the television. Loud and stupid.

Chapter 46

Miracles Can Happen

In the box, the last one, Vivi finds the china or what is left of it. There is a set of twelve plates still, and soup bowls. She knows this because she has never opened the box that Shelley shipped to them soon after they were married. This box full of Shelley's mother's china has been dormant for at least twenty-five years. That feels foolish. There has to be a cousin somewhere who could use the dishes. And there is Shelley's fur.

Vivi was going to leave the box on the porch and drive away from New Rochelle quickly but the sickening drone of afternoon television that comes from the front window reaches out and makes her want to wretch. She can't help but lean over the metal railing of the front step to catch her breath and spit just a small acid stream of yellow bile into the dead earth behind the lopsided spruce, standing guard like a dead sentinel.

"Who's there?" Shelley's voice from within.

"A ghost." Vivi calls, caught.

Shelley comes to the front door. "You're not kidding. You couldn't make a phone call?"

"I was just driving through. I didn't know you were home. I finally got the last of the L.A. boxes. I promised you I'd bring back important things so your family can have them." Vivi smiles gamely.

"Are you coming in or are you just going to be a FedEx impersonator?"

"I can't stay Shelley. Really . . . I—"

"Bullshit. Pick up the box and bring it into the dining room at least."

Vivi complies. "So, how are you," says Shelley, who searches for her glasses and the overhead light.

"Actually, I feel like shit. It has been a tough few weeks. A friend passed and I have been dealing with that."

"Oh," says Shelley, listening and eyeing the box. "I don't know what the hell I am going to do with this crap after all this time."

"Well, I can take it to the Salvation Army, if you want. I just wanted to make sure . . ."

"Yes," says Shelley. "You wanted to make sure you don't owe us anything. I know."

Vivi feels a little dizzy. "Can I sit down, please? At least while you're yelling at me?"

Shelley shuffles into the kitchen and brings her a glass of water. "You look like you saw a ghost? Peak-ed."

"A little nauseous, dizzy."

"Ha! You sound pregnant. Now wouldn't that be a miracle? My boy come back from the dead and impregnate you!"

Vivi looks up at her former mother-in-law. "You think that's funny?"

"I don't know. I don't know what's funny anymore, Vivian."

Vivi manages to stay with Shelley for about half an hour. She does so by concentrating on looking at Shelley's hands, which seem to have withered since their last visit. She watches Shelley's hands as they wave and push thoughts away. As she dismisses this cousin and that old friend, as she reaches for her own hair and tries to smooth it though she knows she is overdue for color at the salon. While Shelley's hands are conducting the comings and goings of approvals and disapprovals, Vivi watches and allows herself to slip just slightly out of her body. She has not used this trick in a long time. But somehow, watching Shelley from above allows her to have compassion for her. To view her as a poor lost human and pretend that she, Vivi, has the wisdom of angels.

Finally, she is released.

"Goodbye Shelley. I hope you will drive up to see the new house."

"Invite me. Miracles can happen."

Vivi makes it back to the house and heads to her bed where she flops and gazes out the window. She can just see the shadow of a form on the other side of the doorframe.

"You saw my mother. You could be kind to my mother, she did nothing unkind to you."

"Jake. That you?"

"None other."

"You show up at the weirdest times. Leave me be. I feel sick. I feel lost. I don't know what's going on."

"It's okay, Viv." Jake or his shadow lays down next to her on the bed. She can imagine him trying to whisper into her ear. "It's okay, Viv. You don't get all this transition stuff yet. One life goes, another one comes in. Here, drink this."

Jake offers her a goblet full of a warm, vibrant brew.

"Drink this. Like Alice in Wonderland. Drink me."

Vivi takes the goblet and drinks it down. She thinks she is asleep but can't be sure. That's how it's always been with Jake. She can feel her breasts tighten and her stomach churn.

"Drink it, Vivi. I'm not mad anymore. You deserve another chance at living. I'll help you out."

Vivi can feel herself fall away from Jake and from her bed. She feels herself fully supported by flowing light. She stays there for a moment, the goddess of giving and taking and offering and receiving. Then she gets up and vomits.

"Viv? Vivi? You okay?" It's Cheyenne's voice.

"Oh." She rolls over, groggy. "Stomach flu. It's just stomach flu. You better sleep on the futon."

And she is knocked out again.

Chapter 47

Propulsion

Cheyenne has been pretending to ignore Amanda's sketchbook but he hasn't. He is astonished at what she sees. The boy, the guile, the pretense and the control he yielded. He is not proud of what she saw but he has to admit that she was correct. While Vivi sleeps off whatever she has, Cheyenne sinks into the big chair with his evening drink. He can make out Vivi's arm flung half off the bed. She looks young, open, soft and he knows he is hiding out with her. He wrestles a bit with the possible reasons why he need make no change at all in his life, but he loses all the arguments.

Instead, he makes sure all Amanda's paintings are packed well in their boxes. He packs his own bag and puts it carefully in the car. Then he goes back and enjoys the last of the twilight. Whatever bug bit Vivi, she'll be out for awhile. No need to sneak off in the dead of night. He can make the right decision without stealth or guilt. He throws a sheet and some blankets on the futon and settles in for the night.

At seven the next morning, Vivi is still out. He pens a note. "Ennis wants me in Boston for a few days. Call when you wake up."

When she does wake up, she does not call. She feels her tightening breasts and rubs her hands around her belly.

"This is absurd. I mean, I can't possibly . . ."

At the drug store, she is ready with a story about a young friend being too shy to buy the pregnancy test, but no one asks. When she is alone, back at the house and sees the positive results, she thinks she has no reaction at all. She knows there needs to be more of a reaction to her reported condition, but she feels numb.

Her other pregnancy so many years ago was secret. She needed to hide it until she was ready to accept that she and Jake were a pair, that they were saying yes to their lives together. Now, she is alone. There is no one really who cares about this child shoving itself back into life through her aging body. Except Shelley. Maybe she should call Shelley and give her the grandchild she has always craved? She smiles at the outrage she feels at the prospect of sharing this child with Shelley. And is immediately guilty. What has Shelley ever done to anyone except wanting to love them and receive love in return. Her always open platform of needing and willing to be needed is something that Vivi has never understood or accepted easily. Her own mother was always so busy she never really knew how she felt about Vivi becoming a mother one day. Vivi imagines she would greet the news with a soft smile and a plan for a college fund, and then invite Vivi to the movies.

Vivi is acutely aware of her own ambivalence towards giving life. Yet, she receives this lesson again and again. Giving birth, making life, creating beauty. It is the job, after all. But does everyone do it the same way?

Never mind. She bats away her own feelings. Instead, her logical mind brings up the reams of negative statistics about women giving birth in their early 50s. She knows she is not a hero and would not easily welcome a child with disabilities. Again, her guilt at such a selfish thought overwhelms her.

Fiddle dee dee, Vivi thinks. How does Scarlett O'Hara from *Gone With the Wind* show up at just this exact moment, she wonders? Maybe she had more wisdom than we thought.

The phone has been clattering all morning. Vivi has been ignoring it, consumed with her own attempt to stick to her routine and avoid the hormonal snags that she can already feel in her thinking, in her digestion, in the visual sweep of her beloved one-bedroom house.

She, too, got a call from Ennis in Boston. She is trying to work on a design for a new development they will build in Cambridge. She is intent on figuring out green walls for the Eastern climate and finding the right mix of hard and soft scape to impress the architects. She knows Mark has suggested they call when he arrived in Boston. She's grateful for it but she has not spoken to him. She is too busy and focus is called for with her current condition.

Glancing at her calendar, she sees that this weekend is the gathering of the Labyrinth Society at the college. Mark has been waiting for this Conference since he came back, looking forward to meeting some of the designers and enthusiasts. He's been talking about it ever since she built the house and they planned the gardens together.

"I can't be responsible for his choices!" Vivi says to herself as she ignores the phone once again. And then, she has had enough. The phone is driving her crazy.

"Hello!" she barks.

"Oh. Sorry to bother you but, is this Vivian?" It's clear it is no one who knows her with that greeting.

"Yes. This is Vivi. Who's this?"

The voice goes on to tell her that the Labyrinth Society is gathering at the college and they understand she is a designer and might want to make a presentation.

"Well, I'm afraid I'm not really prepared for a presentation."

"Ah. I received the wrong information,"

"It's a friend of mine. He's an architect and he was interested . . ." Vivi thinks fast. "I have a site, on my land. He thought he might want to create one for the community."

"That's interesting. Really?"

They go on to discuss the legalities of a public labyrinth in a private space and the rest. It is difficult for Vivi to focus on the voice that drones on a little too sensitively on the other end of the line. It is the problem that she has always had with these spiritual types that Vikram champions. They are all so self-consciously modulated.

The voice goes on to chat about the placement of labyrinths, the holiness of land and the rest. All this talk of holy land and green spirits is literally choking her with fertility. Ever since she saw the results of that dipstick she can't stand to be in the garden. It feels like her whole body is sprouting, vines coming out of her nose and ears dripping with nascent Dutch hornpipes. This morning in the shower, she felt the pulsing water making sensitive the mammary glands in her back. This is not a pleasant feeling. She is feeling invaded and a good slug of vinegar sounds perfect to find balance. She is not prepared to think about or deal with this odd circumstance in which she finds herself but her last ditch hormones are having a field day with the surprise deposit in their midst. Her inner landscape is all moss and ooze. She is permeable, inside and out.

"Tell me about the site," the kind voice asks.

Vivi is not sure how to respond. Instead she laughs.

"That good?" says the voice. "By the way, my name is Charles."

"Hi Charles. Nice to meet you." She really wants to get off the phone but instead she says, "The site. Well, it's my home. My new home. I don't think I've really ever had a home except I built this one through a weird confluence of magical events!"

"That sounds promising."

While she talks she is looking for those saltines she left in the kitchen.

"I found the land about a year ago and we built the house so it's sited toward the hills and late sunsets. I've created terraces where I have put lilacs and forsythia. This year I am starting wisteria around the deck that oversees the site."

There they are, the crackers. And there's an inviting can of Canada Dry Ginger Ale right next to it. Vivi is seeing how she can open the can and keep the phone at her ear.

"It sounds like you are making a garden fortress."

"No. Well, maybe. I can't tell." Ah, the can is open and she is pleased with herself that she is speaking normally as she maneuvers her needs. "I think the land has some history. Early American history. There was a settlement here in the early 1700s. I think that's why I was drawn to the place."

"Yes."

"And there is a magic circle, there is a round area that we dug out when we made the terraces. And that's gaping, healing at the moment. Vikram . . . do you know him?"

"Yes, actually. Vikram invited us to the college. I have known him for many years. He actually gave me your name."

"Yes, right. He would do that. Well, Vikram did a kind of mandala ceremony on the land. Made it holy. But it all got very weird and frankly, I think that's enough about all that." Vivi takes a slug of ginger ale.

"Sounds very beautiful and a special spot. I hope you will continue to dedicate it."

"Yes, yes. Dedication is all. At the moment, I am trying to make a living. So, I'll come by and leave a bunch of cards for folks. Maybe if they want to visit my garden, it may inspire them."

"Sure. It's fairly relaxed. Come by and tell us about your work."

"Thanks. Thanks I'll do that." The crumbs from the saltines fall to the floor. "So long. Thanks for calling."

She's not sure but Vivi thinks she agreed to come by and talk about her house and her work. Mostly, she needs to get to the grocery store and stock up on saltines and ginger ale. And that curry relish stuff she used to slather on Bratwurst. That sounds great. And maybe some Bratwurst, too. With sauerkraut. Definitely with sauerkraut.

The group in front of her is three rows of women in tie-dye with rounded breasts, mostly long greyish hair, glasses, plump faces and beatific smiles They are in the fluorescent, downstairs meeting room of the Stillness Center. This is the room that Vikram used for his gatherings and it still has a Buddha statue and curling posters about retreats in India and the Center for Spiritual Studies near Chennaie. Somebody put some pink gel over one of the fluorescents which helps a little but it does rather create a spotlight of sorts over one area. Pink light must have been required for someone, or something. Right now it highlights an empty spot on the well-used corduroy sofa, emphasizing a dip in the cushion. Vivi wonders who is the unseen watcher. The open plastic folding chairs strain to hold the women eager for softer seats and better lighting.

Vivi is showing the photos she has compiled of her garden on a power point presentation and the assembled are responding with appropriate pleasure.

"Well, actually I have an architect friend who has been itching to create a labyrinth on my property for a while. Perhaps by next year it will be done and I can invite folks over for a walk and to admire his handy work."

"What's the history of the land?" A round face with glasses smiles up at her. The face is connected to a pudgy body swaddled in a gray oversized jacket. She has been watching Vivi intently but trying to appear casual. "Oh, I'm sorry. My name is Naomi. I'm interested in the history of this area."

"Hi Naomi," Vivi tries to smile, but she has an uncomfortable feeling that she is in a twelve step program for spiritual addicts.

"Oh, not everything has a hocus pocus background, you know." Vivi laughs, defending herself from what she is not sure. "It's just a pretty piece of land and my friend, Vikram, who you all might know . . ."

"Oh yes, we love Vikram. What a wonderful teacher . . ." Smiles and nods spread through the crowd. Vikram has several admirers here and Vivi is irked by their devotion.

"Well, he's an old friend. I mean I knew him before he was a 'teacher'. I moved here because he was nearby but now he seems to have moved to India or someplace far away from here and me and the college. So, as holy as this ground might be, he sure isn't interested in it. So, for me, this whole idea of dedicating and labyrinths and the rest seem a little silly. I mean, I guess I am just not part of the tribe."

Vivi looks at Naomi's face, which still has a persistent smile. Vivi is amazed at how these words come pouring straight from her, no filter, no functioning frontal lobe doing its job.

"I know there was a settlement in this area in the early 1700s," says Naomi. "It later was an area where some of the women accused in the Salem Witch trials were arrested."

"I wouldn't know anything about that. It's a little too spooky for me."

The group laughs comfortingly.

"Well, it's just that in our experience, when we site a labyrinth or even disturb the earth of a place, the elements can get a little wild. Have you experienced anything like that?" Naomi will not stop.

"I can't imagine what you might mean . . ."

"Well, actually I have known stories of spirits rising and taking over their former life purposes."

Vivi is out of her realm here except that her body, a burgeoning forest, is feeling pretty crowded. She can feel herself start to lift out and above the group. *Damn*, she thinks. *I thought this crap was over! Is this chick saying that all that rebirth bullshit that happened when I dug the terraces was for a purpose? Can she see that I am pregnant again, at this age, and totally unable to hold any of this inside myself? Of course not. I can't be more than six weeks!*

"Are you alright, Vivian?" says Naomi.

It's probably pretty clear that Vivi has vacated the room, she thinks, and is hovering above the overly kind labyrinth lovers. Vivi is fine with that perspective, it feels pretty good actually, except the height gives her vertigo and she wants to vomit all over their heads.

"I think we need to thank Vivi for coming and telling us about her site and her plans for the future. Thank you, Vivi." Charles has come forward and now is clapping weakly to end the encounter. "Lunch is at the Commons. And we'll all reconnect here at two for the afternoon session."

As the group begins to scrape back their chairs and leave the room,

Vivi can feel Naomi's nosy energy, but Charles takes Naomi by the shoulder and they walk to the door together. "I'll check back with you, Naomi. You make some interesting points."

"Well, it's irresponsible to just dump things without some oversight!" Vivi can hear Naomi's officious authority come snarling out of her nose. Vivi has no staying power and knows it is time to leave. Vivi feels herself slam back into her body, her hand on her computer. She quickly dissolves the Power Point images she has brought with her and jams her things in her backpack, looking for her purse.

"Thanks so much, Vivi," says Charles. "I apologize for Naomi's . . . um . . . enthusiasm. She can be like a dog with a bone."

"I am not really like all of you. I was Vikram's friend and not his follower." She is surprised at how angry she sounds.

"I will thank Vikram for our introduction."

"Yes, Good. Thanks. Have you been in touch?"

"Only an email now and then. He sent me your name some time ago. He seems quite busy with his work at the Center."

"Oh," says Vivi. "Good for him. Busy, busy." She tries not to reveal how much she could use a friend at the moment. Charles is steady as he watches her. He doesn't seem to miss any of it.

"I'll tell him he should be in touch."

"He can do what he pleases, I suppose." Again, Vivi realizes she is losing the upper hand in the mask and bury contest. Vivi smiles in a way that she hopes is vibrant and healthy. "I'll take off now. I left some cards on the table."

"Yes, I see them. You want to sit for a moment? You feeling okay?"

"Oh, of course. Just fine. Goodbye." And Vivi somehow makes it to the doorway, stops on the path back to the parking lot just in time to let go with a small vomit behind a tree. She looks around like a thief and hurries back to her car. She does not know why she is angry and confused.

Charles watches her in her hasty retreat and then spots her computer briefcase. He finds her sitting in her car in the parking lot, windows open, trying to re-center.

"You forgot this." He presents her backpack to her through the window.

"Oh, gosh. I guess I did. I'm a little foggy."

"I appreciate you coming today." He smiles at her.

Vivi looks up. She wants to change the rhythm of their encounter. Her mood is certainly not this nice fellow's fault. "I'm sorry if I was rude. I'm not feeling very well."

"No explanation needed." Vivi could tell he really meant that. He was a kind man.

"It's just that."

"Naomi can be a pain in the ass and you're not available for recruitment at the moment," he says.

"Something like that." She softens. "Thank you, Charles. Nice to meet you."

"Nice to meet you, Vivi. I look forward to meeting again soon."

With that he pats the side of her car and heads back to the meeting room. This time Vivi watches him walk away, hands in pockets, easily striding back to his work. It's an effortless, measured stride. She likes the way in which his feet hit the earth solidly and with no fuss. She puts her car in gear, the wheels turn and she heads back home.

Chapter 48

Mark in Boston

"Good you could come in for the project." Ennis speaks around Mark, but Mark gets the distinct idea that Jim Ennis is surveying him as he would a potential site for construction.

"Thanks for asking me," Mark responds, available and enjoying the attention.

"We're on a crunch to finish and I was hoping to be able to count on you for a month or so. Can you arrange for that? You can stay in the client apartment, and the pay will be better."

"Sure. That would be great."

"Dustin told me you used to help him with compliance issues. The codes are different here but if you can study up, it would be a terrific help to have someone dedicated to that area. Pilar can help you."

Pilar is that sloe eyed dark beauty that Mark had caught sight of the first time he came to the Ennis Studio. He glances now into the back of the open loft and she is sitting quietly over her drawing.

"Okay. That's great."

"So, you're good to go. See what you can find out about . . ." And Ennis hands him a sheaf of papers and directions to the construction site he will be working on. "Take a look at the real thing, today, yes? Then see you tomorrow at ten."

Mark heads to the address Ennis gives him. He navigates Boston streets easily and is soon across the bridge and feeling competent. He slings the car up the drive to the chained link fence and parks. The site is in an industrial part of Cambridge and was once a large warehouse. The building is mostly gone, bowing to the wreckers who have already started their work. In the middle of the large concrete yard, the aging cement is cracked and crumbled. An errant tree has taken root in the lonely soil, itching to get some air. Ivy ripples along another fissure that runs the length of what was once a parking area. He can see the outline of old embedded tanks, once full of fuel, now a toxic nuisance. He marvels at how alive and challenging the greenery that has forced its way back to life seems against the concrete expanse. He remembers how the earth at Vivi's had a spirit of its own as he ripped it up with the Bobcat last year. Even here the earth has its own priorities. Mark wonders about what secrets it holds, but quickly moves his head back to the problems of how many feet he can squeeze out in his plans to allow for building a compliant residential building on a former toxic site. He is not hired to deal with "life force" issues. His job is to make it possible to bury earth and memory so somebody new can make more money and so it goes. The rest is for 'pussies', he thinks. From somewhere deep in him, before he had his 'spiritual retreat', he recognizes the familiar brutal heave of emotions over a cliff, and the powerful feeling he has at the thought of burying and building walls. Excavation is too careful for him. He wants to build and conquer. He knows somewhere how silly that might sound to some, but it comforts him.

"Dougie! This is Amanda's friend. He lived with her out in the country." Pegg is speaking very loudly for Dougie's benefit. "The hearing aids don't do anything but buzz. Doug? Dougie? Did you hear? I said this was Amanda's friend."

Mark has finally delivered the paintings to Pegg in Boston. Her octogenarian husband, who doesn't miss a trick, has been impatient all through dinner.

"That so?" Dougie looks up with a twinkle. "You like aged meat?"

Pegg smacks his arm. "Shut up, Dougie. He rented a room from her. That's all, right? Right, Mark?"

Pegg looks at Mark from under tattooed eyebrows. She wanted Dougie to see the person that Amanda lavished her last crush upon.

"Never mind. Sometimes experience makes for a better lover than the fresh young things. Take it from me." Dougie lets out with a wise old hoot. Or maybe he was farting. Mark isn't sure. "Now roll me into my television, will you? I want to check the money scores!"

"I'll take you," says Mark, eager to get the evening finished.

When Mark returns to the dining room, Pegg is looking at the paintings he has brought.

"These are the pussy paintings?"

Mark still can't bring himself to describe them in that way.

"They were the first pieces she did when she got the cabin, she told me."

"I like the pine cones better. But we'll see if they sell."

"It's good you're here, you know." Pegg says, certain that he needs her opinion. "In Boston. I'm not your mother but I can tell you it's time you came back into the world. What happened to you, made you hide so far away with those women?"

Mark smiles. "Don't mince words, Pegg. I mean I wouldn't want you to be considerate of my feelings or anything."

"Cut that crap. I mean, really. The only good thing about getting older is that you know stuff. And in knowing stuff at least you have to open your mouth and say it. So what happened to you that hasn't happened to every other living soul?"

"Nothing you'd be interested in, Pegg." Mark is really ready to get out of there though Pegg wants to talk.

"When Amanda left me, time after time, and I kept letting her return and then leave me again, all I really wanted to do was hide away in between times. I figured it made no sense to heal my heart because I knew she would be back and why go through all that healing when you just have to rip off the scabs in a few months anyway. At least that's how I played it."

"Gotta head out, Pegg. Work tomorrow," says Mark. Pegg's eyebrows shoot up, but before she can speak again, Mark says, "I took a little time to recover. I've learned a lot from spending time with Amanda."

"And now Vivi, right." Amanda lifts her glass while Mark puts his down.

"We're friends. We're good friends. There's nothing wrong with that."

"You're twenty years younger than she is and of able mind and body. Vivi is a nice gal but I bet you could have your own life instead of crowning hers. Just saying."

"Thanks for the advice, Pegg." Mark rumbles to his feet, feeling a slight buzz from the wine.

Fumbling with his key as he gets to his own apartment door, he realizes he misses that Vivi won't be in his bed when he collapses into it. He sets his alarm and sleeps anyway. He dreams of making money instead. That serves as his lullaby.

Mark dives into his work. He is happy for the break from drafting and seeing a city at work, out his window, energizes him. He works the phones, finds the files, consults the project managers, and drinks lots of cappuccino. He's in a brand new movie with ringing phones and emails and messages at the office when he comes back from a break. His first Saturday in town, he cruises by Brooks Brothers and finds himself happy to purchase a casually elegant tie and a sports jacket on sale. He doesn't miss the flannel shirts and jeans he has been wearing for the last months. He gets a haircut and lets the hip barbershop sell him a fifteen-minute neck massage designed for "busy professional guys."

Pilar is indispensable. Every morning she greets him with the large compliance files and outlines the priorities for the day.

"Here are hard copies of all the permits. It's a complicated mass!" she says. "I was analyzing the documents but I am afraid my English is not good enough for all this legal mimbo-jimbo."

Mark likes looking up at her big black eyes. Likes that she is not trying to be cute and likes the fact that her look pierces him. He will not correct her English. She means business in a friendly kind of way.

"I am here to assist you in your endeavors," she smiles.

"Good to know."

"Yes, knowing is good," she grins. "Good luck. I take you to dinner sometime!"

And he grins back.

"I would be honored."

Mark's friendship with Pilar is playful and convenient. They work late together. They like the same white wine. And they make love like feral rabbits. It surprises and delights both of them. This is as close to a summer romance as either of them have enjoyed in a few years. They dive in. There's something of the 'rough trade' they inspire in each other and it makes it all the more fun.

Mark lets Vivi know he'll be in Boston for a couple more weeks. She seems distracted and fine with that information. She is working hard on designs as well, she says. Besides, her friend Tara will finally be back from Florida so she'll have a pal at hand. He is free.

Chapter 49

Bringing Home the Fiance

Two weeks later, Vivi is into her routine. Working well and gathering clients. Making adjustments to plans. She even closed two jobs. She is pleased that this garden business has a real shot at being successful. And with the referrals from the Boston office where Mark has been working, she is in good shape.

She has mostly ignored her physical situation. She figures she is almost two months pregnant. She's sure that she'll see spotting every morning but it all seems to be holding. She remembers how she kept her first pregnancy a secret from Jake for the first two months as well. Never trusting that she would be willing to be a mother. And not sure she wanted to have Jake's child in the first place.

This is different. This is a waiting game. Every morning she wonders what she will feel today. How she will react. Whether she will be brave enough to talk to Mark and make some kind of a decision. When he called and said he was heading back for the weekend, she felt relieved.

"Have you seen a doctor, yet?" Tara asks her. Tara knew almost immediately that something was up with Vivi. Maybe it was all the saltines and ginger ale. Or the fact that Vivi had a certain "glow" around her. "Have you called that Mark Cheyenne yet? What's going on?"

Vivi takes another sip of tea and looks out her kitchen window.

"You are being a romantic fool, Vivi." When Tara gets no response, she says, "Give me another cookie."

"I am not being a fool. I am letting things settle. I have an appointment for next week, after Mark shows up. We'll talk and I'll make a decision."

Tara rolls her eyes at her friend and gets to her feet. "Give me a call when you find your marbles."

"Tara. The chance of this situation turning into a viable pregnancy is very low. And the chance that I can carry to term is lower. And the chance that I am prepared for anything like a pregnancy at this point is lower still."

"What about what he wants?"

"Mark and I are not prepared to parent a child. I am pretty sure about that."

"So."

"I think I should tell him. At least tell him before I go ahead and do what I think is best."

A low summer storm has been brewing all day. At five o'clock, all hell breaks loose and the heavens open with a biblical deluge. Vivi is glad she has decided to head home early. She confesses to herself that she is looking forward to seeing Mark this evening. Her garden has been generous and she has a bounty of heirloom tomatoes with basil ready for a salad. A bottle of white is chilling. She has that great Italian olive oil in her pantry. And she bought a couple of baguettes, some excellent cheese and a fragrant pile of peaches, ready early this year. He has said he would arrive around eight, so Vivi plans an early bath and fresh sheets. She knows that they are "friends," but they are also lovers, and they can at least celebrate that friendship together tonight. She admits she misses him. And he said the same in his phone call. Said he had been busy, that Boston had been good for him, that he's making some decisions about next steps.

Cautioning herself against adolescent tendencies, Vivi wants, at least, to celebrate this pregnancy with Mark first, before she says no to it. And no to them. In the end she knows that is what is necessary but she wants very much to acknowledge the fact that whatever they have is potent. It is something to admire, be grateful for and honor. That's what she's after this evening. An opportunity to honor this moment.

The rain continues throughout the evening. There is no cell reception and Vivi assumes the rain has delayed him. She bathes slowly, enjoying the sensual privacy and the sound of the rain on the roof. She wonders how long this time with Mark will last. When he arrives, wet, bedraggled and with a small, dark eyed woman in tow, she has her answer.

Vivi is shocked when they troop in, like kids coming home for a college break. Mark even brings a bag of laundry with him. The girl is polite enough. She clearly adores Mark. Vivi is surprised how quickly she can turn her own emotional availability off. How quickly she arms herself in her matronly cloak. How she says a swift goodnight and hides behind her bedroom door letting Mark fend for himself. How she catches her breath with surprise at this turn of events, which she should have anticipated, of course. How she puts an extra blanket on the bed and a long T-shirt over her shoulders. How she rocks herself on the bed, petting her belly.

"Of course," she says to herself over and over, rocking up and back, up and back. "Of course. Of course," shaking her head.

She hears Mark flatten the futon in the living room and find sheets in the bathroom. He and Pilar whisper conspiratorially until they settle in together.

She thinks that is enough to endure. And then she hears a slow rhythmic moan and the slight squeak of the futon. It is everything she can do to keep from rising from her bed and hovering over them like Anna Elizabeth, that child she birthed that weird night at the mandala, and shower down roots and earth and blood and dirt. To command they stop conjuring life when there is too much of it, undervalued, around. But she knows she cannot do that. She knows she is part of the debris of creation just like they are and there is nothing to be done but endure this next coming forth.

"So, Pilar, is it?" she asks over morning coffee.

"Yes, ma'am."

Mark laughs. "Ma'am is hardly necessary, Pilar. Vivi is one of us!" He grins round the table at the women he has brought together.

"Just trying to be respectful."

"You work at the Ennis Studio?" Vivi goes into hostess mode.

"Yes. I have a seven-years-old boy and I support him. I am from Barcelona."

"Great architecture there," says Mark. "Gaudi was a genius."

"I prefer the United States," Pilar says. "More interesting people."

Mark smiles. "Hope we didn't freak you out last night, Viv. We didn't know if Pilar could come along til the last minute and by then the cell phones were down and I wanted you to meet her."

Vivi looks around at Mark. Even he knows that story is bullshit. He sees what he has done. He has set his boundaries. He has taken Vivi at her word. He has tested friendship and ignored whatever may have been deeper, may have bonded them past Pilar and Amanda and Vikram and Jake. Vivi realizes that there may not have been much more than the casual friendship that Mark is "honoring" by being comfortable enough to bring his new lover to Vivi's table. It is not a new story. Vivi marvels at all the ways in which women must maneuver their feelings to continue to move forward without losing a leg in the craters that litter an interesting path.

And this Pilar. She has her own plans. She has a seven-year-old child already in the world. Maybe Mark is heading straight to fatherhood one way or the other.

"We'll head off this afternoon, Viv. Sorry to barge in on you. I wanted to introduce you to Pilar and had to pick up more of my stuff."

"Sure. Of course. You have all of Amanda's paintings in Boston now?"

"Yes. All of that is done."

Vivi looks at Mark again. "It seems to be. Congratulations."

Vivi wonders if she should bring up the Labyrinth Society. She decides that if her own news can wait, that can wait.

"I'm not sure how long I'll be there." Mark is focused on wiping down the kitchen counter.

Pilar smiles. "Well, I am!" They laugh and she puts her hand on his ass. It's like an imprint. She's claiming territory, too.

"Right. We'll be in touch." She is done with this pissing contest. Vivi grabs her purse and her file from her desk. "Drive safe!" She closes the door on the two of them in her home, folding his laundry, and washing the breakfast dishes. She gets into her station wagon to head to her Saturday morning appointment and feels another wave of nausea.

Chapter 50

Get a Dog

Vivi knows she has to make some choices soon. She places a call to her old friend, Jean Taub, her doctor for over twenty years in L.A. It was Jean who helped her with her first miscarriage so many years ago. They had both been young and sad and tender around the loss. Jean is probably the only person to whom Vivi can present her current situation without assumptions and judgements rocketing toward her. Jean knows her. Jean is still her friend and Vivi is happy when she calls her back.

Jean is practical and impatient. The years have taught her a few things and she sounds surprised that Vivi hasn't learned some of the same hard lessons.

"Well, I'm not fifteen," Vivi says to Jean defensively. "I don't need 'support'."

"I realize that." She can hear Jean take a piece of Kleenex and blow her nose. "Sorry. Allergies."

"Sure," says Vivi.

"But there's nothing new under the sun. A woman has a baby. A woman needs support. You ready to set up a team in your new territory? And, of course, we know from our history together that pregnancies can be problematic."

"I have no desire to return to an Earth Mother phase, I never embraced it when it might have been appropriate."

"Yes. So, now? At this point?" Vivi doesn't answer her old friend. "What's really going on, Viv?"

"I'm not sure," says Vivi. "I just wanted to talk with you. I mean, I can't think of anyone else to work with on this . . . situation. I mean, we go back."

"We do." Jean is quiet. "Do you want to make a decision? Do you want me to make one for you? Are you ready?"

Vivi blinks as Jean talks on. She really wants that feeling of floating upward and away from this conversation but somehow she is bump stopped. She cannot leave. Whatever the hormones that are floating around inside of her, they insist she stay put and deal directly with what they are cooking.

"How far along are you?"

"Maybe two and a half, three months. I mean. It's early. I have time," says Vivi.

"For what?" Jean would rather tell Vivi to end the pregnancy now, and then go home and watch the news. But there is enough of her old reflex to hold her tongue and allow her patient, her friend, to make her own decision. "You do know how difficult a pregnancy for someone of your age might be." Vivi does, of course. "Do you want a child now, Viv?"

Vivi knows but she cannot say it out loud. But then, she hears herself say this.

"You know, Jean, having a child has never been a priority for me. Not since I was young. I mean, I could have adopted if I wanted to be a mother. But something, something inside of me now is looking down the road ahead of me and having no one else to care for, no one else to base a decision upon, all that freedom stretching out like a wind tunnel . . . All of a sudden, it exhausts me. I just wonder how I am going to hold up the sky for just myself. Or why?"

Jean takes a breath. She knows this one. "That's another conversation, Viv. We are having a conversation about the viability of a three-month old fetus. It's health. Your health. The rest is what women deal with, what we all deal with, as we walk down the road. It's another conversation."

Ending the pregnancy now means she has to build the rest of her life, on her own. No one else depending on her and she depending on no one. Suddenly, Vivi is so exhausted at the thought she sits stunned and thick in the chair.

"If you're lonely, get a dog, Viv. If I was there I would hug you long and hard. But you know that wouldn't be enough."

"Thanks, Jean. It's good to hear your voice."

"I have another patient," Jean says. "I'll be in touch."

Vivi turns from the phone to settle in the large Adirondack chair on her deck. The late afternoon sun tries to sneak under her blouse and warm her belly, newly alive with shifting possibilities. Vivi allows her left hand to settle on her stomach. It is a reflexive moment that surprises her. Until now, the idea that this feeling of invasive energy had never coalesced into a real image of a possible life. Vivi allows this quickening to happen under her palm. It is a greedy moment for her, all of her hungers, lined up to chomp on this feeling.

"Stop it!" she hears herself say. "Cut it out! You knew from the beginning that this was not going to happen!"

Her voice floats across the deck and she can see the words and sounds float into the well of the mandala below her. The planted forsythia, lilacs and butterfly bushes straighten in the breeze. They are listening.

Vivi looks out into the sunset, to the bushes, to the squirrels that skitter up the oak and sit watching her with big eyes. The leaves flutter a bit. One squirrel looks on steadily. He keeps listening for something more. Vivi says nothing. The clouds begin to leak and small spittles of rain slip from the sky.

Chapter 51

And Then He Comes Back

A week later, Mark shows up again. This time he's alone. And his face is scratched. Band Aid over his right eye. He smells of stale beer. She's never seen him quite this off center. She doesn't react. Instead she says, "You might want to let me know when you're planning to drop in," when he rumbles through the door and comes straight to her at her desk.

"I got fired and I couldn't stay in the Ennis apartment. So, I came back."

"Oh. That was quick." Vivi looks away

"Yes," Cheyenne answers. Mark is gone. "Yes. Oh."

"And your new love? No room at her inn?"

"Very funny, Viv." She doesn't answer him. "I mean, you can't be jealous." She doesn't answer him. Is she jealous?

He is pacing the room. They don't really need to talk about this. He knows. "I'm sorry," he said. "I wanted you to meet her. I wanted you to see me with her, somehow. I'm sorry if it was a stupid move." He is talking to himself as much as to Vivi.

"It was a stupid move." Vivi goes back to the papers on her desk. "Shall I ask what happened?" She turns in her chair and addresses him directly. "Stop pacing. You're making me crazy."

He stops but doesn't look at her. "It seems Pilar gets around. Her seven-year-old kid. He was fathered by Jim Ennis."

"The boss?" Vivi starts to laugh. "You're kidding me!"

"I am not kidding you." Mark does not join in her laughter. Instead he starts moving again, wondering what he should be feeling about any of this.

"And he didn't want you stepping on his territory?"

"Something like that."

"Nice work."

"Fuck you, Vivi. So easy to sit here all set up in your new beginning. I wanted one too."

"So, you've toddled yourself back to your old woman." She realizes that's a cheap shot and truthfully, she has never felt that he rejected her, rather, that he wanted to accept something else.

"I beat the shit out of Jim Ennis. He called the cops. I spent a night in jail. And I came back here."

Mark is quiet. He stands and looks through the big windows into the garden. "I told you I was sorry, Viv. I'm just not sure what's next." He moves away from her. "I liked the idea that she had a kid. I liked that." Vivi is surprised by that one. Mark is on a roll. "Haven't you ever wanted a kid? To make a family? To build something to care about?"

Vivi is nonplussed by this ridiculous question. It comes at her from a place of such inexperience and lack. She sees Mark. She sees Cheyenne in all his youth, his need, his lack of life force. He has been defeated so young, she thinks.

"You really want me to answer that question? I have had a long marriage and a whole other life. I guess this is my second coming of age cycle and you're just stuck on round one. Get tough, Mark. Life will come at you with bowling balls a lot more complicated than a broken heart. You can count on it."

Vivi doesn't want to heave the fact that she is holding a life he helped to create as some kind of revenge or reward. She wants to honor it. She will not react. When she does tell him, she will act and offer. That's what she learns from his desperate face, guilty like he ate too many cookies.

"I'm going for a walk," she says to him. "I need some air."

There is a jerky continuum to the life that Vivi and Mark take up again for the first week.

She is quiet and distant and spends time sketching and making calls for possible design gigs she can grab. Mark is sleeping on the couch and spending his days outside, skulking around the terraces, shoring up misplaced bricks and diligently searching for weeds and anything he can grab and destroy. He starts on a patch of land behind the house that is full of low tree sprouts and bramble. He decides he will clear this and put in a patio, though he does not discuss this with Vivi.

Maybe he can put in a little sleeping shed where he can work, he thinks. The fact that they have not discussed their next steps floats like a sprouted potato losing volume in the atmosphere. Neither are ready to acknowledge the changes that have happened since they have been together.

"I thought I'd make a chicken. Lemon and rosemary. And maybe a salad. And maybe some beans." Vivi is trying to determine the way in which she and Mark can speak to each other. She thinks that talking about dinner might be easy. She rehearses these words in her head but they don't work. They have been eating at odd times since his return. He usually disappears for a few hours in the evening and she has a bowl of soup and whatever else she can find that appeals to her. Breakfast is coffee at odd times. Lunch is grab and go with leftovers and yogurt taken in corners. Mark sometimes retreats to his truck to eat in peace. He brings back a case of beer and bags of chips from town excursions. He leaves them in the truck for easy access.

Vivi notices that there are frozen pizzas in the freezer though she has not smelled the oven at odd hours so she is not sure if he is making this his main source of nourishment.

Winter is coming in now and the first snowfall will eliminate hiding places. Soon the ground will freeze, the freeze will come and they will be here for the winter. Growing nothing, building snow caves and deciding whether the waiting for spring is worth the effort.

Finally, Vivi speaks. "Mark, I'd like to talk to you about something." She says this in the morning. "I have to make some calls, but I'd like to talk with you. Maybe around one o'clock? Will you be free?"

Mark looks at her. "Free? I think I can make room in my schedule."

Vivi says, with a hardening of the arch of her eyebrows, "Don't be an asshole, Mark. Nobody likes an asshole." He says nothing. His city veneer has not left him yet, nor his hangover headache which he nurses every evening with a visit to the local workingman's bar in the next town. Vivi does not mention it except to ask him to shower a couple of times when the alcohol sweat becomes a bit too obvious to ignore.

With Mark foraging in the back of the property, Vivi sits at her desk and makes calls.

One of them is to the Women's Clinic in the next town. Planned Parenthood seems like a place for young women so she has asked them for the name of another private provider in the area.

"I am confirming my appointment for next Friday," she says into the phone. "Yes, I have had my preliminary intake meeting this week." There is a silence as she listens to the voice on the other end of the line. Then she says, "Yes. I am fifty-two years old. Yes, a D and C."

"Then we will see you next Friday at eleven. Please do not eat or drink before the procedure." The voice comes at her like a power screwdriver.

The tangle of bramble, sprouts and dead trees reminds Mark of a fairytale forest. He briefly entertains the idea that he is clearing debris and will find his Sleeping Beauty in the middle of the jungled, overlooked foliage. Instead, he finds a stash of old stepping stones. They are piled neatly and overgrown with moss and worm rot. The flat cold surfaces are satisfying to the touch. He places his naked hand against them one after the other and feels the way in which life has rusted and rotted them. He feels where the bridges of mineral will not give way. He pulls at long roping roots to free the stones. He edges his boot against lichen and mossy tree trunk, slipping and rutting into resistant, petrified soil. He is not sure what is malleable and worth cracking or what needs to be left as evidence of his failed effort. After two hours, he has freed about ten stones and dragged them out into the small clearing he has made. His hands are crossed one side to the other with welts and rivulets of blood. He realizes his jaw hurts with the effort. He stands and looks at the pile still there to be released and decides that their imprisonment will have to be negotiated. It is worthy, mindless, body-engaging work and it keeps his mind from digging into the stone of his heart, that place in him that he cannot access, not since he left here and went to Boston.

Vivi sits across from him. She is lovely this afternoon. She is soft around her chin and though tired, she is warm and round to Mark's eye.

She is not rigid though she does not welcome Mark as they finally sit at the table across from one another.

"You've been working hard." Her look is steady and questioning.

"I found stepping stones. I will bring them down to the Garden. Finally place your labyrinth." Mark doesn't look at her. He drinks his coffee.

Vivi can't maintain the chill. "We are a miserable mess," she says.

Mark looks up and smiles. He laughs a little. "I guess so."

Vivi nods. "You spoke to Ennis."

"Yes."

"He pressing charges?"

"Not unless I hang around Pilar again."

"That's okay with her?"

"Yeah. That's okay with her. She sure as hell didn't choose me." He walks across the room. Brutally humiliated. Trying to shake off his own stupidity. Vivi watches as he twitches with the mantle of the fool. She can see how he knows the whole episode was ridiculous and how smothered he is in figuring out where he stands. Not only with Pilar or Vivi. But with himself. As himself. He takes a deep breath and sits on the couch. He looks up.

"I guess I should apologize. But not sure to whom. So, let me start with you. Thanks for letting me come back here."

Vivi stirs her cup. "Sure. Yes. Is this home?" This sounds presumptuous even to Vivi. "I mean where is home for you?"

Mark looks at her like he has never considered this. "I don't know. Do you?"

"Of course."

"Really?"

"I built this house. I am building this home."

"This is not quite home yet, is it, Vivi. I mean, you're still new. You're always so new."

"What does that mean?" Vivi is not sure why they are perhaps fighting.

"It means, you always seem to be starting each day with no memory—or nothing that impedes you. You're like a clear cipher."

"Mark. Snails move with their whole lives on their backs. If I brought everything of my life with me, I'd never move an inch."

He is not sure what she means but she is just realizing this truth herself so she can't really explain. "I built this house. This home. I am now filling it with what comes next."

"Vistas? Flowers? Heirloom tomatoes?" he says, mocking her.

"Not so easy finding what works for me now, at this time in my life. There was Amanda for a while, there was you . . ."

"Vivi, you can't count on me."

"That is abundantly clear. That is absolutely clear. My entire life I have been trying to create a home, a community, something or someone that can be trusted, that can share experience, that can know me and that I can know. I have not been skillful at choosing partners, places."

Mark gets up. Washes out his coffee cup. "You're not depending on me, I hope." He makes the point a second time, as much for himself as for her.

"No. I am not depending on you." She says this clearly and he hears her, a little disappointed. She ignores his pique. She doesn't want to get caught on that thorn either. "That is not what I want to talk with you about."

"What? What do you want to talk to me about?" he says belligerently.

"My God, Mark. What the hell is wrong with you?"

Mark looks up at her. "I am so fucking furious. So fucking pissed off that every woman I meet has to have it her own way. Like I have no say in the way we love, in the way we . . . plan things."

"Really?" Vivi is quiet and then she says to him. "The last year or so that we have known each other I see you like a pinball. An unreliable pinball. Ringing bells where you can, sneaking down alleys that give you a free pass, disappearing down chutes and then reemerging again."

"Unreliable. You just told me you don't count on me. You know better."

"You like being a fascinator. Both Amanda and I hadn't, haven't, been fascinated in a while. Perhaps you have been our last best hope."

"That sounds depressing."

"Factual. Not depressing."

Mark moves to get another cup for coffee. He deliberately fills it. Slowly, he sits back at the table with a full cup. He is unable to process what he wants from Vivi. He just knows he has to come up with something new.

"Can we start again? As friends, real friends this time. I found some wonderful stepping stones and we can finally complete your home. Complete your vision."

Vivi looks at him and her eyes brim. "Mark. Cheyenne. Mark. Things have consequence. Caring has consequence. Time spent has consequence. I don't know what one is supposed to do with all that, but it's true."

"I know. I know that, Vivi. I am your friend. That I know. And I have loved being your lover. You are open and passionate and more possible than any woman I have met in such a long time."

"Mark. I am fifty-two years old, you know. I am just on the cusp of so many things I don't understand."

"That goes for two of us." Mark looks across the table at Vivi. Her eyes are red and he is not sure why she is crying. But, his heart opens when he looks at her. And he too feels tears coming from a place he does not know. "Vivi, I learn things from you. I learn how to start again. I learn how to begin at the beginning again. To make beauty. To create something, anything."

Vivi's eyes are streaming as she speaks steadily. "There is nothing to do but start again. But, when you have to meet reinvention over and over again, it chips at nerves and chunks at courage."

"But, you do it. You do it every day. I have watched you."

Vivi is in a vortex here. "I could never carry a child to term. I lost two with Jake. I somehow think it's the same one eating at me, demanding me to give them a life, a living, a way to be. And every time I say no. What's that about? Either they are lost or I am."

Mark looks at her. He has no idea why he is loving her at this moment but he can see her raw pulse. He can see her simple struggle to just be. He says, "You are meant to bring things to life. At least that is what I think. And I say that knowing that I barely have the courage to make up a new way to drive to work, let alone figure out what's worth living for."

Vivi looks at him. "It's hard to know what is ours to create. And what is not." Vivi smiles at this handsome young man. He has a beautiful face. Then, she sobers. "I'm having a D and C next Friday. I am pregnant. I am too old for this dream and I guess you are unlucky once again. "

Mark is stunned. "You're pregnant?"

Vivi looks away. "The chance that the fetus is healthy is very low. It needs to come out. It needs to try again with someone else. I'm sorry."

"Oh my god," Mark says. "Oh, Vivi." Mark gets up from the table and reaches for Vivi. She stands thinking she will go elsewhere, stoic, mature and in need of nothing. But she walks right into his arms. And he embraces her. His head at her neck.

They stand for a very long time, swaying and trying to bury their hearts somewhere where they won't ache so badly. They aren't sure that that place is within each other.

The sun moves lower in the sky.

He takes her hand. "Please sit with me," he says. "Please."

The two of them go to the porch and watch the late afternoon come in. He won't let go of her hand.

"We are so broken, babe. God are we broken."

Vivi looks at him and knows that he is speaking about himself because, of course, he does not know her.

Chapter 52

The Clinic

They drive to Boston to the same hospital that had cared for Amanda. Mark pulls away from the entrance in Vivi's car and vows to be in the waiting room in thirty minutes. When Vivi wakes up in the clinic area recovery room Mark is sitting beside her.

"Jake?" Vivi says as she looks at the man sitting next to her bed. "Is Jake here?"

"It's Mark, Vivi. Not Jake."

"Right," says groggy Viv. "No, of course not."

She falls asleep again.

"You okay there?" says Mark. He has positioned her on the couch looking out to her garden. A favorite view. Next to her, he has set up a little table with a pot of tea and a book, her sketch pad and the remote for the television. He has been by her side since they let him come into the Recovery Room.

"What did you do all day?" Vivi asks him.

"I was there. I sat right there all day. Boston tends to get me in trouble."

"Yes. Sure. Thanks, Mark. I am fine. I just need to rest for a day or two. That's all."

"Yes," he says. He looks at Vivi and sees her for the first time a bit haggard. Hard on the edges. Sloppy in the middle. He shakes away the idea that he is judging her at this juncture.

"Jeesh," he says out loud.

"What?"

"I feel like I had the thing done to me, you know? Like they cleaned me out, too,"

Vivi doesn't answer him but she can't help thinking it might not be a bad idea for this young man to get a good solid gut cleanse. His sadness and anger has already morphed into trouble. Vivi knows that his trouble doesn't have to be hers.

"Mark?" Vivi says. "What will you do now?"

He is taken off guard. "Well, what do you mean?"

"I mean it's great that you have stuck with me through all this. But I wonder if it makes sense for you to stay?"

"You kicking me out?"

"No. I'm just wondering if it makes sense for you to stay." Vivi looks away and Mark does too. He shuffles out of the room.

"I guess I'll come up with a plan," he says.

Resting on the couch, Vivi slips in and out of sleep. She clicks on the remote but the mindless television doesn't engage her. She can still hear Mark working outside, and moving in and out of the house during the day, so she doesn't need the extra sound to float her until the evening news. She sits herself up, slurps some tea and notices that her phone has a message.

"Viv? It's Laura. Cousin Laura. I hope this is the right number. Listen, Bernie died. He died yesterday and he's being buried today. I'm East with Shelley. I tried to reach you. Can you call?"

Chapter 53

Holding Hands

"Hello, Tatehleh." Shelley looks up with rheumy eyes when she sees Vivi enter the front door. She doesn't get up. She is sitting at the dining room table next to a large platter of cold cuts with a pencil in hand, scratching at a crossword puzzle book. She crosses out a word and looks up with a sigh. "I guess we finally have something in common." She looks Vivi straight in the eye. Before Vivi can turn tail and run she hears Laura's voice.

"Shelley! For God's sake, say hello to Viv and be nice," Laura comes out of the kitchen holding a dishtowel. "Vivi, darling! Give me a hug, sweetheart. Give me a hug!" Laura grabs her friend and gives her a bear hug. "I'm glad to see you! How are you, sweetie? Thanks for coming."

"Of course." Vivi turns to Shelley. "I'm sorry I couldn't make the funeral, Shelley. I had a procedure. Was in the hospital for a day. You okay?"

"I'm fine, as you can see. I'm glad you're fine." Shelley tries to smile but can't muster the interest. She goes back to her puzzle book.

"Everything, okay?" says Laura to Vivi.

"Oh yes. Just maintenance," Vivi says.

"I'm glad you're fine, too," says Laura. "Okay, come in here and help me wash some dishes. Tonight's the last night of shiva and there will be quite a crowd. Free food has them crawling from the woodwork. I swear I saw Judy Kramer take home a whole Tupperware container full of chopped liver with her last night!"

"That's not true," Shelley yells from the living room. "She was hungry, she made a couple of sandwiches. What do I care? Herb left her bubkes." The front door opens again. "Oh, hello Stanley. Thanks for coming again."

"Of course, Shelley. Of course." Stanley's gentle deep voice is warm and easy. Laura and Vivi can hear him take his old friend aside and make her laugh.

The Rabbi is matter of fact and helpful. The group of friends from the Temple distribute the prayerbooks to everyone, make sure those who want yarmulkes get them. They efficiently open the piled folding chairs at the side of the room and place them in small neat rows so everyone can sit together, in attention, not all conscious that just their presence helps to fill the hollow house where it gapes.

Shelley can feel the absence more than the others, of course. She is aware that the scent of Bernie's cigars is already dissipating from the corners of her living room, from the upholstery of his favorite chair. The house smells sour without the cigar smoke. It's the stink of the roses that someone has set on the side table that are turning her stomach. She moves across the room and opens the front door, fanning air into the room.

"I'm gonna get a headache from all this perfume and crap." She mumbles. "No offense anyone. It's just when was the last time anyone here smelled roses and corned beef more than cigar smoke." The rabbi looks over at her and gently motions for her to take her seat. "Oy," she sighs.

Standing together as a cohort against the absence of Bernie's cigars and big personality, the group chants the Kaddish together. The rhythm of the prayer rocks the room like a rumbling cradle. Shelley can't say the words. Her eyes dart from corner to corner, unable to settle until they collide with Vivi's. For the first time, they see each other under the masks, below the posing, and directly onto the nerve that joins them, the physical place where loss resides. Quietly, Vivi moves from her place next to Laura and stands next to Shelley. Shelley reaches up and takes her hand and squeezes it hard as her tears wash away her black mascara. Shelley can't raise her head, let alone her voice, so Vivi prays for her. She prays for herself, for her mother in law, for Jake and for the reminder that the only thing to count on is change.

Driving home, the feel of Shelley's imprint stays on her palm. Her hands were dry and surprisingly small for a woman with such personal expanse. Vivi has never really liked Shelley and knows Shelley feels the same. But Shelley reached for her hand and neither of them would let go. Vivi's hands, now resting on the steering wheel, feel Shelley's pulse, she feels the pulse of her own mother tapping her heartbeat at the root of her thumb. Women's hands hold each other. Imprints through time.

Chapter 54

Winter

Mark is gone when Vivi returns. She can see the tire tracks out of her driveway. He has left the stepping stones in a neat pile at the base of the terraced garden. She wonders if maybe she should make a brick patio. But she leaves the pile alone. She leaves the plans alone. It's November. She can wait until spring.

"Now's the hard part," says Tara, when she shows up a few days after Vivi is back from the shiva. "Fill your days. All by yourself. I dare you."

It's not that the hours she logs at Home Center to keep her sane through the winter have no meaning, it's that the imprint of Shelley's hand remains with her as she hauls plants, sets out the turkey lawn ornaments, prepares winter poinsettia's again. It's the way Shelley grabbed for her hand and how she held it. How her own mother held her hand. How she sometimes held Jake's hand. And Vikram's. The way Shelley needed her touch to remain steady.

This stays with Vivi as she goes through the motions at work, nods to Cheryl, appreciates her co-worker, Robert. How that touch, that hand, reminded her of the small hand her magical child Elizabeth Ann had given her. How that touch had grown into a roar of need and want and steady sustenance.

She keeps her own hands buried in work gloves these days. It helps with the work. But when Charles, the man who ran the Labyrinth conference, shows up at the Home Center and extends his hand to hers, she strips the leather glove and offers him a human touch.

"Hello Charles. It's Charles, right? From the Labyrinth Society."

"That's right," he grins at her. "Nice that you remembered. You work here now?"

"I work here off season. Until summer gardens come back and people are ready to think about cleaning them up, planting them again, making a new start."

Charles smiles at her. "That's a mouthful," he says. "You like what you do."

Vivi smiles herself. "Yes. I guess I do. It's winter and I need to remind myself sometimes what matters."

"I actually came to look for you. It's the only garden center in the area."

"Really? I don't know if I am happy or not that my cover is blown."

"No shame in earning a living. I'm trying to do the same myself. I'm here interviewing for a job at the college."

"Really? That's great. Congratulations."

"Here for two days. Will you have dinner with me?"

Vivi is surprised by the invitation. "I mean, I'd like to know more about this area. And you're my only contact. Will you?" Vivi finds Charles charming. He is short and has a bottle brush mustache and a corduroy jacket that has seen better days. He is also resolute and clear. He seems to be exactly what he presents.

"Well, I work from three to eleven. I can do lunch, or even breakfast. Maybe come to my place and I'll fix you pancakes?"

"I'd like that." And as easy as that they have a date.

Charles arrives at 8:00 a.m. with a jug of Vermont maple syrup from his hometown.

"Did you tap it from your own tree?"

"Will you let me in if I tell you the truth?"

"Sure," she smiles.

"It's from the co-op. But it's local."

"Good for me! Thanks."

The coffee is already on and Vivi is happy to see him. She remembers how measured he was the day at the college when she was making her garden presentation. The morning light is strong and the dusting of snow and frost out the window has outlined her terraces like an etching. Vivi can see his breath as he comes up on the porch to knock on the door.

"Oh, it's such a beautiful day, yes?" says Vivi, as he brings in the crispness of the day with him. "Let's go for a walk after breakfast and I'll show you the terrace plantings."

"And we can talk about the labyrinth site as well," says Charles. "I haven't forgotten." He looks around. "It smells great in here!"

And they fall into easy conversation. Vivi pours coffee and soon Charles is mixing the pancakes and Vivi is cutting grapefruit. They speak of favorite breakfasts. Charles always had a full one growing up in Vermont, Vivi rarely had more than a glass of milk and a piece of toast rushing off to get to the school bus while her Mom struggled to get to work on time. Charles confesses to Mickey Mouse pancake expertise as his wife taught an early class at Johnson State and it was his job to get their son, now in his late 20s, off to preschool and all the schools to follow. Vivi offers her expertise at bagels and cream cheese for writer meetings at her place, and how Jake appreciated that she made a great spread and then usually disappeared so the guys could work out their ideas on their own. Charles listens to that one.

"When did he die?"

It stops Vivi. "It's been five years."

"Diane died about the same time. Breast cancer. It ravaged her. Us."

Vivi doesn't look at him. "Yes. It tends to do that."

"My son left college. Went to Japan to teach English. He met a girl there. Hasn't been back since."

Vivi looks up. "That seems tough."

"He's young. Time is not the same for him."

"Time is pretty precious."

"For both of us," says Charles. "I'm not always sure I am honoring it enough."

He grabs his coat. "Show me your garden."

They leave the plates on the table and head out. Vivi loves the sound of the crunchy snow beneath her boots. Charles paces the mandala at the base of the terraces. He is measuring off the path. Checking the angle of the morning sun. The proximity to the main house.

"This would really be perfect for a labyrinth and look, you already have the stepping stones. Would that do?" Charles looks up at her. "Honor time?"

"We do what we can do. I'm never quite sure."

Charles comes over to the neatly piled stones Mark left. "I had thought maybe a patio?" she says.

Charles smiles. "No promises. No worries."

That's how the morning went. Vivi smiles easily after her leaves, as she does the dishes, looks out across the mandala. It is an easy lifting of weights and measurements of time, need and obligation.

She is surprised when she sees it's already one in the afternoon and she hustles to finish up the kitchen, take her shower and start her shift.

Chapter 55

The Game is On

"So, they offered me the job during the meeting and I said yes! I am just a one semester replacement but I get to teach through summer and look forward to it!"

Sitting in Vikram's old office at the college is odd. Vivi hasn't heard a word from him in almost a year. Charles has invited her over for a chat and as she sits here she remembers how tall Vikram is and how small and compact Charles is, dwarfed in Vikram's throne-like desk chair. His size is not lost on him.

"I feel like the little king in this chair! I've ordered an ergonomic ball to sit on. It will come soon!"

He is elated at his good fortune. His eyes twinkle as he crows about his plans. "It's a mix of urban planning, spiritual spaces and landscape design," he says, without needing her question. "I'm calling my class 'Walking the Labyrinth: Being in Place.' What do you think?"

"Sounds great." Vivi smiles at his delight at his own cleverness. Charles had been rather subdued when she had met him a few months back. A quiet, patient, shepherd, she remembers, as he navigated the wild women and old goat labyrinth enthusiasts. She is lost in this thought and when she turns a corner in her mind, there is Charles, his kind eyes resting on her face. His gaze is easy, relaxed and open. She is startled looking back at him and stumbles where there is no stone. "I'm . . . I'm not real sure where I come in," she says.

Charles has moved to his electric teakettle by the window and is now pouring them two mugs of Lavender Mint tea, Vikram's favorite.

"Walking the labyrinth is a terrific practice . . ." He hands her a large blue mug, "because it is all about the journey not the destination. It's walking the labyrinth, the actual doing of it step by step, that allows you to be exactly where you are and begin to recognize the wisdom and fullness of that choice."

"That sounds impressive."

Vivi is charmed as Charles brings out books and his computer to show her images. "Here's what I want to build," he says simply, offering her a photo of a large expanse of green meadow with stones and grasses intermingling. "The students will do it. We can start as soon as its warm, and until then, we can do the sketches, choose the plants, compare ancient designs, create a liturgy for the walk! It will be glorious!"

Vivi confesses that she has never conceived of creating a liturgy and the idea that this man finds the prospect glorious is disarming. When Vikram spoke of his Buddha and his path and refuge and dharma it was always his personal road to salvation. Vivi was never included in his way forward.

"So, you with me?" He grins at her and takes a breath. "Sorry to be so boisterous," he says, not sorry at all. "I just am so delighted that it's possible."

"What's possible?"

"You. You have a piece of land, yes?"

"Yes."

"You told me that you are wanting a labyrinth built there, yes?"

"Yes."

"And you are a wonderful gardener. A giver of life, yes?"

Vivi smiles. "Well," she says. And he smiles again. "Sure."

"Okay! We're on."

Chapter 56

Stone by Stone

Vivi is surprised that the wheeziest of the kids taking Charles's class is the one who starts the hauling of the stones from their spot at her doorstep down to the mandala.

"Careful there!" she yells over to the skinny boy struggling with balancing her blue wheelbarrow. The kid laughs. "It's fun!" he says. "Being a manly man! I'm so queer and I hate the gym! Maybe this will get me closer to the muscly men that make me skyrocket!" He laughs again at his own wit and Vivi watches as he turns the corner and heads down the slight incline to the magic circle at the root of the garden. It looks like the wheelbarrow is pulling him but then who knows what needs who to make things work.

It's finally spring again and the April rains have marbled the soil with rivulets and openings, which another team of kids are now smoothing and turning. Charles is there in corduroys and a tucked in plaid shirt. He really wanted his corduroy jacket on as well, but Vivi convinced him to leave it up here at her table overlooking the site.

"I'll take care of it, Charlie! You'll be fine!"

Charles gives her a confessional smile, "I'm nervous. And totally aware that corduroy jackets are a 70s crutch. Take good care of it for me."

Vivi is sitting at her desk where she has been sketching and visualizing the stones in patterns, the bushes in bloom. She has ordered the grasses from an online nursery far away and Cheryl called her to ask why Home Center is not getting a piece of the action.

"I'll give you a great price. We can use juniper for shrubs. I can get you bayberry and chokeberry. Sumac is great for color. And you can put that other stuff here and there wherever you want!" Vivi shakes her head as she listens to her former boss on the phone. "I'll throw in delivery and Jorge and Esteban are dying to get back over there and see what you've done with the place."

Vivi can't say no to Cheryl but they settle on softer vines and a few rhododendrons. They are being delivered later today. Vivi looks now through her big windows at the work being done below and she can feel the breeze and see how the grasses will hide and invite walkers along the path. She has spent the last month poring over classic patterns of labyrinths with Charlie, her new best friend.

"You have to bow to the land, Vivian," he says sternly. "But then, you know that. Tell me what you see here. Tell me what we are bringing."

Vivi would always start with the wind, the angle of the sun and the shadows from the terraces above. Charlie would push her to the experience of the stones, the step-by-step encounters she and others might find as they navigated the path.

"I plant flowers. I create landscapes. I want them to grow" she says to Charlie when he finally pins her down. "I can't create experience. The things that happen. God knows I am not in charge of any of that!"

"Okay, you create the frame," he says thoughtfully. "I get that. But when you bring this labyrinth, this experience right here at the foot of your home, you are going to receive lots of people's dreams and confusions. They will float up in bubbles. They'll get caught in the lilac sometimes."

"Maybe they'll get brushed away by the grasses!" Vivi says, trying to get into the swing of Charlie's vision.

"Nobody has a clue what's going to happen," he says, "despite the best efforts of tarot readers and spirit animals. Or spirits from other dimensions or rule makers or breakers. Nobody really knows how they can live with what happens—with what they think they create or what is created for them. But here, creating a frame for the acknowledgment of steps, of stones, of maybes and 'yesses' . . . and lots of 'oh my god, noes', you receive that experience, too. It will float up from the earth before you and whether you want to or not, you become the custodian of other people's stories. Just sitting right here at your desk, looking at the view and thinking about lunch. And because you can make beauty."

Vivi smiles. "My husband who died—Jake—he used to say that. He used to tell me I had to safeguard his story for him so he could figure out what he was living, who he was in reflection, I guess."

"How'd you do?" asks Charlie, smiling.

"Not so great. I just loved him when I could and kept holding a vision of him I thought he'd be proud of."

"And?" asks Charlie gently.

"He followed me around for a while. I mean after he died. I mean. if you believe in that kind of thing. And then he kind of lost interest, I guess, and we both got on with the rest of our . . . lives . . . jobs . . . tasks . . . who knows? No easy wrap up, there."

"Oh good! Now this!" says Charles.

Vivi looks up quizzically.

"Well there's a chant that someone devised like that. I always liked it. You take a step. You try not to fall into the pit. You get brave enough to look to the next step. You take a deep breath and let yourself find the next stone on the path. And you take a big deep breath and say, 'Oh good! Now this.'"

"That sounds awfully brave," says Vivi.

"Maybe it's because I am a bit older than you, Vivian. But, I am finding that making plans is foolish. It's like, we're here for the ride and we've already put what we can into the soup and now we will drink what we've created . . . and that will have a life of its own. On and on it goes. Just take the next step."

Vivi has been troubled by her lack of plan for the rest of her life. Charles knows this. He just laughs at her when she wonders if she should get a Master's Degree, or start a homeless shelter or, or, or.

"No matter," says Charles as he watches her calibrate all her possibilities once again. "Let's build the labyrinth. Okay?" he smiles.

"Sure," says Vivi. "But can we have a sandwich first? I made extra bacon at breakfast and would love to make you the best BLT with early heirlooms. It's seeming to take preference." He grins.

"Oh good!" says Charles.

And Vivi grabs her bottle of water and heads to the task at hand. "Now this!" she says.

She heads to the kitchen. She listens to the sounds of people stepping forward, laying stone, stubbing their toes, slapping at flies, and then opens her jar of mayo and sets herself to the task in front of her.

Epilogue

After Midnight and Before Dawn

It is like a landing strip that waves at her when she is looking the other way. The round stones that circle her terrace, the spiral path that leads inward and out again. On the path she takes a step and often finds Jake's footprints, but that's all. And she encounters her mom, Beverly.

Beverly is always smiling. Sometimes, Vivi can still see the bloody bandage around Beverly's forehead that the EMTs put in place to stop the oozing of her brain. This is where the tire of the car crushed her head. It does no good, the bandage, but Beverly is smiling anyway, like a secret homing beacon, letting Vivi know she can come home anytime and she we will be welcomed. There is even a shadow of a hulking fellow with a strong jaw grinning behind Beverly. If Vivi reaches deep she can recognize that jaw as part of her own, and realize that she never saw her father grin when he was with her. He seems delighted to be near Bev again though, even with her messy headgear.

Jake shows up once by himself. Standing at a distance. He has given up looking for or offering forgiveness. He stands at a distance and observes, finally seeing the movie he always wanted to make. Way behind him, Vivi can sometimes make out the shadow of Bernie, Jake's dad, still not giving up on the dream of his only son being a mensch. Shelley never comes, even though, Cousin Laura told Viv that Shelley passed over about a year ago. Shelley doesn't show up at Vivi's labyrinth, except maybe as that bruised cloud way to the west of Jake and resting just above Bernie's shoulder. It always looks dark and full and sad, leaking red rain.

A baby sometimes cuddles compliant, in Jake's arms, but more often has its own flotation device, a patient pink. It is buoyant on unseen gases and leaves its options open. Sometimes the baby's face changes from a blonde and blue eyed beauty to a face with eyes slit from Mayan stone and a square resolute jaw. Sometimes, the face morphs into a tortoise waiting for adoption at a suburban pet store or even a mosquito, that catches a ride on an imported rug and hopes to inoculate someone else who will birth it and let it be alive in human time. One time it showed up as a squashed roach, once again choosing the wrong channel into the planet. But it won't give up. Vivi can see that.

Tara floats by, but not with the dead ones. She brings a bench with her and makes Esteban install it so she can come and sit any time she wants. She always wears flowy orlon muumuus, which catch the wind and make her smile like the Oracle she is. She sees the parade of visitors, spirit walkers coming in, and observing Tara from Vivi's office perch, Vivi can see Tara chatting and gathering info like Western Union. Vivi hopes this gives Tara an edge with her channeling, mediumship and card business. In the several years they have now been friends, Tara has never figured out how to fully monetize her gifts, but it's still enough to live on, she tells Vivi. Her visits to the labyrinth make Tara chuckle, and that chuckle is welcome as it gets caught in the bushes, is spread by the breeze.

Vikram does not appear. Not in spirit or in flesh. She can feel his will to be elsewhere.

When light comes again and the spirits are quiet, Vivi ventures down with her clippers, some twine, a spade. She tends the grasses, trusses the waving branches, protects the occasional bird nest that appears in spring.

One year, she keeps careful watch over easy blue eggs that warm in the sun when their mama is off getting worms or organic birdseed. That year, Vivi comes every day. She notes how the mama bird gives the little eggs just enough warmth to flourish but not enough to smother them. Vivi is there when one of the eggs starts to move from within, a tiny beak stubborn and thorny poking through the shell. Vivi stands and watches. She isn't sure if she should root for the beak and its progress but she can tell that beak has a mind of its own and doesn't really need her help. Slowly, methodically, it makes a hole, and then a larger one. It pecks away at the opening, then it flexes a wing and breaks a larger portal, and the other wing stretches as well. Now, the neck is stretching, determined to show up and take its place.

Vivi is there. Vivi is watching it birth itself. It is not a miracle. It is accepting what's next and when the small creature makes its way through the shell, and feels the sun hit and dry its feathers, and it starts to grow and crow and sing, finally in the right place, finally in life, finally near enough to Vivi to share her spirit. When this happens and it hops from its perch, the small creature lights itself on Vivi's shoulder. It moves spindly and determinedly to Vivi's ear. It nips the lobe, not knowing how to kiss, and whispers in her ear as it splits itself into more and more prisms of beauty, "Oh Good Now This!" the creature says in Vivi's ear! "Oh Good! Now This!"

And takes off and lives.

THE END

[blocpress] is a small press that supports the work of the writers of the New York and Los Angeles Writers Bloc.

Originally founded in the 1970s by playwright and critic Jeffrey Sweet, the New York Writers Bloc, is a supportive safe haven writers group growing from a small group focused on work for theatre practitioners only—with actors and writers offering support and development—to work supporting fiction, non-fiction, memoir, television, film and theatre. Original members included Jerry Stiller, Anne Meara, Percy Granger, Donald Margulies (Pulitzer) and Merson, among many others.

In 1984, Susan Merson, Jane Anderson and Tony Shultz established the Los Angeles group which became home to several award-winning writers including Jane Anderson (Emmy), Noni White and Bob Tzudkier (Tony for *Newsies*), National Book Award Finalist, Janet Fitch, Kim Purcell (YA NPR Award), Jennifer Castle (Disney Books) and Barbara Bottner (Award-winning children's book author and YA honoree for *I am Still Here*).

The Bloc is still active on both coasts, moderated by Susan Merson in New York and Barbara Bottner in Los Angeles.

Made in the USA
Columbia, SC
26 February 2021